***"Someone ough[t to...] hand,"* Cooper m[uttered.]**

Tess stared at the hard, tan line of his throat. "I think it's way too late for that...."

The next moment, he was kissing her, hard. She jerked back, clamping her lips together. But instead of releasing her, Cooper held her still closer, his mouth hot and commanding.

Tess paused. She didn't mean to. It just happened. One second she was about to fight with all her strength, and the next her knees had turned to water. Her hands were still clamped around the rail behind her, but they itched to reach up and wind themselves around his neck.

At last she tore her mouth from his, gasping when he pressed hard kisses against her jawline. "Stop it," she breathed, hearing the quaver in her own voice.

His answer was a whispered challenge. "Make me...."

Dear Reader:

Romance readers have been enthusiastic about the Silhouette Special Editions for years. And that's not by accident: Special Editions were the first of their kind and continue to feature realistic stories with heightened romantic tension.

The longer stories, sophisticated style, greater sensual detail and variety that made Special Editions popular are the same elements that will make you want to read book after book.

We hope that you enjoy this Special Edition today, and will enjoy many more.

Please write to us:

Jane Nicholls
Silhouette Books
PO Box 236
Thornton Road
Croydon
Surrey
CR9 3RU

The Princess of Coldwater Flats

NATALIE BISHOP

SILHOUETTE

SPECIAL EDITION

*All the characters in this book have no existence outside the imagination of
the Author, and have no relation whatsoever to anyone bearing the same
name or names. They are not even distantly inspired by any individual
known or unknown to the Author, and all the incidents are pure invention.*

*First published in Great Britain in 1994
by Silhouette Books, Eton House, 18-24 Paradise Road,
Richmond, Surrey TW9 1SR*

© Nancy Bush 1994

*Silhouette, Silhouette Special Edition and Colophon are
Trade Marks of Harlequin Enterprises B.V.*

ISBN 0 373 59315 5

23-9409

Made and printed in Great Britain

NATALIE BISHOP

lives in Lake Oswego, Oregon, with her husband, Ken, and daughter, Kelly. Natalie began writing in 1981 along with her sister, Lisa Jackson, another Silhouette author. Though they write separate books, Natalie and Lisa work out most of their plots together. They live within shouting distance of each other and between them have published over thirty Silhouette novels. When Natalie isn't writing, she enjoys spending time at her mountain cabin at Black Butte Ranch, where she catches up on her reading.

Other Silhouette Books by Natalie Bishop

Silhouette Special Edition

Saturday's Child
Lover or Deceiver
Stolen Thunder
Trial by Fire
String of Pearls
Diamond in the Sky
Silver Thaw
Just a Kiss Away
Summertime Blues
Imaginary Lover
The Princess and the Pauper
Dear Diary
Downright Dangerous
Romancing Rachel
A Love Like Romeo and Juliet

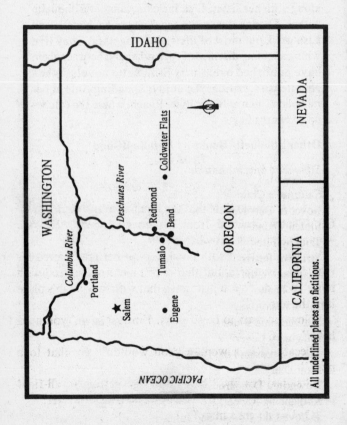

All underlined places are fictitious.

Prologue

" . . . I'm just sayin' that the ranch is tough work, girl,"
Gil Whalen declared from his hospital bed. "No one
woman can handle it by herself."

Sammy Jo glared with mock fury at her gray-haired father. She loved him, but that didn't mean she agreed with
him. "Why don't you just finish that with 'a woman's place
is in the home'?"

"Now, no need to be so sassy. I'm just sayin' you need
help."

"Because I'm a woman. You wouldn't say that to a
man."

Gil sighed heavily. "Now, don't go getting so all-fired
prickly. Good Lord, girl, you gotta be a little sweeter."

"Or I won't get a man."

Gil drew a deep breath, then wheezed slightly from the
exertion. His lungs were slowly failing him and these bouts
in the hospital were becoming more frequent. It worried

Sammy Jo, but there wasn't much she could do but humor him. However, in direct opposition to Gil's declining health was his fret over Sammy Jo's future. His obsession made her crazy. Lord, he was worse than an old hen!

"You're going to be around a long time yet," Sammy Jo told him.

"You have to make plans." He yawned, scowled at the white identification band on his arm, then turned back to his favorite subject. "That's why I've taken care of things."

Sammy Jo didn't like the sound of that at all. "How?"

He waved her away. Feebly. Sammy Jo swallowed. His emphysema was very real, and she knew he wouldn't be around much longer. And though a part of her couldn't help being annoyed with her irascible father, another part dreaded that day when he wouldn't be there to harass and teach her. She'd learned everything she knew about ranching from him. He'd been father and mother to her since she was three.

"Get some sleep," she said softly.

"You've been a good daughter, Sammy Jo. And a good rancher. I just want everything to be right for you."

"I know."

"That's why I'm getting your future set." He patted her hand and closed his eyes. "You'll thank me one day, Sammy Jo, girl. You surely will...."

Gazing fondly at his weathered face, Sammy Jo couldn't shake the uneasy feeling that not only would she *not* thank him, she might even rue the day.

And as it turned out ... she was right.

Chapter One

Booted footsteps pounded across the rustic plankwood floor of Valley Federal's central lobby. Heads turned. The row of tellers looked up from their cages and watched the determined young woman striding toward the archway on the north side of the bank. Lithe and tall, with sun-bleached blond hair and jean-clad legs that never seemed to stop, she beelined for the manager's corner, unaware of the small commotion she created.

Valley Federal was Coldwater Flats's one and only bank, and it boasted an interest rate one percent lower than those other, bigger, national banks. It also suffered from bad loans since the town was a ranching and farming community and times were tough. Times were darn near always tough.

"I want to see Matt Durning," she said icily to the new accounts clerk. The woman's nameplate read, *Hi, I'm Donna. How can I help you?*

"Well, hello, Sammy Jo," Donna said, recognizing her instantly. Sammy Jo was a bit notorious in Coldwater Flats. "Now just sit yourself down, 'cause Mr. Durning's in a meeting."

"Who with?"

"Well, honey, I don't think that's . . . Sammy Jo!"

Her snakeskin cowboy boots stomped determinedly past Donna's desk, scattering dust motes into the air-conditioned splendor of the bank. Sammy Jo felt no qualms about barging into Matt's office. She was too burned to pay attention to anyone who stood in her way.

Those who knew Sammy Jo—and practically the whole town did—recognized the signs of her infamous temper. Her face was flushed and her green eyes sparkled with suppressed fury. She'd snapped her blond hair into a ragged ponytail, but loose, broken strands flew around her face. Her blouse was denim, sleeves pushed up to her elbows. Dirt smudged one forearm.

"Damn it all, Matt," she greeted the bank manager as she rounded the corner to his private alcove. Matt's desk, a refurbished antique of mammoth proportions, sat squarely in front of huge floor-to-ceiling, paned windows. "What's the meaning of this?" Sammy Jo demanded. From a back pocket, she pulled out a rolled-up document and tossed it across the banker's cluttered desk with disdain.

"Sammy Jo, you can't just charge in here like this."

"And you can't take my property away from me, either!" she yelled right back. "I own Ridge Range Ranch. The Triple R is mine. My dad left it to me, damn it!"

"Gil also left a lot of unpaid bills." Matt Durning smoothed his string tie and glanced anxiously toward the only other occupant of the room. A man stood at the windows, his back to them, apparently oblivious to the interruption. Matt's mouth compressed.

"Make an appointment, Sammy Jo," he said in a low voice.

Sammy Jo flicked a glance at the stranger, then stared Matt down. "Two hundred thousand dollars in unpaid bills?" she demanded.

Matt sighed. Now, he liked Sammy Jo okay, but there was no denying she could be a real pain in the tail end sometimes. "No one's paid on that mortgage for months. I'm sorry, but it's the bank's policy—"

"Don't you spout policy to me! You know I can run that ranch. Better than my dad did. I've got a few hospital bills to pay off, but I'm still standing."

"Sammy Jo, honey, not financially, you're not." Matt couldn't help a second glance to his other customer. "Maybe you ought to go back to rodeo-riding. Or check with that rich uncle of yours."

Sammy Jo glared at him. That was a low-down, undeserved comment if she'd ever heard one. Matt, like everyone else in town, knew that after Gil's death Sammy Jo had been approached by her Uncle Peter Whalen from Linn County. She'd never really known him; Gil and Peter hadn't been on speaking terms. But when he'd come to the funeral to pay his respects, she'd been so hurt and broken and glad of the company that she'd forgotten all those rumors of bad blood between the brothers and embraced him with open arms.

Well . . .

It turned out Uncle Peter was a stingy opportunist who'd carried a grudge against Sammy Jo's father ever since the day Gil Whalen married the prettiest woman in town. Good old Uncle Peter had never forgiven him, and the day Irene Whalen left her husband, Uncle Peter came to Coldwater

Flats to laugh in his brother's face. That had been the last time the two men had seen each other.

But Sammy Jo didn't know any of that at the time Uncle Peter appeared. Well-spoken, well-dressed and plainly well-off, he'd thrown a line to Sammy Jo, hooked her and reeled her in before she knew what had happened. She almost lost the ranch to him right then and there. That's what the old crook had been after. The Triple R. He'd promised her he'd pay off the mortgage. Sure, she could stay on. She was his only niece, wasn't she?

Sammy Jo's suspicions grew when Peter kept leaving her out of negotiations. She made an appointment with Matt Durning at Valley Federal and learned some very bitter truths. A few phone calls to "friends" of Uncle Peter's and she learned the whole story about the brothers' feud. Gil had never told her. He'd tried to spare her again. Sammy Jo was pretty damn sure if one more man tried to spare her, she'd be penniless.

Matt was waiting for a response. He didn't know the extent of Uncle Peter's greed and deceit. He only saw the money. To him, Uncle Peter had been a godsend—one Sammy Jo had deliberately kicked in the rear end and bounced out of town.

"Oh, Mr. Durning, I'm so sorry!" Donna cried. She'd finally squeezed her plump shape out of the chair and had pumped her way to Matt's office. "I tried to stop her."

"It's okay, Donna. Sammy Jo was just leaving."

"The hell I am! I'm going to park it right here until you listen to me." With that, Sammy Jo dropped into one of the wooden swivel chairs. A puff of dust rose from her jeans.

Matt closed his eyes. The man at the window hadn't complained about the interruption, but if Sammy Jo didn't stop raising holy hell soon, Matt could lose the one customer he was desperate to keep. "Check with my secretary, Glenda, and make an appointment, Sammy Jo.'' He waved away Donna who pursed her lips at Sammy Jo and puffed out of the office.

''I'm not going to lose my ranch,'' she said stubbornly.

The man at the window shifted his weight. He seemed to be concentrating solely on the sun-baked central Oregon countryside beyond but Matt had the feeling he was keyed in to this conversation. He frowned. He'd like to strangle Sammy Jo for this!

''I'm in a very important meeting,'' he told her warningly.

''Matt, you're going to have one heck of a time evicting me off my rightful property. Now, I came here at your summons.'' Wrinkling her nose, she glared at the rolled-up paper as if it gave off an offending smell. ''The way I see it, that's nothing less than a declaration of war between me and Valley Federal.''

''Why don't you help the young lady, Matt?'' the man by the window suggested without turning around. ''I can wait.''

Matt gnashed his teeth. He stared at Sammy Jo. There was no denying Sammy Jo Whalen was a natural beauty, but that sure didn't make up for how headstrong she was. She couldn't accept the fact that her father had run the ranch's finances into the ground. Almost purposely so, since he'd been sick, or so it seemed to Matt. The old man had invested in every losing venture that had come Coldwater Flats's way the past few years, and the ranch was teetering on the verge of bankruptcy. It was a shame, really, because Sammy Jo was a good rancher.

''I hate to put you out, Mr. Ryan,'' Matt said.

''No problem.''

"Sammy Jo." Matt turned back to the cool, blond beauty in the chair. "Don't make things worse on yourself."

She laughed. Actually threw back her head and laughed until the musical sound rose to the rafters. "Worse? You're threatening foreclosure! How can I make things worse?"

"Sammy Jo..."

"Give me some time, Matt. Three months. I'll fix things."

"You can't." Matt was exasperated. Didn't she know how bad Gil had left Ridge Range Ranch?

"Three months."

"No."

"Come on, Matt. What's it going to hurt Valley Federal? Give me 'til the fall. I've got livestock I can sell. And I've got my rodeo horses. I teach an awful lot of kids to ride."

"You'd be better off to sell those nag—horses," Matt corrected himself. "The Triple R's a fine piece of property. Maybe the finest around. A lot of people are interested in it already. Your uncle, for one, but then you—"

"Don't talk to me about Uncle Peter," she said through gritted teeth.

"Sammy Jo, you can't hang on to that ranch!"

"Three months," she pressed.

Matt Durning desperately wanted to say yes. Just to get her off his back, if nothing else. But he knew he couldn't.

"Give her the three months," the mysterious Mr. Ryan advised.

Sammy Jo narrowed her gold-tipped lashes at him, really noticing him for the first time. She didn't need any help. Especially from a man. It annoyed her to see that at *his* request, Matt was wavering.

"Two months," Matt said through his teeth.

"Three or I stay and listen to the rest of your meeting with him," Sammy Jo said, hooking her thumb toward the stranger. The man wore jeans and a work shirt, but something about him looked too citified for her taste. His black hair brushed his shirt collar smoothly. Maybe it just fell that way, or maybe he worked at it real hard. She didn't trust men with perfect hair. Uncle Peter had perfect hair.

"Three! Fine. Now talk to Glenda and make another appointment," Matt barked.

Satisfied, Sammy Jo jumped to her feet. She shot one more suspicious glance at Mr. Ryan, then shook her head and strode to Glenda's desk. Glenda was as thin as Donna was fat. A cigarette smoldered in an ashtray beside her.

"Those things'll kill you," Sammy Jo told her.

"Don't I know it." She dragged deeply on the cigarette until the end glowed a virulent red. "But I am so stressed, I've picked up all my vices again."

"What's the matter?"

"You name it. Carl's out of a job and drinking to boot. The boys want new shoes, those air-pump kind that cost a fortune, and Lord, if I don't think I'm pregnant again."

Sammy Jo blinked in amazement. Glenda had to be forty-five. "Then what in the world are you doing smoking? It's bad for the baby."

"Don't I know it," she repeated as she held the cigarette out in front of her and gazed at it longingly. "This could be my last one. If I get the positive report today, I quit right now. I quit when I was having the boys, I can quit with this one, too. But I'm not quitting 'til they tell me." With that, she stuck the cigarette back between her lips and flipped open the appointment book. "You can see Matt on Friday. Would that be all right?"

Sammy Jo shrugged. "Every day's the same to me."

"Fine, I'll pencil you in."

"If Carl's looking for work, I could use some help around the Triple R. I couldn't pay much right now, but I'm good for it, you know that."

"I know that, Sammy Jo. And thanks." Glenda smiled. "I'll kick his butt out of that easy chair in front of the TV and send him over to you."

Feeling someone's gaze on her, Sammy Jo glanced around and encountered the intense blue eyes of Mr. Ryan. She felt that same stare follow her out as she strode toward Valley Federal's double doors. For no good reason other than she felt full of vinegar and frustration, she shot him a dirty look, then felt like an idiot as she stepped into the baking heat of the afternoon. She darn near burned her hand on her old pickup's door handle it was so blasted hot. Swearing beneath her breath, she yanked several times to open the stubborn thing, then jumped up to the ripped seat to settle herself behind the wheel.

"Probably miserably rich," she muttered, remembering the way Matt had fawned over him.

"Sammy Jo!"

Glancing up, Sammy Jo saw Lorna Miller, her one true girlfriend from childhood, come hurrying toward her in a pair of three-inch, red heels. Marveling how Lorna mastered a half run without teetering, Sammy Jo rolled down her window and rested her arm on the hot metal door.

"Hey, Lorna," she said apologetically. "I gotta get going. I've got a ton of work waiting for me."

As curvy as Sammy Jo was lean, Lorna waved her friend's excuses away. "I've been on a break that's been a little longer than it should," she revealed, shooting a guilty look toward the bank. Lorna had worked at Valley Federal since she graduated from high school. She'd married a trucker named Larry who'd made her life miserable for six long years before she'd kicked him out. Now Lorna supported herself and her daughter, Karen, on her salary at Valley Federal, and occasionally dragged Larry's sorry behind into court for another round of trying to get back child support out of him.

But nothing fazed Lorna for long. She was as happy and carefree as Sammy Jo was worried and frustrated. "Did Bev call you?"

"Bev Hawkins?" Sammy Jo asked in surprise. Bev didn't run in Sammy Jo's circle. Bev was a few more important rungs up the Coldwater Flats society ladder—or at least that's how she came off.

"She wants to get Karen and Emmy riding lessons. I told her to call you."

"What kind of riding lessons?"

"Trick-riding."

"Oh, Lorna. I can't teach kids tricks!"

"Sure you can. You're the Princess."

Lorna grinned, and Sammy Jo managed to hold back the few choice words she desperately wanted to spit out. Her reputation as a rodeo trick-rider was more bother than help.

"It'll bring in a little income," Lorna added.

Sammy Jo grimaced. "I gotta go."

"I'll call you. Hey, there's something else! Did you see that Mr. Cooper? Was he still here?"

Sammy Jo shook her head. "There was a Mr. Ryan at Matt's desk."

"Oh, that's right. It's *Cooper* Ryan! Man, is he something, huh?"

"Lorna," Sammy Jo murmured impatiently.

"He's got lots of money and wants to spend it here." Lorna raised her eyebrows and looked at her friend as if Sammy Jo ought to start thinking how to avail herself of some of Mr. Cooper Ryan's cold hard cash.

Sammy Jo's answer was a sharp grinding of gears as she wheeled from the lot. Through the back window, she saw Lorna race on her red heels to the interior of the bank.

Sammy Jo smiled to herself. Lorna had always meddled in Sammy Jo's life. When they were kids, Lorna had envied Sammy Jo's slim shape and easy rapport with the boys their age. Rounder and shorter, the then Lorna Dunsworth had been unfortunately tagged Lorna Doon by those same boys she'd so desperately wanted to impress. But as they grew up, Sammy Jo's mercurial temper and tough ways had put off interested members of the opposite sex, and it was Lorna who'd been chased and lusted after. Lorna whose breasts had developed at an alarming rate until Sammy Jo had wanted to scream at the way the guys all howled and drooled over her. Lorna who'd learned about sex and told Sammy Jo all the particulars.

Sammy Jo shuddered. Thinking of those particulars was the reason she was a virgin to this day. That, and the fact she believed men couldn't be trusted to treat a woman fairly. Witness how her own father had treated her!

Shoving that thought aside, Sammy Jo skipped ahead to the next, most immediate crisis of the day, which in her case gave her a choice of three: the broken fence at the north end of the property; her favorite mare who was nine months pregnant and off her feed; or her new neighbor who didn't seem to care a whit if his cattle roamed with hers because the damn things leaped fences as if they were half-deer.

"Thanks, Dad, for making this all possible," she muttered dryly, slamming her foot down on the accelerator.

Cooper Ryan watched Sammy Jo Whalen's blue pickup tear out of the parking lot and screech onto the street. An ironic smile touched his lips. Talk about stubborn! That woman gave new meaning to the phrase "hard to get along with."

Unfortunately, "that woman" was his neighbor. A neighbor he had a desperate need to stay on good terms with. Good terms because he intended to buy her out.

Too bad his Limousin cattle had already created a problem. He was in the process of selling the whole damn lot; the previous owner of his property, who had revoltingly named the spread Serenity Ranch, had purchased the lean, nervous breed for reasons which escaped Cooper. He'd spent the last few months trying to keep them penned in, but they invariably jumped the fence that separated Serenity from the Triple R, and Cooper's ranch foreman, Jack Babbitt, had received more than one blistering phone call from Sammy Jo Whalen.

Profuse apologies weren't enough, apparently. Jack had asked Cooper to leave it up to him, but Sammy Jo wasn't easily appeased. Cooper had been meaning to meet with the woman personally but hadn't yet had the chance; he was still in the process of moving from southern California. Now, however, he'd gotten his first glimpse of her, and he was seriously rethinking his approach. She clearly didn't want to sell. And it didn't take a brain surgeon to recognize she was stubborn as a bad cold and maybe just as nasty.

But Cooper was going to own that ranch. He had a plan, one he'd formed months—years—ago, really. Even before he and Pamela split up, he'd decided he wanted to own land, lots of land, the biggest spread around. And when he'd happened upon Coldwater Flats and knew he could buy up both Serenity and the Triple R, he'd started making his dream happen.

Except Sammy Jo Whalen had proved to be a more prickly thorn than he'd anticipated.

No problem, he thought with his usual arrogance. It was just a matter of time. Three months, to be exact.

"If there's anything else Valley Federal can do for you, Mr. Ryan?" Matt Durning finished on a questioning note.

Cooper examined the bank manager's obsequious smile. Durning clearly liked the sum of Cooper's collective bank balances.

"I think we're all set."

"Are you planning to relocate to Coldwater Flats completely?" Durning could hardly contain his excitement. He was as transparent as glass. Cooper could practically see dollar signs flash in his eyes.

"Thinking about it," Cooper answered in blatant understatement. Like Sammy Jo Whalen, he was dressed for ranching. As soon as he'd bought Serenity Ranch, he'd tossed off his city clothes with unrestrained relief. Growing up in a small Idaho town hadn't prepared him for his years as a southern California corporate rancher. Oh, he'd been successful. More than successful, really. But talking about profit and loss with ten other men and women in sterile, air-conditioned offices on the thirtieth floor of some skyscraper, enduring meeting upon meeting with a host of bank managers and vice presidents and assistant vice presidents and assistant-assistant vice presidents, then going home to an equally sterile apartment with piped-in Muzak... well, his patience for the rat race hadn't been much to begin with. Now it was nil. Zippo. Nada. It had died an unlamented death when he'd turned thirty-five, looked at himself in the mirror and asked, "When am I going to get what I want?"

The answer came on a weekend trip across Oregon on his way back to Idaho. On a lark, he'd taken a side road and unexpectedly bumped into the hamlet of Coldwater Flats. Clean, open, uninhabited spaces and a horizon that stretched endlessly east one way, and to the Cascade Mountains, west and south.

Love at first sight.

He purchased the ranch next to Gil Whalen's that very week though he'd thought the place was poorly named. Serenity Ranch? Good grief, it sounded like a substance abuse center! Cooper determined he would change the name as soon as possible, but then a myriad of responsibilities got in his way. He couldn't move as fast as he wanted. Too many loose ends to tie up. Hell, he'd had a corporation to sell. Consequently, it had taken the better part of a year to divest himself of his old life and in the interim he'd let Jack Babbitt and his wife, Lettie, take care of Serenity until he got here. They'd done a decent job and had been the ones who'd unwittingly let Cooper know about the neighboring Triple R's rocky finances.

"The old man's gone stark out of his skull," Jack had reported with a bewildered shake of his graying head. "Ain't buyin' any new livestock. Sellin' off that prize bull. His daughter's scramblin' around, tryin' to put things right, but every time she plugs a hole, Gil punches two more open."

"It's affected his mind, sure enough." Lettie pursed her lips, folded her arms under her ample bosom and nodded as if she'd uttered the definitive last word.

"Will the Triple R be sold?" Cooper had asked, already knowing the answer. He'd planned to buy the ranch no matter what; money was a big talker. But this state of affairs made things so much easier he almost laughed aloud in delight.

"Gonna have to be, I'm afraid," Jack murmured sorrowfully.

But Cooper hadn't heard a word after that. Plans filled his head. He would expand his own property and have one of the area's largest ranches. Maybe he'd make money; maybe he wouldn't. It hardly mattered. He already possessed more than any decent soul had a right to. He only wanted to ranch. Hands-on. His palms wrapped around a shovel, his throat choked with dust. It was his dream. It had just taken him a decade or so to figure it out.

How many nights had he stood at his office window, staring across a smog-gray moonscape of the Los Angeles skyline? How many times had unnamed longing filled him? How many times during his ill-fated marriage to Pamela had he asked himself if anything else was out there? Something better. Something good.

Now he knew. He wanted earth and dirt and aching muscles and plain, hard work.

But Sammy Jo Whalen was going to be a problem. *That* he could tell straight away. Was it worth his while to try to get to know her, to soften her up, so to speak? Or would it be smarter to just wait for the inevitable to happen and let the Triple R fall into his lap? She wouldn't be able to make those payments for long, and Matt Durning was more than anxious to be rid of her bad loan. Three months? From what Cooper could see, she'd be lucky if she managed to make it for one.

But there was no doubt she'd go down kicking and screaming.

"You know, you ought to think about acquiring the Triple R," Matt Durning suggested, unwittingly reading Cooper's thoughts. "It's a nice piece of land. Folks around here have always known that if Serenity and the Triple R were combined, it'd be the biggest ranch for three, maybe four, counties."

Cooper hid his feelings on the subject. "Think Sammy Jo'll sell?"

"She won't have any choice," was Matt's grim prediction.

Sammy Jo's pickup bumped up the long driveway to the Triple R's ranch house. Dust plumed out the back like the tail of a comet, which was about the speed Sammy Jo was traveling. She absently waved to the huge oak that stood like a sentinel at the turn, a ritual she'd begun as a child. Her mind churned in turmoil. Damn, damn, *damn!* How could Gil have been so foolhardy?

I'll take care of everything....

"Yeah. Right."

Yanking on the wheel, she rounded the final turn, screeching to a halt in front of the house, a sprawling, slightly dilapidated building with one shutter hanging drunkenly and about to fall off completely. Yes, the place wasn't pretty. It never had been. Her father had built it himself and, as a carpenter, Gil Whalen made a good rancher.

Only he really wasn't much of a rancher, especially these past few years before his death. In fact, he was about as bad a rancher as you could be.

"What did you think you were doing?" Sammy Jo demanded, slamming open the front door. Tears stood in her eyes. She was so angry at him, she could spit nails. "How could you do this to me?" she cried to the empty house.

Plunking down on the footstool, she dropped her chin into her palm, feeling like a child, an idiot and a complete failure. She'd been snookered. Snookered by her father and now by Valley Federal. It was all an elaborate plot. Gil Whalen hadn't thought his only daughter could take care of the ranch so he'd made certain she wouldn't get a chance.

In fury she stomped her foot on the faded hooked rug her grandmother had made. Dust soared into the air and she waved it away, coughing. For the first time that day, she saw the terrible shape her boots were in and she stomped off to the back porch and the bootjack.

Evening shadows striped the fields behind the house, companion to the striated sunlight that glowed on the burnished hides of the horses and cattle and sparkled on the smooth water in the trough. The air smelled hot and dusty and tangy with the not unpleasant scent of the animals. Not unpleasant to Sammy Jo's way of thinking, anyway.

Tugging off her boots, she stood in her stocking feet, leaning against the porch rails. Her chest was so tight she could scarcely breathe. Anger consumed her. How could Gil have done this? *How?*

Worst of all, she missed him, anyway. Missed him desperately. She hadn't known she would feel so alone, but loneliness filled her up inside.

And that made her mad, too.

She flung herself onto the cushioned porch swing and pumped furiously with her legs, forcing the sluggish, mammoth thing to creak and sway. Gil had done it on purpose. She knew it. Matt Durning knew it. Heck, the whole town knew it! It had been a last ploy to force her into marriage with Tommy Weatherwood, Coldwater Flats's only eligible bachelor—at least in Gil's biased opinion. Tommy was a cowboy through and through. He could rope and ranch and generally swagger his way through life with the best of them. He was good-looking, too. Women flocked to him. Of course, Tommy couldn't stick with one woman. No way, no how. But he sure knew how to drink, and when he drank, he was downright mean-tempered and vile.

Yup, he sure was good husband material. Gil could sure pick them.

And what if she'd actually sold out to Uncle Peter? What then? Gil clearly hadn't thought of that alternative.

"Damn you," Sammy Jo muttered softly to the slowly darkening sky. She said it without heat, her anger spent. She wasn't really mad at her dad's ill-conceived plans to marry her off. She was hurt that he'd left her.

"And it certainly didn't help that you left me in such a mess," she added sternly, just in case he was listening.

Trigger, Sammy Jo's black-and-white Border collie, loped from the fields, tongue lolling, and dropped at her feet. Nose protected by her paws, she eyed Sammy Jo expectantly, eyebrows waggling. Sammy Jo absently scratched the dog's head.

There had always been a dog, just as there had always been horses and cattle. Ridge Range Ranch, the Triple R, had been around since Sammy Jo's great-grandfather, Jessup Whalen, had homesteaded the property. It had also always prospered, and Sammy Jo was bound and determined to keep things that way.

Narrowing her eyes, she pushed her father's warped logic out of her mind and thought long and hard how to hang on to the ranch. Teaching little hopefuls how to stand on a pony while it was galloping, or how to barrel-race, or generally how to look cute while doing rodeo didn't exactly bring in the big bucks. Matt had been right on that score: she ought to sell the horses.

Sammy Jo's gaze slid over the fields to the distant brown and black specks huddled together by a small grove of pines and aspens. A couple of Shetlands and several small quarter horses were her rodeo *nags*—thank you again, Matt Durning—and these days they preferred to wile away the hours grazing and silently communing with their friends than perform.

Well, she hadn't lied about the livestock. The Triple R had some of the best beef cattle around. What was left of them, that is.

Sighing, she recognized the truth. The land was the most valuable asset. The *mortgaged* land.

"I ought to marry Tommy Weatherwood just to show you what a miserable loser he is," she grumbled, turning one eye to the dusky blue heavens. "Except he drinks away every dime he earns, and I don't believe that story about his having some money stashed away."

Stomping back inside the house, she swiped the sweat from her forehead and poured a glass of lemonade. As she stood in the kitchen, her gaze arrowed through the archway to the living room and centered on her trophy case. She'd won enough blue ribbons to make a satin quilt. At one time, she could rope and ride with the best cowboys around. But a good fall off nasty old Knickerbocker, and a broken collarbone and wrist to boot, had cured her of wanting to barrel-race competitively anymore. Besides, she loved ranching. It was her life. And she was as good as any man. Better, really. She'd sure as hell been better than her father.

Her gaze settled on the tiny gilt-framed photo next to the case, her one and only reminder of her mother. Gil would have done about anything to get rid of it. Ever since Irene Whalen had run off with a man half her age, leaving Gil and three-year-old Sammy Jo behind, her name had never been mentioned again. When Gil referred to her at all, his kindest label was "that tramp." His vocabulary deteriorated from there. Sammy Jo didn't feel too kindly toward Irene, either. The woman hadn't exactly been flowing with the milk of human kindness, especially in the maternal sense. But she was Sammy Jo's mother, and therefore Sammy Jo hung on to the photograph.

Sammy Jo made a face. She couldn't remember that long-ago time when reportedly Uncle Peter had stopped by to gloat that Gil Whalen's pretty wife had left him flat. Now, knowing the facts, she shuddered at the thought of that scene. Their fight must have been a doozy. Uncle Peter's involvement certainly hadn't helped her father get over her mother. And Sammy Jo suspected that the whole unfortunate series of events had shaped how her father had treated her from then on.

Gil had raised Sammy Jo as if she were a boy, and a boy is what she'd fervently longed to be. But she hadn't been, and in the end, Gil hadn't trusted his only daughter to run the Triple R. He wanted a man in charge, and to that end he'd argued loud and long about why she should get married. His efforts merely convinced Sammy Jo that she would never tie herself to a man. Gil, however, was as determined as Sammy Jo, and knowing her the way he did, he'd run the ranch into the ground, thinking he could force her to marry. Without another income, Sammy Jo was sunk, and in that, Gil was right.

Sammy Jo tossed back the rest of her lemonade and slammed down the glass. It was damned annoying! Gil's outdated, old-fashioned, chauvinistic values had landed her in a heap of trouble.

"Even if I wanted to get married, no man would look at me," she declared, half-challenging, half-afraid it was true.

Glancing at the clock, she realized the chores wouldn't wait. She needed help but couldn't afford it. Glenda's husband, Carl, would be a godsend, but Sammy Jo felt guilty that she wouldn't be able to pay him right away. That's how she'd lost her ranch hands, even the most devoted of them. Slow payment. They hadn't been able to afford to ride out the bad times with her.

Depressed, she grabbed her hat off a peg by the back door, whacked it several times on her thigh, ostensibly to remove dust, but partly out of frustration, jammed it on her head and strode into the blazing, orange sunset of a mountain-high summer evening.

Cooper leaned his arms on the top rail of his fence, the fence he shared with the Triple R. A stream meandered along the fence line, branching off and cutting beneath it at one point to wander across the southwest corner of his property. Cotton Creek it was called, according to Jack, and to the north it ducked under the fence to cut across the vast acreage of the Triple R.

He'd been standing here for a good half hour. Sammy Jo Whalen was doing chores. From a distance he'd watched her walk into the barn, and he imagined she was feeding the horses. He had half a mind to ask her if she needed help because her body language said she was about done in.

But then, if her performance at the bank was any indication, she'd probably scorn his offer and make him feel like an idiot for even trying to help.

So, he stood at the fence, his fertile mind trying to come up with a way to take control of the Triple R without evoking Sammy Jo Whalen's ire. He didn't doubt that she could be a regular she-cat.

There wasn't a whole lot of light left. As he watched, Sammy Jo stepped from the barn and headed toward the house. Her weariness communicated itself to him as she refilled the trough with the hose.

He was in the process of lifting his arm to hail her when movement caught in his peripheral vision. Turning slightly, he saw one of his cows sail over the connecting fence, land on Whalen property and bound into the gathering darkness.

"Damn," Cooper murmured, but his one slight imprecation couldn't match the stream of profanity that suddenly issued from Sammy Jo's lips. Cooper leaped over the fence with nearly as much grace as the cow. Unfortunately, he landed knee-high in the stream, and his one tiny, "Damn," changed to language almost as ear-singeing as Sammy Jo's.

"You!" Sammy Jo yelled, recognizing him as she stalked furiously toward the fence.

"I'll get the cow," Cooper said as he staved her off.

"Yeah? How? It took off like a jackrabbit, and if history repeats itself, the damn thing'll send my cattle frantically in all directions. Is that Bambi-wanna-be your piece of livestock, Mr. Ryan?"

"Look, I'm selling off the Limousins as soon as—"

"So, *you're* Serenity's new owner?"

"That's right, and I'll make sure I make it up to you. I just need a little time and—"

"Just get that thing off my property," Sammy Jo snapped, hands on her hips. "And then do the same yourself!"

Cooper stared. He hadn't expected her to be out-and-out rude. "That's the thanks I get for helping you today?"

"Helping me?" The tone of her voice warned of danger.

"At the bank."

"The bank?" Her lashes narrowed. "All I saw was interference."

"Fine," Cooper said, sorry he'd brought it up. "I'll get Jack, and we'll chase down the cow."

"I'll get the pickup. I know where they all are."

"I don't want your help," Cooper said, annoyed.

"Too bad."

She stomped off toward the house. Cooper waded back through the stream, climbed the fence and stalked toward his own house, full of growing fury. Okay, so the cow had leaped the fence again. Big deal. It wasn't as if he wasn't going to take care of it, for Pete's sake.

He slammed through the back door. "Limousin's jumped the fence," he growled to Jack who was standing by the stove, examining the stew his wife was stirring.

"Lemme get my hat," Jack said, following after Cooper. "Does Sammy Jo know?"

He couldn't quite hide his anxiety, and that annoyed Cooper even more. "She knows," he muttered through his teeth.

"Bad luck," Jack said, and that was really all there was to say about that.

An hour and a half later, Jack had the pesky cow by a halter and lead rope and was trying to lead her into the back of one of Serenity Ranch's trucks. The stubborn beast was having none of it, so grumbling all the way, Jack led the cow down the Triple R's long driveway and then back up the adjoining driveway to Serenity Ranch.

That left Cooper standing in Sammy Jo's front yard with the Triple R's blond owner beside him.

"Sorry for all the trouble," he told her.

They'd barely spoken three words to each other during the search. Still, he'd told her his first name and she hadn't seemed to mind that he called her Sammy Jo.

"So, you bought the Riggs place, huh?" She brushed blond strands away from her face. Several strands clung to her lips, drawing Cooper's unwilling gaze to a pink mouth set in stubborn lines.

She was too damn pretty for someone so prickly, he thought. "Yup."

She gave him the once-over, from the top of his dirt-spattered cowboy hat to the tips of his worn boots. When her green eyes met his, they were cloudy and full of mistrust.

"Lettie says you hail from California."

Her tone suggested he was probably an ax murderer. "That's right."

"And you've... retired... to Serenity Ranch?"

"Not retired. I plan to expand the current operation."

"But you're a corporate farmer."

Mistrust wasn't a strong enough word. The lady's voice dripped sarcasm and disgust. "Why do I get the feeling that's a dirty word?"

She was frank. "Because it is."

"Ahh..."

"Look, Cooper," she said coolly. "I've got things to do. As you've probably guessed, I'm in a bit of a money bind. I can't waste time talking to the neighbors. Good luck to you, and I'm sure by the next time we meet, you'll have built a taller fence...."

"Have you had dinner?" he asked quickly, before he thought.

Sammy Jo slid him an assessing look. "No. Why?"

"Thought I might take you out. Try to pay you back for all the trouble."

"What are you really after, Mr. Ryan?"

"It was Cooper a minute ago," he reminded her. "And all I want is to even the scales."

"They're even."

She was one stubborn piece of work, Cooper concluded, wondering why in the world he was trying so hard. There was no chance for friendship. He didn't want it, anyway. He just wanted the ranch.

"Look," she said, "I've had a heck of a day. I had a piece of broken fence that I've just finished jerry-rigging together. I've got a lot of other chores, and I'm tired. Why don't you just . . . go away?"

He could see she was exhausted. For reasons he couldn't explain, he wanted her to just give in. "If you won't accept my invitation tonight, then we'll do it later. I mean to have my way," he told her.

That comment earned him her full attention. She walked right up to him, and if she'd been six inches taller, they would have been standing nose to nose.

"That's the first thing you've said tonight that I totally believe. I bet you mean to *always* have your way."

"What did I do to get you so riled up?"

"I don't know. I've just got a feeling about you, and I trust my feelings. Good night, Mr. Ryan . . . Cooper," she corrected herself. Then, to Cooper's intense surprise, a dimple suddenly peeked out beneath her stern countenance, cute and sweet and entirely at odds with Sammy Jo Whalen's rigid manner.

Before he could respond, she'd walked up to her door and shut it behind her, and he was left alone in her front yard, surrounded by summer heat, the lusty song of the crickets and a powerful need to know a lot more about the owner of the Triple R.

A lot more . . .

Chapter Two

A second trip to the bank proved as fruitless as the first. Sammy Jo waited impatiently in one of Matt Durning's client chairs while he spoke on the phone to another of the bank's VIP customers, or at least that's what it sounded like based on Matt's wheedling tones.

"I'll have Glenda express those forms to you today, and never mind about the appraisal fees." Matt smiled as if the VIP were sitting in front of him. "We'll take care of everything...."

He hung up and stared blankly over Sammy Jo's head, a million miles away. She said distinctly, "I believe we were having a conversation before you were interrupted by that phone call."

"Sorry, Sammy Jo." He jumped visibly. "Where were we?"

"If you can't remember, I think we're already done." She got to her feet. Today she was dressed in a denim skirt, white full-sleeved blouse and paisley vest, an attempt at showing Matt Durning she could be a lady when she felt like it. But it had been wasted effort. Matt had barely glanced her way except to frown at her beloved cowboy boots as they'd clattered across the plankwood floor.

"If I could help, Sammy Jo, I would," he said sincerely.

"Thanks."

Passing Glenda's desk, she gave the secretary a faint shake of her head. Glenda was still smoking, and she waved Sammy Jo over.

"Test was negative!" Glenda revealed. "I'm so relieved!"

Sammy Jo managed a smile. "That smoking's still going to kill you."

Glenda scowled. "Not for long. The bank's gone totally nonsmoking. So far, nobody's forced me to stop yet, but it's coming. Oh, and honey, Carl will be there tomorrow if you still need him."

"I most certainly do."

"Good luck," Glenda said, meaning it.

Lorna waved Sammy Jo over to her teller's window. "Have you met your new neighbor yet?" she asked.

"Oh, yes." Sammy Jo's voice was dry.

"And?"

"And nothing," she told her sternly.

"Handsome as the devil and twice as rich." Lorna waggled her eyebrows, and Sammy Jo couldn't help laughing.

"Give it up, Lorna. I've got a heap of trouble already. But you're welcome to him. As I understand it, he's available."

"How do you know?"

"Well, he asked me to dinner, and I didn't get the impression it was to meet the wife."

"Really?" Her brown eyes sparked with anticipation. "He asked you to dinner?"

"Don't make more of this than there is," Sammy Jo warned, mentally kicking herself for giving Lorna more ammunition. "His cattle jumped the fence, and we had a heck of a time separating mine from his. The invitation was offered as a thank-you."

"Sammy Jo, this is perfect. If he thinks he owes you something, maybe you can get him to invest in the Triple R! I mean, the man's a philanthropist, for Pete's sake. I heard Matt talking. Mr. Cooper's got lots of money and he plans to invest it all right here in Coldwater Flats!"

"Mr. Ryan," Sammy Jo corrected.

"Ask him for a loan. If he feels guilty enough, maybe he'll help you."

"Dream on."

"Hey, it's worth a try, isn't it?"

"No one in their right mind is going to lend a virtual stranger two hundred thousand dollars just because they need it."

"Then *get* to know him. He doesn't have to be a stranger forever."

"Forget it, Lorna. There's got to be another way."

"When you think of it, let me know."

Sammy Jo walked into the hot afternoon, wishing for a breeze. The air was chokingly hot, and still as death. Drawing a breath, she climbed into the pickup, then stared through the windshield, completely at a loss. What should she do? What *could* she do?

Praying for divine intervention, she drove home slowly, passing all the familiar landmarks of Coldwater Flats: the split-rail fence that surrounded the shopping center; the ancient clock tower, which was annually adorned with a six-foot-high cowboy hat over the Fourth of July; the walk along the creek, which edged the little town with its metal, inlaid stars, denoting the names of the rodeo queens all the way back to 1968. Yup. It was a great place to live.

What am I going to do?

Passing the lane to the Riggs place—she could hardly stand to call it Serenity Ranch, and it sure didn't feel like Cooper Ryan's spread yet—Sammy Jo slowed to a stop, letting the engine idle. As she recalled that last conversation with Cooper, she actually shuddered, still acutely embarrassed. Why had she smiled? She knew why. She'd found him attractive in an untamed, hard sort of way.

"Blast it," she cursed softly, remembering how she'd kicked herself for not accepting his dinner invitation, how she'd lain awake all night, tossing and turning and worrying and thinking about her new neighbor. He'd looked so taken aback and kind of cute when she'd flat out refused him, as if he'd never been turned down by a woman before.

And what if she had gone out with him? He'd said it was just a thank-you. Why hadn't she agreed to go? Heck, she could use a free meal, if nothing else!

Because he's trouble. I feel it already.

Sammy Jo threw the pickup in gear and bumped onto her own lane. She wasn't superstitious or particularly religious, but she trusted her instincts implicitly. And man trouble she didn't need!

Halfway down the lane, she yanked the wheel and screeched to a stop beside the gnarled oak tree. Climbing out, she closed her eyes and took several long breaths. Sammy Jo had spent half her childhood, it seemed, high up in the sky, safely concealed within the oak's spreading branches. When other girls' mothers helped out at school and crowded together, chatting and familiar with one another, giving Sammy Jo a glimpse into the kind of dream family she constantly wished for, she ran from the school bus for the oak tree. When she heard girls whisper about her tomboyish ways and laugh and giggle and point, she learned to answer with flying fists instead of tears, and as soon as she was alone, she beelined for the oak tree.

Sammy Jo had spent hours in the tree, working through some of her loneliest, most miserable moments. Silly though it might seem to others, this therapy still worked, and now and again she simply sat down on the root-bumped ground and leaned against the trunk, content to let her friend, the oak, comfort her.

Today, however, she stood to one side, just looking at the tree. There were too many problems at the ranch to waste time soothing her tired emotions. After several minutes, she climbed into the pickup and headed for the house.

When she pulled to a stop, she saw Doc Carey's familiar white horse trailer pulled up next to the gate at the side of her house.

"Well, it's about time," she huffed, venting her fury on the unsuspecting veterinarian. She'd called the man this morning when Tick-Tock, her pregnant mare, had taken a turn for the worse. Off her feed for the better part of two days, the animal had gone head-down and listless this morning, looking for all the world as if she were about to give up and die. In a panic, Sammy Jo had phoned the vet who'd been up to his elbows in surgery in Bend. His assistant had been called to some emergency, as well, so Sammy Jo had stood on one foot, then the other, and tried to make the mare comfortable while she waited. The appointment at the bank had been, in its way, a welcome diversion, but now her worries rushed back, and she barely threw the truck out of gear before racing pell-mell toward the barn.

Doc Carey, sixty, white-haired and the most notorious gossip in the county, had a hand against Tick-Tock's sweaty neck. His expression was grim.

"Well?" Sammy Jo asked. The mare's head was even lower and she shifted her weight constantly. Sammy Jo swallowed, thinking of the unborn foal.

"Looks like some kind of bowel obstruction."

"Serious?"

He grimaced. "Gonna take surgery to get it out."

"Oh, God."

"She'll have to go to the hospital in Bend, but Sammy Jo, her chances aren't so good. And it'll be risky and expensive."

"Everything is," Sammy Jo answered bitterly.

Silently, Sammy Jo weighed the alternatives. The procedure would undoubtedly cost thousands of dollars, and she could still lose the horse and the unborn foal. Tick-Tock wasn't worth that much to the ranch.

But the mare was a personal friend of Sammy Jo's.

Wrapping her arms around her waist, Sammy Jo strode to the other end of the barn and gazed unseeingly across the fenced paddock. Several horses stood together, flicking flies away with their tails. Tick-Tock was only one of several mares due to foal. The Triple R could absorb the loss.

Except . . .

Doc Carey came up behind her, dropping a comforting hand on her shoulder. "I could handle another surgery today if Tick-Tock can handle the ride to Bend."

"Thanks." Sammy Jo swallowed hard against the lump in her throat.

"No problem."

Twenty minutes later, Tick-Tock was bumping her way down the lane and getting ready for the hour's drive to Bend. It was lunacy to think she would pull through. Sheer madness to even try to save her, especially given Sammy Jo's financial situation. But what was life for, if not to try for something better and hope for the best? Quitting seemed so wrong.

Tick-Tock's situation threw Sammy Jo's problems in her face. Hard. She had to come up with an alternative. She had to save the ranch.

As Sammy Jo stood at her bedroom window and glanced across her property to the fence that divided her land from the Riggs place, she chewed on her lower lip. No matter what she thought of Cooper Ryan as a man, he'd been friendly enough, and he sure as hell had enough money. He'd talked Matt Durning into giving her some extra time to get back on her feet. Maybe he'd help her some more, if she asked. Lorna sure seemed to think so. Maybe he got off on that damsel-in-distress stuff.

"Don't be crazy," she reproved herself, but the wheels in her mind kept churning right along. She wasn't exactly the damsel in distress type, but hey, it was worth a try, wasn't it? She didn't have to actually *like* the man, and she never planned on trusting him. But if he could get the bank off her back, she'd give an Oscar-winning performance!

With that in mind, she strode determinedly toward her antique cheval mirror. A little lipstick? Some blush, perhaps?

Moving closer, Sammy Jo critically examined her skin. She was deeply tanned from working outside all summer, and tiny freckles dotted the bridge of her nose. She'd showered right before heading to the bank, so there were no visible dirt smudges, but Sammy Jo considered showering again. A second later, she snorted at herself. What was she trying to find, an investor or a *suitor?*

"Get over yourself," she muttered, brushing her fine blond hair with vicious abandon until it flew and crackled around her head. Dropping the brush, she swiped at the strands that practically stood on end around her face, uttering imprecations all the while. A second later, she'd snapped another rubber band around the mess and was stomping to the door. She stopped herself, infuriated, then reluctantly turned back. Checking her appearance in the mirror once again, she pulled out the rubber band. With difficulty, she tamed her blond hair, then added that blush and a bit of mascara. The clothes would work. She looked feminine and that was a first order of business for this plan.

She actually chuckled as she climbed into the pickup. Immediately, she sobered. This Cooper Ryan fellow might toss her out on her ear. The plan wasn't foolproof.

But...

There were still a few other people in town who might help her. She just hadn't wanted to ask them because she didn't want to owe anybody anything.

For instance, she might get a loan from Tommy Weatherwood. Okay, sure, she didn't believe he'd actually inherited that money, but he had managed to buy himself a place down at Shady Glen, hadn't he? And though he never seemed to work, he sure managed to keep himself in beer and women and still have change left over. She and Tommy weren't all that close anymore, but maybe he'd be interested in a little investment.

Sammy Jo wrinkled her nose. Having Tommy as a business partner was hardly an appealing thought. Well, what about Brent Rollins? He'd been sweet on her for a long time. He wasn't exactly rolling in the green stuff, but he was honest and kind and willing to work hard. And he did own Rollins Real Estate, which seemed to be limping along all right. Brent wasn't too interesting, but maybe he'd see the investment potential of the ranch.

"Oh, nuts," Sammy Jo grumbled, yanking the wheel toward Serenity Ranch's driveway.

Better to start with her new neighbor, she determined, shooting a last glance at the lowering sun.

He wasn't home. Jack and Lettie were there, seated at the table over heaping helpings of strawberry shortcake, but Cooper Ryan was nowhere to be seen.

"Sit down, Sammy Jo," Lettie invited, scraping back her chair.

"No, thanks, I'm kind of in a hurry," Sammy Jo demurred, but before she could say any more, Lettie had plunked a mound of strawberry shortcake on a plate in front of Sammy Jo.

"You lookin' for Mr. Ryan, then?" Jack asked as she sat down.

"I was hoping to talk to him," she admitted.

"He went into town a couple hours ago," he mumbled around a mouthful of whipped cream. "He told me and Lettie about the cattle gettin' out. Heap o' trouble."

"You said it," Sammy Jo agreed.

"Mind now, he's gettin' rid of them hoppity beasts." Clearly, Lettie was waiting for Sammy Jo to dig in.

With a sigh, Sammy Jo complied. She wasn't very hungry. "What's he planning on doing?"

"New livestock. And makin' Serenity a real humdinger of a ranch," Jack revealed.

"Are you two staying on to help?" Sammy Jo asked.

"Sure enough." Jack nodded. "It's a big place. You got a big place, too."

"I know." Sammy Jo heard the implied criticism even though she knew Jack wasn't meaning it that way. "Carl Murdock's coming to help. Glenda told me he's been laid off and was looking for work."

"Good, good." Jack nodded again.

"So, do you know when Mr. Ryan will be back?"

"No. . ." Lettie gave Sammy Jo an assessing look. "The man's got a lot on his mind."

"Oh?" Sammy Jo swallowed some strawberry short-cake. The strawberries were sweet and fresh and the biscuit melted on her tongue. She groaned with appreciation and Lettie's face brightened. "Wow, this is good."

"The best in three counties," Jack said, shooting his wife an amused look.

"Mr. Ryan's been askin' a lot about you," Lettie reported, watching with satisfaction as Sammy Jo scooped up more strawberries and whipped cream.

"Really?" Sammy Jo's heart jumped.

"Now, Lettie," Jack admonished. "Don't start somethin'."

"I'm not startin'. I just know when a man's got a woman on his mind."

"Oh, and how do you know that?"

"He's just got a certain look."

"Well, I think you've got that 'look' wrong," Sammy Jo interrupted this exchange, her voice bubbling with laughter. "I don't even know him very well."

"Who needs to know?" Lettie lifted her shoulders dismissively. "He's sweet on you, Sammy Jo, my girl."

"Oh, please!"

"Lettie's just yakkin', you know." Jack threw his wife a quelling look, which she ignored completely.

"He's been askin' lots of questions. Wants to know all about Sammy Jo Whalen of Ridge Range Ranch, don't you know. But I was careful. I didn't say too much. A woman's got to have some mystery."

Sammy Jo shook her head, grinning with embarrassment. She didn't believe a word of Lettie's fantasy, but the idea made her feel good, anyway. Men didn't look at her that way. They looked at Bev Hawkins that way, but then who wouldn't? Bev oozed sensuality, and even though she was supposedly happily married, men's gazes lingered on her hips and legs whenever she sashayed by. Sammy Jo had a tendency to clump through a room and she'd heard the remarks that followed her passing.

" . . . stubborn as sin . . . not quite pretty enough to make up for that fast mouth . . . shoulda been born a boy . . ."

"You'd better not let Mr. Ryan know what you think," Sammy Jo advised, fighting back the little spurt of pain those memories caused. "He might figure you lost your mind."

Jack laughed aloud and signaled Lettie to serve him up some more. His wife merely glared at him.

"I know what I know," Lettie insisted stubbornly.

"You're an old woman with a big imagination," her husband told her.

"You can just get yourself some more shortcake!"

Jack laughed.

Sammy Jo scraped back her chair, deciding she'd better get out of here before World War III erupted. "Thanks. It was delicious."

"You want to find that man?" Lettie's hands were on her hips. "Go on in to town. You can't miss that shiny black truck of his. You'll catch up to him."

"I can talk to him later."

"Go on, now." She shooed Sammy Jo outside. "Mark my words. He's a man who's lookin' for a woman like you."

"A woman like me," Sammy Jo repeated, not sure she liked the sound of that.

"Someone who knows her own mind. None of that namby-pamby stuff. Go on after him. It'd be good for both of you."

Ten minutes later, Sammy Jo found herself parked in front of the Triple R, a frown darkening her pretty face. She didn't believe Lettie for a minute, but that didn't mean she'd changed her mind about finding Cooper. But was she being too anxious? She knew enough about human nature to know that nobody wants to help someone who's so desperate. She had to play it cool, be aloof.

But sitting at home wasn't going to solve her problems.

You can't get too mad if things don't go just your way, she reminded herself.

With new resolve, Sammy Jo ground the gears and tore away from the Triple R toward the streets of Coldwater Flats. Correction. The *street* of Coldwater Flats. The town was really just one long main street with a few little arterials that meandered aimlessly out from the center like crooked spokes. Spying her cowboy hat resting on the seat beside her, she jammed it on her head.

"Be cool," she told herself again, practicing a smile of pleasure and surprise when she "accidentally" ran into Cooper Ryan.

Cooper leaned across the scarred bar of the Last Stand Saloon and said quietly to the bartender, "Know anything about a woman named Sammy Jo Whalen?"

"Sammy Jo?" The bartender grinned, showing spaces where there should have been teeth. "You mean the Princess!"

"The Princess?" Cooper repeated blankly.

"Who's askin'?" a deep voice growled from the end of the bar.

Cooper peered through the haze of smoke to the hulk of a man seated on the last stool. A thick red beard covered a weathered face. At first glance, he appeared to be in his forties, but as Cooper walked down the expanse of the bar, he realized the man was probably around thirty.

"Cooper Ryan," he said, thrusting out his hand. The man shook it, nearly crushing the life from Cooper's hand as he did so. Cooper raised his eyebrows, wondering if he'd offended the man by asking about Sammy Jo and if he and Red-beard were about to end up in a fight.

But apparently Red-beard just liked to crush bones because he said amiably enough, "Sammy Jo Whalen's a rodeo princess."

"*Ex*-rodeo princess," a feminine voice corrected somewhere to Cooper's right.

Glancing around, Cooper saw a woman in skintight jeans hunched over her pool shot. A cigarette was clenched firmly between hot-pink, lipsticked lips. She squinted against the smoke, lined up the shot and smoothly pocketed the number twelve ball with enough English on the cue ball to set herself up for three more straight shots.

Red-beard watched without much interest. "Sammy Jo Whalen's a regular tigress. Took down my little brother in a wrestling match when they was at Harding Elementary. Humiliated the hell out of him. He won't talk to her 'til this day."

"She's a pain in the butt," the woman added with a sniff.

"Ginny, there, don't like her much. But then she's just jealous." Red-beard grinned.

"I ain't jealous of nobody!"

"Except Sammy Jo. Ginny can't never forgive her for stealin' Brent Rollins's heart," Red-beard added for Cooper's benefit. "Josh Johnson," he said by way of introduction. "So, what'cha askin' about Sammy Jo for?"

"Probably got an itch for the Princess, too," Ginny declared, slamming a ball into the pocket.

"I bought the Riggs place. Sammy Jo is my new neighbor."

"Serenity Ranch?" Ginny looked up, impressed. "They was askin' a lot for that place." For the second time since arriving in Coldwater Flats, Cooper got the once-over from a woman, but unlike Sammy Jo, Ginny's gaze lingered on a few spots that both amused Cooper and made him slightly uncomfortable.

"So, you're that corporate rancher, huh?" Josh regarded Cooper with a frown.

"Word travels pretty fast around here," Cooper said dryly.

"There's more going on in Coldwater Flats than anything you can catch on them soap operas," the bartender chimed in, sliding Cooper a beer across the bar's nicked finish.

Cooper took a long draft. It had been a week since his meeting with Sammy Jo, a week in which he'd rounded up his cattle and sold them off, bringing in the new herd he'd acquired over the past few months. Everything had gone like clockwork. His plan was moving right along.

Except Sammy Jo Whalen hadn't been far from his thoughts, and he wasn't certain which way to jump when it came to her. He wanted the ranch the easiest way possible, but that meant booting out Sammy Jo. Tonight he'd wandered into the Last Stand Saloon intending to get more information. It was the only tavern in town that looked as if the windows had ever been cleaned. He hadn't wasted time; he'd asked about Sammy Jo Whalen straightaway, and once again, the people spoke right up about her.

That was something he'd learned. The good folks of Coldwater Flats were more than willing to talk about

Sammy Jo. Everyone had an opinion. Whatever else you could say about Sammy Jo Whalen, she was unforgettable.

Ginny laid down her pool cue and walked up next to Cooper. Her sharp eyes sized him up. "So, you bought the land next to the Princess and now you're askin' about her."

"Well . . . yeah."

"Was I right?" she demanded.

"Right?"

"About that itch . . ."

Cooper smiled. "I was just curious."

"Ahh . . ." Ginny lifted a knowing eyebrow.

He could practically smell the interest growing. If he wasn't careful, Sammy Jo would hear of his questions, and he had a feeling she was smart enough to put two and two together and get at least four. It seemed safer to let them believe what they wanted to believe. "She's a very pretty woman."

"Ain't that the truth!" Josh snorted.

"Stubborn as sin," Ginny stated flatly.

"A lot of guys have looked at her," the bartender offered, putting in his two cents' worth. "But then she starts in bein' all bossy and stubborn and they hightail it fast."

"Gonna take a real man to tame that wildcat." Josh grinned at Cooper.

Cooper didn't respond to that. "I saw her at the bank the other day," he said casually.

"Oh, yeah." Josh nodded sagely. "Money troubles, and lots of 'em."

"Old Gil liked the smell of a bad investment," the bartender said.

"Bees to the honey," Ginny agreed.

"What happened?" Cooper asked, settling himself on a bar stool.

"The old man always wanted a boy." Josh leaned back as if preparing for a good, long yarn. Ginny hopped onto the stool on Cooper's left, and the bartender, who introduced himself as Sam, leaned forward, showing annoyance when a couple strolled in and looked at him expectantly. Muttering beneath his breath, he went to serve them, as Josh continued, "Gil treated Sammy Jo like a boy, and she acted like one, too. Learned to rope and ride from the ranch hands. Free as the wind and rawhide-tough. When all the other girls were gettin' into nylons and hairspray and boys, Sammy Jo was herdin' cattle and gettin' sick on rotgut liquor down at Shady Glen with Tommy Weatherwood and a few of his friends."

"Tommy ended up buyin' hisself a place at Shady Glen," Ginny interjected.

Josh glared at her for interrupting. "'Course, Sammy Jo never took to liquor, not like Tommy, anyhows." Josh glanced at Ginny, who snorted and muttered something into her beer glass. Cooper decided Ginny must have liked Tommy Weatherwood at one time as well as Brent Rollins. Whether Sammy Jo meant to or not, she'd made an enemy of Ginny just by being more attractive.

"You wanna know about Sammy Jo, you should talk to Lorna Doon," Ginny told him.

"Lorna works at the bank," Josh supplied. "Name's Lorna Miller now. She and Sammy Jo are friends. Lorna's got a daughter the same age as Ginny's," he added for reasons Cooper didn't quite understand until Ginny blasted Josh with a hard, cold glare. Apparently, Ginny didn't want Cooper to know all the facets of her personal life.

"Sammy Jo took to animals," Josh said picking up his story. "Half the time she was tryin' to give away barn kittens when old man Riggs tried to drown 'em."

"Riggs drowned kittens?" Cooper repeated, appalled. He was no cat-lover, but good Lord!

"Riggs didn't have no heart," Ginny explained. "Had a lot of cats and just did away with 'em. Probably did the same to puppies, but no one knows for sure. Named that damn place Serenity Ranch, too. Now, ain't that funny?"

"I'm changing the name," Cooper told them as Sam returned from serving his other customers.

"To what?" the bartender asked.

The Triple R. "I don't know yet," was the only answer Cooper could give. When he bought out Sammy Jo Whalen, he'd adopt the name for the whole spread, but until then he had to be mum.

"When Riggs up and died, we thought Gil Whalen would buy Serenity," Josh said. Cooper hesitated, his beer halfway to his lips. "Combinin' those two ranches would make it the best darn place around. Prime ranchin' land. A bunch of developers looked at Serenity, even made offers to Gil for the Triple R, too. Gil practically ran 'em off with a shotgun. Then he let the whole damn thing slip away. Don't that beat all?"

"Sammy Jo seems to want to make a go of it," Cooper said.

"Well, she ain't but one bitty girl. She can't do it."

Cooper didn't think Sammy Jo would like being called a girl, let alone a bitty one. She was ranch-tough and a woman through and through.

"Her uncle came down to buy the place after Gil's death," Sam revealed. "Don't know what happened, but he left with smoke comin' out of his ears, he was so mad at Sammy Jo."

"She certainly knows how to win friends," Cooper remarked dryly.

"She's trouble," Ginny remarked flatly.

"You know, you oughta make an offer on the Triple R, if you're interested," Sam suggested. "Sammy Jo has got a lot of financial problems. You might just be the answer to her prayers."

"She's probably waitin' for some Prince Charming to save her." Ginny smiled meanly. "Go on, mister. Make her an offer. I bet she snaps it up without even a thank-you."

A vision of Sammy Jo Whalen crowded inside Cooper's mind: slim, volatile, headstrong, willful and sure of herself. But she had the softest-looking lips, and a mouth, though stubbornly set, that seemed to want to smile. Her hair was that natural yellow blond, just shy of golden, and her irises were the brightest, most luminous emerald he thought he'd ever seen.

And she possessed two of the most charming, irresistible dimples he'd ever laid eyes on.

Some strange, deeply buried, chivalrous part of himself wanted to help her, but he shoved those thoughts aside and concentrated on his own self-interests. And the patrons of the Last Stand Saloon had just given him a reason to make an offer.

"I don't know," Cooper said, playing along. "Buying the Triple R might be more than I want to bite off right now."

"Oh, go on!" Ginny waved at him. "You can afford it."

"It's not a matter of money," Cooper said.

"What, then?" Sam asked.

Three pairs of eyes regarded him with frank curiosity. "I got the impression she really loves that ranch," Cooper said, treading carefully.

"She's gonna love it right into the ground," Josh snorted.

"You'd be doin' her a favor by makin' an offer," Sam added.

"You really think so?" Cooper asked innocently.

"I know so!" Ginny jumped down from her stool and headed back to the pool table. "Not that I give a damn what happens to the Princess."

"I do," Josh disagreed. "I like Sammy Jo a bunch."

"Me, too," Sam declared. He pulled two more beers without being asked and slid them to Josh and Cooper.

Cooper rubbed his jaw reflectively. "Well, she sure doesn't need that ranch. It's an albatross around her neck."

"Huh?" Josh looked across the top of his beer and licked foam from his beard.

Ginny came back, snapped her fingers at Sam who pulled her a beer, too. She took a long swallow.

Deciding it was time to lay his cards on the table, Cooper took a stand. "She'd be better off selling the place, paying off her debts and buying herself a whole new life," he proclaimed decisively.

A tad too decisively as it turned out, because Ginny commenced to choke and sputter, coughing so hard Cooper had to slam her on the back a couple of times.

Gasping, she came up for air. "You go tell her that, mister! And after you do, come back here and let us know how she took the news!"

Josh, Sam and Ginny suddenly broke into uproarious laughter. They might all agree that Cooper ought to buy the Triple R, but convincing Sammy Jo of that fact appeared to be another matter altogether.

"Sounds like Ms. Whalen doesn't take kindly to advice," Cooper said.

They all doubled over again. And that's when Sammy Jo Whalen herself strode into the Last Stand Saloon.

Chapter Three

Conversation stopped as fast as flames doused by a bucket of cold water. Sammy Jo looked around in confusion. You'd think the patrons of the Last Stand Saloon had never seen a woman in a skirt before.

"Well?" she demanded of the room at large. Immediately, everyone's nose went back to their beer glasses, pool balls clicked and the din of conversation returned.

Sam scurried over to her end of the bar. "What would you like, Sammy Jo?"

"I don't really want anything, Sam. I was looking for…"

Her gaze landed squarely on Cooper at that moment. He was leaning against the curve of the bar at the far end, elbows back, chest thrust forward so that his denim jacket revealed the straining buttons of his shirt. There wasn't an ounce of fat on the man's body. She didn't have to stretch her imagination much to know how hard those muscles must be.

"I was looking for Doc Carey," she lied, switching gears.

"The doc don't drink," Sam said, regarding her curiously.

"One of my mares is sick and me and the doc have been missing each other. Just thought I'd look here."

She wasn't fooling anyone, but Sam wasn't sharp enough to get the picture. She hoped Cooper wasn't paying close attention to their conversation. He had ears that heard too much and eyes that saw too much. She knew that for a fact already.

"Hi, there, Sammy Jo," Josh Johnson greeted her, rising from his stool and gesturing her to take it.

"Hi, Josh. Thanks, but I'm just stopping by."

"Have you met your new neighbor?"

Sammy Jo spared a glance at Cooper whose eyes slid her a disinterested look in return. "We've met. How are those cattle doing?"

"All taken care of," Cooper answered.

"Meaning?"

"They're gone." His voice was tight and Sammy Jo couldn't help flushing, mad at herself for antagonizing him right off the bat. What was she thinking of?

"Is there a problem?" Cooper drawled. Everyone looked at Sammy Jo expectantly.

"Not that I know of. Sam, I'd like a beer, after all," she called to the bartender.

"What brought you to the Last Stand?" Josh asked her.

"Oh, nothing much."

"Said she's looking for Doc Carey," Sam supplied, handing her a foaming glass.

Sammy Jo ground her teeth together as Josh said, "Now, you know the doc don't drink."

She could feel Cooper's heavy, assessing gaze. Her flush deepened, hot and embarrassingly red, she was sure. "Tick-Tock's got a problem. Some kind of bowel obstruction."

The men instantly forgot their needling and offered words of worry and consolation. Cooper looked from one face to another, until Josh explained, "Sammy Jo's mare, Tick-Tock, is pregnant. Bowel obstruction...sounds bad."

"Where's the mare now?" Cooper asked.

She could hardly mention Doc Carey had taken the horse into Bend without revealing she'd made this stupid little lie up in the first place. "I got her to the veterinary hospital in Bend," she said dismissively.

Josh wouldn't let it go. "Who's working on her? Timmy?"

Timmy was Doc Carey's assistant vet and more butcher than surgeon. No self-respecting livestock owner would trust him. "Lord, I hope not," she muttered fervently.

A round of "Here, here" followed with lifted glasses and nods of agreement. Cooper's mouth quirked in amusement but he raised his beer along with the others.

"So, Sammy Jo, why're ya all dressed up?" Ginny Martin asked, leaning on her pool cue and slipping Sammy Jo a mean-mouthed look.

"I've been to the bank." *Just my luck,* Sammy Jo thought with an inward sigh. She and Ginny's rivalry went way back, ever since Brent Rollins chose Sammy Jo in the sixth grade as his junior court rodeo princess. It had been her first crown, a kind of foreshadowing of the future, but Ginny had never forgiven her. Sammy Jo hadn't bothered to mend fences. What was the point? Ginny wouldn't believe Sammy Jo didn't give a damn about Brent then, now, or ever.

"That the only reason?" Ginny persisted, eyeing the open-throat of Sammy Jo's white blouse. "I've never seen ya dress up for anything, 'cept'n maybe to accept a trophy. Did ya know Sammy Jo here's a local celebrity?'' Ginny turned to Cooper with a not-so-nice grin plastered across her face. Sammy Jo wished she'd just shut up. ''Barrel-racing mostly, but she's collected some trophies for trick-riding and other things. Even won a heart or two, though she'd like to tell ya different.''

Burning inside, Sammy Jo wondered what was going on between Ginny and Cooper Ryan. Not that she cared. Much. But she hated being a source of amusement to any-one. ''If you're talking about Brent, why don't you just spit it out?'' Sammy Jo challenged.

Ginny's lips tightened and she turned back to her game, slamming several balls into the pockets.

''So, how did it go with Matt Durning?'' Cooper asked casually.

Sammy Jo sipped at her beer, trying hard not to even look at Cooper. She didn't know why, but it bothered her to meet him eye-to-eye except for brief little glances. ''It went bad.''

''He's calling the loan?''

''He's called the loan,'' she corrected. ''I've just been begging for more time. It really burns me up. We've never missed a payment to anybody. He has no right!''

''We?''

''Gil—my dad—and I. My dad raised me.'' Why she'd added that bit of trivia, she didn't rightly know.

''How's your income statement look?'' Cooper asked. ''Bankers like fat, healthy income statements.''

Sammy Jo met his gaze squarely this time. An ironic smile lifted one corner of her mouth. ''It sucks,'' she ad-mitted.

He grinned. And then he laughed aloud, the sound deep and musical, reaching into Sammy Jo's insides and mixing them up in a way that made her uncomfortable. His teeth were white and straight, his lips thin and yet, sexy and appealing, in a way no man's had a right to be.

Sammy Jo yanked her thoughts back hard, annoyed at this flight into fancy. She felt like a teenager, for God's sake, thinking about the man's body parts while her heart fluttered and trembled as if it were about to quit altogether. Good Lord.

"That's too bad, Sammy Jo," Josh commiserated.

"A real bitch," Sam added.

If Ginny had heard this exchange, she gave no sign of it. For that Sammy Jo was glad. That "real bitch" comment was just aching to be interpreted in other ways, and Sammy Jo didn't feel like getting into it with Ginny.

"What do you plan to do with Serenity?" Sammy Jo asked.

"Before or after I change the name?"

Sammy Jo laughed. "Thank God!"

"Seems to be the general consensus around here," Cooper observed with a good-natured drawl.

"When Ethan Riggs named the place Serenity Ranch, my father nearly took a shotgun to him," Sammy Jo said, her voice bubbling with amusement. "It used to be called Cotton Creek Ranch, after the stream, but it's been years since Riggs bought it from the family that first homesteaded the place. I don't suppose you'd be interested in changing the name back?"

"You never know," Cooper said, sidestepping the question.

"Whatever you'd choose, it's bound to be better than Serenity Ranch." She snorted. "Sounds like a retirement home for has-been rodeo stock."

"Mr. Ryan's bound to come up with something," Ginny interjected.

Her tone caught Sammy Jo's attention. There was something so calculating and slithery about it. Was Ginny interested in Cooper? She certainly acted as though she was, Sammy Jo thought, watching Ginny lean over the pool table once more. It irked her that Ginny played such a mean game of pool. Sammy Jo was hopeless at it. But then, Ginny didn't know the first thing about ranching, so maybe they were even.

"Care to play me?" Ginny asked Cooper suggestively.

Sammy Jo burned. With difficulty, she kept her feelings out of her face. If Cooper Ryan fell for Ginny's games, he wasn't the man she thought he was.

"Can't right now," he told her. "I've got to be somewhere."

"You meeting someone?" Ginny asked quickly.

Sammy Jo wanted to hear the answer to that, too.

"No, I've just got work to do."

He scooped up his hat and headed for the door. Sammy Jo followed him.

"I know you're in a hurry, but I wanted to talk to you," she said.

"What about?"

"Oh . . . well . . ." She darted a glance to Josh, Sam and Ginny who were all staring unabashedly. "The Triple R."

Cooper's gaze followed hers. After a moment, in that slow drawl she was becoming familiar with, he said, "I skipped out on dinner tonight with Lettie and Jack. Thought I'd grab something in town. You want to join me?"

Sammy Jo's breath caught. This was the perfect opportunity. Better than she could have wished for.

"I owe you a dinner," he reminded her.

"Yes, you do," she agreed with a smile.

She didn't turn around, but she could well imagine the annoyance that must be sharpening Ginny's face. Her smile widened into dimples.

Cooper held the door for her, his gaze rapt on her face. Uncomfortable under that frank appraisal, Sammy Jo instantly sobered, wondering what he found so keenly interesting about her face. "Tell me about the Triple R," he invited as he strode past his truck and her pickup and they meandered down the street to a steak house, little more than a hole in the wall but renowned for its grilled T-bones.

"You're pretty familiar with Coldwater Flats already," Sammy Jo remarked as they stood outside the restaurant.

"I know this place and The Riverside are the only restaurants in town worth speaking of. I haven't been to The Riverside yet."

"The Riverside has better atmosphere, but more of the locals come here."

"If you want to switch...?"

"I'm really more interested in conversation than food," she admitted candidly.

For an answer, Cooper inclined his head and held open the door. Smoke hung in the air, as much from the wildly sizzling grill at the back of the place as from cigarettes. Sammy Jo found a spot as far away from the smoke as possible and Cooper stretched out in a chair opposite her. His legs were long, lean and seemed to surround her. Sammy Jo tucked in her knees and felt intimidated.

"You really don't have to buy me dinner."

He shook his head. "It's payback time."

Staring at the menu, which she knew by heart, Sammy Jo said, "I'm not all that hungry. I think I'll have a salad."

"You're not one of those women who starve themselves to save their figures, are you?" he asked curiously.

Sammy Jo shot him a look. "Do I look like the type?"

He grinned. "No."

Her hands were sweating. Wiping them on her skirt, she dived in. "I've just got some things on my mind, and food's not one of them."

"Y'all ready?" the waitress asked, pen poised. Dressed in jeans and a plaid shirt, she shifted her gaze from Cooper to Sammy Jo and back again.

"I'll have a T-bone and the lady wants a salad," Cooper said.

"Ranch dressing," Sammy Jo told the woman before she could rush away. The place wasn't known for its congenial staff.

"Back to the Triple R," Cooper said, settling still deeper into his chair. He still wore his cowboy hat and it settled low over his eyes, making him seem half-asleep though Sammy Jo was certain he was as awake and alert as an eagle.

"You already know that I'm having some financial trouble. My father died a while back and well, you heard Matt Durning…I've only got a few months left before the bank takes over."

She felt like an idiot. Her heart was pounding so loudly she could scarcely hear herself, and what she did hear worried her. Was that really *her* voice, so breathy and filled with desperation?

"Three months," Cooper said.

"If I'm lucky. So, I was thinking…"

"Go on," he said when her voice faded out.

"I was thinking…" Sammy Jo didn't know if she could go through with this. It was ridiculous to believe he would help her. Insane!

A vision of Uncle Peter's gloating face crossed her mind. She could practically see him shaking hands with Matt Durning as they finalized a deal over the Triple R. As soon as the bank took over, she had no doubt Uncle Peter would be at Valley Federal's front door, scooping up *her* ranch and enjoying the last laugh against her father.

"I was thinking maybe you could help me," she blurted out.

Cooper Ryan's blue eyes bored into hers. "How so?"

"You seemed kind of sympathetic at the bank," Sammy Jo rushed on, "and I just thought . . . maybe . . . you'd be interested in helping me out."

"You want to sell?"

"No!" Sammy Jo gasped. "Oh, no. The ranch is mine. I just thought I could talk you into investing."

"Two hundred thousand dollars?"

She shrugged unhappily. He'd heard every word in Matt's office. "They've called my loan."

"Not interested."

His cold answer took her breath away. Sammy Jo stared into his dark blue eyes, totally annihilated. She'd pegged him wrong. An aborted spurt of laughter sounded behind her. She turned slightly and looked up. Ginny and Josh had made their way over from the Last Stand, and were standing by her table. Ginny was laughing.

Sammy Jo's cheeks flamed. She'd made a fool out of herself in the worst way.

"Sammy Jo, honey, not all guys are as gullible as Brent," Ginny stated smugly.

"Mind your own business!" Sammy Jo seethed.

"You can't always get your way just because you think the world owes it to you."

"Did Mr. Ryan give you his advice, Sammy Jo?" Josh asked. He wasn't laughing like Ginny, but he wasn't helping the situation, either.

"Advice?" Sammy Jo stared bleakly at Cooper.

Cooper hesitated, shooting Josh a look so dark Sammy Jo wondered what was really going on. "I suggested you sell the place,'' Cooper told her, but his gaze was sharp on Josh.

"Over my dead body."

"I'm serious, Sammy Jo," Cooper responded, his gaze softening.

The way he said her name made her stomach twist and her throat tighten. She didn't like the feeling. And she didn't like what he was saying.

But he kept on saying it, anyway. "You've got a big place to run there. It's hard enough for a whole crew of ranch hands, but for one woman it's impossible."

All she heard was *woman*. Woman, as in weak, incompetent, unworthy and prone to hysteria. Oh, she'd heard it all from her father a hundred times. A thousand times.

Ginny's smile was so big Sammy Jo could practically feel the waves of amusement it emanated. "Do you mind?" Sammy Jo demanded of Ginny and Josh. Ginny looked as if she were planted for the next millennium, but Josh hustled her to a table out of earshot.

"Thanks for that unsolicited advice, Mr. Ryan," Sammy Jo told Cooper through her teeth. "But I've got someone to help me around the ranch."

"Who?"

"None of your business!"

"One person? You've got one person to help you?"

Oh, he was pressing it! Why was he being so awful now? She could have sworn there was more to him the night that he'd asked her to dinner. He'd seemed so sincere. So friendly. But now he was as cold as a rattler! "I've got a whole army to help me, as a matter of fact!"

"Really?"

"I'm *not* selling."

"When you change your mind, let me know. I'd be more than willing to help out."

"I'll bet," she muttered. She had half a mind to kick him in the shins. He was just like all the rest of them. Worse. What had ever possessed her to think he might be interested in helping her? Really helping her?

Lorna. Lorna had told her the man was a philanthropist. Hah! Opportunist, more like it.

"You're going to have to make a decision soon," Cooper went on. "Don't wait until the last minute. You'll go under. You need to deal from strength."

"I think I can get by without the patronization," she squeezed out through her teeth.

His dark eyebrows snapped together. "I'm just telling you to be smart."

"Why don't you go tell it to somebody who cares?"

The waitress clattered Sammy Jo's salad down so hard the lettuce leaves jumped onto the table. Sammy Jo stared at it, seething. Without another word, she slid out of her seat and strode through the front door. On the street, she stopped long enough to take a deep breath. Blasted men. They all thought the same way! Nobody wanted to help her. They just wanted to steal from her. And why not? Women—no, *girls* like her!—were easy pickings. The men in this town were all counting on her to fail by virtue of her sex alone!

"The hell I will!" she said.

Smoke-filled air swelled around her as the door opened again and Cooper followed her outside. Sammy Jo stiffened, refusing to look at him.

"You don't want to sell, I can't blame you," he said reasonably. His very reasonableness infuriated her further. "And I don't like being the one to make you face reality, but Sammy Jo, you're out of options."

"I know my situation."

"Nobody's going to help you," he observed flatly. "People don't have money to waste. You've got a losing enterprise going there, and in my experience, women are too tenderhearted to make the really tough decisions in business that need to be made."

She turned slowly, her expression full of scorn. "What do you know about women?"

"A lot. And they all react the same way."

"Do they?" One blond eyebrow arched.

Cooper's own temper was getting the better of him. Had Sammy Jo known him better she might have been surprised. Over the years, he'd learned how to be a sphinx when it came to hiding his emotions. His ex-wife, Pamela, had cured him of ever showing any feelings. If he did, she'd pounce on him, carving up his heart in tiny little pieces, taking a part of his soul each time she succeeded in wounding him, fooling him yet again.

"Yes, they do," he said forcefully. "And just because you think you're different, you're not."

"Wait 'til the feminists find out about you." Sammy Jo's nostrils flared in outrage. "They'll hang you by your... well, I'm sure you get the picture."

"Insulting me isn't going to save your ranch. There's only one way to come out of this alive and that's sell. Sell to the highest bidder."

Harsh words. Words it hurt to utter. Cooper clamped down on his emotions and tried to ignore the piquant face turned up to him.

"You really are a corporate rancher, aren't you?"

That stopped him for a moment. "What does that mean?"

"No heart."

"Bankers don't care if you've got heart," he observed tightly. "They only want cash. Now, can we go back and have dinner? I'm sorry to be so tough, but I can see there's no other way with you.''

"I'm not hungry anymore, Mr. Ryan,'' Sammy Jo told him, her green eyes shaded in the half-light. "And I'm going to hang on to the Triple R. Just watch me.''

"You're too damn stubborn for your own good.''

"Maybe so. But you're wrong. I'm not out of options yet. There's still another way.''

He shook his head a bit regretfully. "No, there isn't.''

"Oh, yes, there is.'' Sammy Jo swept away toward her pickup, her denim skirt billowing, the white sleeves of her blouse bright against the darkened sky.

"What is it?'' he called after her.

She yanked three times on her pickup's door, but when he started to come to her aid, she quelled him with a cold glance he could feel from ten feet away.

"When I think of it, you'll be the first to know. . . .''

It was all well and good offering a challenge to the likes of Cooper Ryan, but Sammy Jo learned it was a lot tougher to follow through. Days passed with no relief as bills piled up, and she felt the unseen breath of Matt Durning of Valley Federal heating the back of her neck. The only positive note was that after surgery, Tick-Tock had come home minus a two-foot length of intestine but otherwise healthy, happy and still pregnant, and she'd been shipped home with a clean bill of health. However, the bill from Doc Carey hadn't arrived yet, which was just as well since she had absolutely no way of paying it.

Despair filled her as she trekked up Cotton Creek, searching for the reason the water had slowed to a sluggish trickle down below. As furious as she'd been with Cooper, she couldn't fault his logic—though it nearly killed her to admit as much. She did need to sell.

"Damn it all." She sighed heavily, then swore more violently as her foot slipped through the mud into the stream. Cold water streamed over the top of her boot, filling it up. *"Ecch!"* she yelled, pulling it off. Picking up the mud-covered, sorry-looking snakeskin boot, she poured filthy, brown water from it.

Suddenly, she could stand it no longer. Flinging herself onto the ground, she stared at the dusky blue sky, then threw her arm across her eyes, fighting back the unaccustomed sting of tears. Why did it have to be so hard. *Why?* She'd wanted to hit Cooper Ryan for verbalizing the truth. It wasn't his affair. He had no right.

But he had spoken cold, hard facts, and though Sammy Jo had wanted to slam her fists into his broad chest and make him take them back, she wasn't stupid enough not to admit the truth to herself at least.

So, how, *how,* could she save the ranch?

A meadowlark sang, sweet and pure. Sammy Jo listened dully, consumed with her problems. She *was* out of options.

"Might as well sell the place to him," she whispered, a lump hard in her throat. Better than letting Uncle Peter get his greedy hands on it.

Rubbing her hot neck with one hand, Sammy Jo grimaced. Next week was the Fourth of July. She'd promised herself that if she didn't have her problems solved by then, she'd go to Brent Rollins and have Rollins Realty put her ranch up for sale.

Except she just couldn't bear it.

After a few more moments of self-pity, she jumped to her feet, scrubbing at her cheeks, angry with herself for giving in to despair. Yanking on the soaking boot, she gritted her teeth and followed the winding, gurgling stream until it slid under several felled aspens and twisted into a copse of trees.

Sammy Jo climbed over a dry, beetle-infested log and fought against a canopy of twisting blackberry vines. Swearing to beat the band, she pulled thorny branches from her hair and suddenly swept in a breath. Hidden in the trees, a beaver dam stood proud and strong, a magnificent structure of mud and branches, looking as sturdy as the Rock of Gibraltar.

Pure pleasure shot through her as a flat tail slapped the water in warning. Instantly, ripples stood in the pool, the only remnants of the furry creatures whose heads had been sticking up only moments before.

"Oh, ho," Sammy Jo said, grinning. "So, you guys have been busy little beavers, huh? No wonder I can't get any water down below. You little monsters have been hoarding it!"

The only answer was the soft ripple of water where the stream continlued, a weak stepdaughter to its robust mother now trapped in a huge, tranquil pool above the dam. The dam itself was mud and stripped aspens, and some of the branches were six inches in diameter.

Sammy Jo enjoyed the moment, then reality slowly intruded again and she considered the extent of the problem. She needed the creek to run free and full. She needed the water for her fields.

And the beavers weren't planning to make it easy for her.

Sitting down on a grayed stump, Sammy Jo tucked her chin into her palms and sighed. She'd never felt so tied up before. Action was her strong suit, and Gil had wound her up so good and tight she couldn't breathe, let alone move.

Absently, Sammy Jo watched a water skipper skim the pond's glasslike surface. Gil. Her father. Who'd wanted the best for her, misdirected as his vision might be. He'd wanted her to marry. To start a family and have a man to help her run Ridge Range Ranch.

A man. A partner. A husband...

"A husband," Sammy Jo said aloud, rolling the words on her tongue, tasting the idea. She shuddered. It was a terrible idea.

Unbidden, a vision of Cooper Ryan's strong arms filled her mind. She could see them so clearly, to the dark dusting of hair, the deep veins, the masculine hands. And his eyes. So cold and hard and blue, and yet, somewhere in their depths she'd seen more, a passion that had reached out and touched her.

"You idiot!" She clapped her hands to her face, horrified by her thoughts.

A husband. Not a lover. Good grief! Whenever she thought of Cooper, she saw him in blocks of body parts. Hormonal influence?

"Blast it!" Sammy Jo leaped to her feet. She'd never had these problems before. But that's how she thought of Cooper, she realized with self-disgust. Arms, legs, eyes, hips...

Shuddering, she made her way back to the house, lost in thought. A husband. A man to share the running of the Triple R with. Someone strong, but not too strong, not as strong as Cooper Ryan anyway. Someone like Brent Rollins, or, if she was really in a pinch, Tommy Weatherwood.

She inhaled deeply, closed her eyes and fought back a stab of conscience. It could work. She could make it work. And, by God, if that's what it took to save the ranch, she *would* make it work!

Chapter Four

"A husband!" Lorna clapped her hands to her sumptuous bosom. "Oh-my-God!"

"Shh." Sammy Jo glanced guiltily down the street as she and Lorna sat on a bench outside the bank and shared deli sandwiches for lunch. "Keep your voice down."

"Who? Who? *Who?*"

"I don't have anyone special in mind," Sammy Jo admitted.

"You mean, you want me to help you pick one?"

"No!"

Sammy Jo deliberately bit deeply into her turkey sandwich. She should never have confided in Lorna, and she wouldn't have except that Lorna had been teasing her about her drop-dead gorgeous neighbor who looked like heaven in bleached-out denim and it was enough to afflict Lorna with a serious case of "chills, fever and a desperate need for a long recuperation in bed." To shut her up, Sammy Jo had changed the subject by asking if Lorna thought it was time for Sammy Jo to find a husband.

Lorna's dark eyes danced. "Is your sudden decision out of lust, or to save that ranch of yours?"

"I don't have the least interest in lust," Sammy Jo declared primly.

"Shoot," Lorna said, disappointed.

"Gil made certain I'd be forced to turn to outside financial help. He did it because he wanted me to get married. After raising me like a favored son, he couldn't trust me enough to make my own decisions."

"You're pretty mad at him, aren't you?"

"I sure was." She shrugged. "But it's time I got married, anyway."

She wrapped up the remains of her sandwich and threw a few bits on the ground for the birds skipping along the grass, then dropped the sack into a nearby garbage can. Lorna did the same.

"Well, I wish I'd been right about Mr. Cooper. I thought for sure he'd help you." Lorna sighed.

"Mr. *Ryan* thought he was helping me by giving me some advice."

"Nobody who offers free advice is helping. Free advice is just what it's worth—nothing." They walked toward the front doors of the bank. "Are you really thinking about marrying some guy just to save the Triple R?"

"I'm thinking about marriage to get married," Sammy Jo corrected firmly, though she knew it was a lie. A half lie, anyway.

"Well, you must have somebody at the top of your list."

"My dad favored Tommy Weatherwood."

"Oh, Sammy Jo!"

Lorna's look of sheer horror made Sammy Jo grin. "Actually, I was thinking about driving over to Rollins Real Estate."

Tucking her arms beneath her breasts, Lorna gave Sammy Jo a long look. "Brent's been sweet on you since sixth grade. You be nice."

"What do you mean?" Sammy Jo demanded, affronted.

"You better be serious about this, or someone's like to get hurt."

Sammy Jo stared after her, openmouthed. She had no intention of hurting Brent or anyone else. Unless that last remark had been meant for her. "I'm not going to get hurt," she muttered, striding toward her pickup.

It was scarcely necessary to drive the five blocks to Granger's Shopping Center, home of Rollins Real Estate, the local Safeway and various other shops, but Sammy Jo felt like having her newly washed blue pickup close by. *Expecting the need for a fast getaway?* she chided herself, pulling into an empty spot in front of the shoe repair shop. Across the street was Bentley Feed and Grain. Grimacing, Sammy Jo made a mental note to stop by soon though she already had a substantial bill there.

A bell tinkled above the door to the real estate office. Ducking her head inside, Sammy Jo saw there was no one at the reception desk.

"Yoo-hoo!" she called, leaning around the counter. Presently, a flustered-looking woman, Brent Rollins's younger sister, Connie, appeared.

"Hi, Sammy Jo," she said. "I was moving some boxes around. Old files. Did you want something?"

"I was looking for Brent."

"He's sitting an open house down in Shady Glen, at 874 Dellwood Lane."

"Thanks."

"Any particular reason you want to see him?" she called after Sammy Jo, her curiosity apparently getting the better of her.

Only to ask him to marry me.

Sammy Jo didn't bother stopping long enough to answer. She ground the pickup's gears as she turned its nose toward Shady Glen.

It was a stupid plan, but it was all she had. And anyway, marriage wouldn't be so bad. Besides, Brent Rollins was just one name on the list of possibles. There were lots of eligible bachelors with enough cash to pull her out of her financial slump.

Sammy Jo wrinkled her nose. That sounded so mercenary! But desperate times called for desperate measures. So, she'd start with Brent and work her way down. Next on the list, Tommy Weatherwood.

"Ugh," she muttered, smoothing back a strand of hair. She wasn't that desperate. Yet.

She thought of Cooper. The rugged planes of his face seemed to continually cross her vision. But he was off limits, out of bounds. She needed someone she could control, and if she were going to sell her soul, by God, it wasn't going to be to some misogynistic, corporate demon with an attitude about women. Uh-uh.

So, Brent Rollins it was.

Pulling in to the tree-canopied driveway of 874 Dellwood Lane, she felt her heart in her throat. She had to swallow several times to work up any saliva at all and was annoyed that she was so nervous. It was just Brent. Heck, she'd held him down in second grade and kissed him until he cried.

"Piece of cake," she murmured, cutting the engine in front of a salmon-pink bungalow that was just too perky for words.

A quick self-assessment preceded her walk to the front door. She wasn't a bad catch; Gil had said so often enough. She looked good and she was intelligent, quick and compassionate. With the Triple R as bait . . . why, any red-blooded, half-alive male looking to improve himself would jump at the chance to marry her!

Except she was stubborn, willful and a general pain in the tail end. Her father had been clear on that, as well.

"Brent knows your good points and your bad," she told herself, rapping lightly on the salmon-and-white front door. She half expected Disney characters to answer.

Brent himself opened the door. "Sammy Jo!" he said with genuine pleasure.

She instantly felt like a fraud. "Hi, Brent. You got a minute?"

"For you, an hour. A week. The rest of my life." He grinned.

"Yeah. Right." Sammy Jo was unusually tongue-tied and she didn't know what to do with her hands. She glanced around the tidy living/dining area. The carpet was white, the walls a light lemon yellow. "How come I feel like I walked into candyland?"

He laughed and shook his head. Sammy Jo wasn't certain he understood her point of view, or whether he was just being polite.

"What's up?" he asked her.

Brent wore a green polo shirt and gray slacks. He was Coldwater Flats's only realtor and he favored the casual look, which was just as well since his clientele favored jeans and work shirts.

For some reason, his very appearance slapped Sammy Jo like a cold shower. She was nuts! Completely nuts! "No reason," she choked out, moving away from him. "How much are you selling this for?"

"You in the market for real estate?"

"Only if I'm selling," she said.

"You'd really sell the Triple R?" His brown eyes brightened with surprise.

"When I'm six feet under. Why? You think there's a market for it?"

"You bet. I'd buy it myself, if I could. It's one fine piece of property as you well know, Sammy Jo."

"What if you could buy it? I mean, what would you do with it?"

"Oh, I don't know. Keep it like you do, I guess. Or at least try to," he added humbly.

Encouraged by his unspoken compliment, Sammy Jo walked through the bungalow's freshly paintly white-tiled kitchen. "That's nice."

He cocked his head. "Something on your mind?"

Sammy Jo leaned against the counter, bracing herself in more ways than one. *Count to ten,* she thought. *Then dive in.* Silence grew as she made the mental count. Gathering her courage, she said, "I've got money problems that you would not believe."

"Try me." He was serious.

"I could lose the Triple R if I don't fix things soon."

"You need a loan?"

She'd thought of that, actually, but Brent lived in a tiny two-bedroom house with the sister he'd practically raised himself. The real estate business wasn't that great in Coldwater Flats. If he loaned Sammy Jo enough money to pay off her debts, she was pretty sure she'd swallow up most of his nest egg.

"No." She smiled with regret. "That wouldn't be fair."

"Don't tell me you're rethinking my marriage proposal," he said lightly, with just the hint of desperation that made Sammy Jo realize how important her answer was.

"Did you propose to me?" she asked.

"About a thousand times."

"I mean, seriously propose," Sammy Jo said, her heart beating in her throat.

That gave him pause. His gaze swept over her tense face. "Yes," he answered quietly.

"Well, then, I'd be a fool not to rethink it. You're the catch of the day."

Brent grinned widely.

"But I just dropped by to say hello," she added hastily, backing toward the door. This wasn't working. What had ever possessed her to think it would?

"Drop by again soon," he said, with just the right amount of accent to let her know he'd been reading her mind. Her face coloring, Sammy Jo made a fast exit after paying a few more compliments over the salmon-colored house.

She passed Tommy Weatherwood's house on the way out of Shady Glen. Tommy himself was in the driveway, washing his glossy red Chevy truck.

Sammy Jo forced herself to slow to a stop and smile and wave. Squinting against the sun, Tommy finally recognized her. When he did, a boyish grin crossed his somewhat dissipated features. The years had not been particularly kind to Tommy.

"Hey, Sammy Jo, you babe," he said, strutting over. He wore jeans and no shirt. Sammy Jo eyed the eagle tattoo he'd added to his bicep since the last time she'd seen him shirtless.

"What's new, Tommy?"

"Same old, same old. You know, it's been a while since you and me put down some of that rotgut liquor." His smile was white, having so far escaped the ravages of nicotine. But then she remembered Tommy, for all his other faults, had never smoked.

"A long while."

"Say, you in this year's Fourth of July rodeo?"

"I retired years ago."

"Prettiest damn rodeo princess this town ever saw. And the best. Sammy Jo, you could always do it." He leered. "You could always do it for me."

"Thanks," she said with a dry smile. At least Tommy could make her laugh. He thought he was God's gift to women, and instead of infuriating her, his attitude generally made her grin and shake her head. There was something of the puppy about Tommy for all his corny lines and low-life ways.

But husband material?

"Maybe I'll see you around on the Fourth," he said in lieu of a goodbye.

"Maybe you will."

The rest of the way home Sammy Jo criticized herself for being such a hypocrite. She couldn't do it. She simply couldn't marry some guy to save the ranch.

She changed her mind half an hour later when she opened Doc Carey's veterinary bill. Gasping, she crumpled it in her fist, then smoothed it out again, chest tight. She was going down for the third time.

Grabbing her purse, she headed back to Shady Glen, got halfway there, stomped on the brake and turned back to town. In front of the Last Stand Saloon, she clenched her hands around the wheel and fought a scream of frustration. Then she slammed out of the truck and stomped into the bar.

The place seemed empty, apart from Sam and Josh who were both at the bar.

"You look mad enough to kill a mountain lion with your bare hands," Josh observed. "Have a brewsky on me."

"Looking for somebody?" Sam asked.

"No," Sammy Jo retorted.

"Here." Sam handed her a frosted mug, which she stared down at uncomprehendingly. "He stopped by earlier," Sam added helpfully.

"Who?"

"Mr. Ryan."

Sammy Jo blinked at Sam. "I'm not looking for Mr. Ryan!"

"Yeah?" Sam seemed unconvinced.

"You must be looking for something," Josh said. "You're fit to be tied."

"If I'm looking for anything, it's salvation! I have got to save the Triple R."

"Sell it to Ryan," Sam said.

"No!"

"You're gonna lose it, anyway," Josh added.

Sammy Jo glared. "You sound just like him. Well, let me tell you something, I'd sell myself before I sold the ranch. Anybody looking for a good woman? How about me for a wife? All you have to do is save the ranch and I'm yours!"

Her words rose to the rafters, desperate, choked-off, embarrassing. Sammy Jo closed her eyes, fighting hot anger.

And it was at that moment that Cooper Ryan chose to make his presence known. He'd been sitting around the corner behind one of the thick, rough-hewn posts that held up the Last Stand's roof. Now, he sauntered over to the bar.

Sammy Jo's mouth dropped in mingled disbelief and horror.

"Is that a proposal for me or the bar in general?" he asked. "If it's for me, I'm afraid I'm going to have to turn you down."

It was the way he said it. One moment she was sick with humiliation and fear, the next she was incensed beyond reason. Her temper, always ragingly healthy, rose like mercury in a thermometer—but at warp speed!

"I wouldn't have you if you were the last man on earth! I wouldn't have you if you groveled at my feet and begged! I wouldn't have you period, mister. Don't you dare listen in on my conversations!"

"I wasn't exactly eavesdropping," he said, enraging her further. "You were shouting. Damn near at the top of your lungs."

"If I were shouting, your ear drums would hurt! I was talking normally! NOW, I'M SHOUTING! I'd rather boil in oil, eat nails and wallow with pigs than even look at you again!"

"Ooooh." Josh grinned, holding up his hands in surrender.

Sam rubbed his jaw, fighting a smile.

Sammy Jo wanted to wring both their necks. And then disaster struck. Ginny unfolded her skinny legs from the banquette seat around the corner and strolled toward them. She'd apparently been cozying up to Cooper when Sammy Jo had banged in, and though Ginny was keeping her expression carefully schooled, Sammy Jo could read the mirth in her eyes.

It was too much, and it goaded Sammy Jo into one more childish and foolhardy remark.

"But if anybody else wants a wife, and therefore a ranch," she challenged rashly, "tell 'em to look me up. I'm available."

With that she slammed through the door without a backward glance, fighting self-recriminations and her still-flaming temper all the way home.

One hell of a woman...
Cooper tossed back the last of his beer and made a face. Josh's words still hung in the air. As soon as Sammy Jo left, Josh had slapped his knee, howled with delight and crowed, "One *hell* of a woman! But she'd make one shrew of a wife!"

"You can't take her seriously," Sam said as he wiped down the bar.

"And why not?" Josh was perfectly reasonable. "She needs the money. And let's face it. She could use a man."

Ginny snorted. "Couldn't we all."

"Sammy Jo isn't that mercenary." Perversely, Cooper found himself defending her. Now, Pamela *had* been that mercenary. But Sammy Jo wasn't Pamela. Not by a long shot.

Josh shrugged. "Who's talkin' mercenary? The girl's in a bind. And she's true-blue. She'd marry to save the ranch in a heartbeat, but she'd stick by the lucky devil. That's how she's made."

Cooper wasn't certain he liked Josh's assessment. Her reason for wanting to marry sounded cold-blooded to him no matter what fancy motivations anyone might attach to it. And he didn't like thinking that of Sammy Jo.

He was surprised to find her pickup parked in front of his house when he returned home later that night. He was even more surprised by his own sense of anticipation. Tamping that down, he entered the front door and followed the sound of her voice to the kitchen where she was leaning against the back door, arms folded across her chest, sharing a cup of coffee with Jack and Lettie.

"This is a surprise," Cooper greeted her. With difficulty, he dragged his gaze from her lean form. What was it about some women that they just looked good in jeans? Slim, long legs capped by softly rounded hips and a firm, flat abdomen. Damn nice. And he wasn't a man who really liked tanned women, either; it seemed so calculated and narcissistic. But Sammy Jo's browned arms spoke of work in the sun, and their sinewy strength was real and therefore sexy. No gym work for Sammy Jo Whalen. Uh-uh. The lady knew how to pull her own weight. Literally.

"I forgot to tell you about the beaver dam," she said coolly. "A family's moved in about a quarter mile up Cotton Creek. That's why everything's so parched down here."

"So, that explains it," Jack said.

"Our furry friends are wreaking havoc," Sammy Jo added, as if Cooper didn't have the brain power to figure it out himself. "We gotta move them."

"You mean kill them?" he asked cautiously.

Sammy Jo's face darkened. "I mean move them! You men always think of killing first!"

"Now, Sammy Jo," Jack tried to intervene.

"I was just making sure of what you meant," Cooper explained in exasperation.

"We'll trap them. Humanely," she added through her teeth, "and we'll ask the forest service to relocate them."

"Okay." Cooper was abrupt, annoyed at her attitude. He didn't need it, and he didn't need Sammy Jo.

"Fine." She set down her coffee cup and headed for the door.

"Fine," he agreed just as sharply.

"Don't you want some dessert, Sammy Jo?" Lettie offered in a rush.

"Looks to me like Ms. Whalen's got better things to do," Cooper cut in.

Sammy Jo wouldn't even honor him with a look. "I'll see you later," she said in a softer tone, and Cooper knew she meant that for Jack and Lettie.

She'd pricked his ego, and Cooper couldn't let it stand. "You know it's not my fault you're trolling around for a husband. You can take it out on me all you want, but you're the one selling yourself."

"What?" Lettie asked, aghast.

Every muscle Sammy Jo possessed tightened until she looked like a steel missile ready to hurl itself into space. Cooper watched in fascination, knowing he'd goaded her, unable to prevent himself.

"Sammy Jo would never!" Lettie blustered, tightening her lips. "You owe her an apology, Mr. Ryan."

"Save it," Sammy Jo retorted, her voice ice. "My business is my business, Mr. Ryan. I'll take care of the beavers by myself."

With that, she was gone in a whoosh of hot air as the front door slammed solidly behind her.

"Mr. Ryan," Lettie said icily to Cooper's broad back, "I'm afraid you've made a bad mistake about Sammy Jo."

"Have I?" He swiveled to look at her, wishing the knot in his gut would unfurl. Outside, Sammy Jo's engine roared to life, angry and hot. Gravel spewed from her tires, pinging against the side of the house as she tore away.

"That girl's seen more trouble and pain than a child oughta," Jack agreed.

"She's not a girl. She's a full-grown woman," Cooper said.

"Sit down," Lettie said.

He couldn't believe it, but he knew Lettie Babbitt was about to give him a lecture. Dropping onto one of the chairs, he wondered if Lettie would offer him some dessert. She was, after all, employed by him and living on his property. To his annoyance and amusement, she carefully wrapped foil over the apple pie on the counter, set it aside, then turned to him, hands on her hips.

"I'm not certain why I'm sitting here," Cooper drawled, "and I don't guarantee I'll stay."

"Gil Whalen was a good man. Hardheaded, but a decent fellow and a good neighbor."

"The hardheaded part must run in the family," Cooper observed.

Jack took the seat opposite Cooper, rubbing his chin and dolefully shaking his head as if Cooper were the most dense, self-destructive human being on earth. Cooper surmised wryly that Jack had probably seen more of these lectures than a man ought to.

"He married a very pretty woman, and I mean pretty. People stared at Irene Whalen when she walked down the street. And she was smart. Real smart. But she kinda liked Irene more than anybody else, and she didn't much take to bein' a mother."

Cooper sat in silence now, both uncomfortable with this window into Sammy Jo's life and fascinated, in spite of himself. He should stop Lettie. Stop her now, before he found himself feeling sorry for Sammy Jo, understanding her more and therefore having to change all his plans concerning Ridge Range Ranch.

Jack got up, poured himself and Cooper each a cup of coffee, then settled down again. Lettie stared at Cooper as if the force of her glare could pound some sense into his thick skull.

"Irene took up with a cowboy a lot younger than herself and she left that little girl in her daddy's care. Sammy Jo never knew her. Gil woulda liked to stamp out every memory. He didn't want Sammy Jo to be like her mama. Nosirree. And she's not."

"Except she's pretty," Jack mumbled.

"She's Gil's daughter," Lettie argued. Relenting, she added, "But she is pretty."

"We all agree Sammy Jo is pretty," Cooper said dryly. "But she said herself she was looking for a husband. I didn't make that up."

"Gil ran the finances into the ground so she'd be *forced* to marry! Sammy Jo's just statin' the obvious!" Lettie sniffed, staunch in her defense. "Gil never really understood Sammy Jo."

"And you do?" Cooper lifted one disbelieving eyebrow.

Lettie wagged a finger in front of Cooper's nose. "I know her uncle shows up like a savior and tells her he'll help. Now, Sammy Jo is ornery and suspicious, but she don't have any other relatives. She welcomed him with open arms. I don't know what happened, but the next thing you know, she boots him out but good. I asked her about it and she said this uncle wanted to get back at Gil. Tried to steal the ranch from her."

Cooper lifted his arms, easing the tension that had developed between his shoulder blades. The knot in his stomach had grown worse, too. Why did it feel as if Lettie was talking about *him?*

"So, Sammy Jo has no one. All she cares about is that ranch and that oak tree. Before you start condemnin' her, you'd better think about her situation. I think she oughta get herself a husband. A rich one."

Cooper looked at Jack whose face was carefully expressionless. He glanced at Lettie. There was no mistaking the meaning behind her last remark.

"I've been married once," he said. "I'm not getting married again. And I'm certainly not marrying a wildcat like Sammy Jo Whalen."

* * *

"Damn the man to hell," Sammy Jo cursed for the fiftieth time as she furiously scrubbed the kitchen floor. "May he die a slow, painful death."

Okay, her idea to find herself a husband hadn't been the wisest plan ever conceived, but he didn't have to be so mean about it. She wanted to kill him!

She scrubbed and buffed and cleaned until she was exhausted and the wooden floor shone with such a high gloss it looked as if it were coated in plastic. Trigger whined at the back door, but after all her work, Sammy Jo refused to let the dog in.

Throwing herself into bed, she ignored the images of Cooper Ryan that seemed to cross her mind like a succession of frames in a film. Cooper's lips quirking in a smile. Cooper lifting one discerning eyebrow. Cooper glaring at her as if she were some kind of noxious bug he couldn't wait to squash.

Blast the man. Did he have to be so good-looking? She hated good-looking men. All they did was stare in the mirror and spout sharp, witty comments about the state of the world as a whole, comments that were generally mean, small and just plain wrong!

Trigger's whining finally got to Sammy Jo. She threw open the bedroom window. "Here, girl," she called, but there was no need. The collie clambered over some boxes that sat against the exterior wall and sailed through the window, curling herself up contentedly at the end of the bed.

Patting the dog's head, Sammy Jo climbed into bed, then spent the next half hour thumping her pillow with her fist and grinding her teeth, mad even at the moonlight that sneaked through her window to trail a soft, blue-white stripe across her grandmother's quilt. Tomorrow she was going to have to approach Brent in earnest. Forget her earlier reservations. She needed someone like Brent, or the ranch was on the Valley Federal chopping block and some eager entrepreneur like Cooper would buy it for a song.

"Over my dead body," she declared, squeezing her eyes shut tightly in a vain attempt to induce sleep.

By the time morning arrived, Sammy Jo was overly tired, grouchy and still just as infuriated. Only her sense of humor saved her when she caught a glimpse of herself in the mirror.

"Ugh!" she declared, laughing shortly at the disheveled sight. "No man in his right mind would look at you, let alone marry you."

A quick shower, a brush of her hair and a clean pair of jeans and shirt and she looked almost presentable. Carl waved at her through the window as he did the morning chores. Sammy Jo's heart twisted. She was thankful for the help but totally stressed over when and how she would pay him.

Grabbing the paper, she headed into town to find Doc Carey and talk about payment of the bill for Tick-Tock's surgery. The one bright spot was that the mare seemed to be feeling well and the pregnancy was progressing on schedule. But that didn't solve Sammy Jo's financial troubles.

A familiar truck sat on the street in front of the veterinary clinic, its shiny black finish glittering under the hot sun.

Cooper's truck.

"What's he doing here?" she mumbled as she slammed her door and headed inside.

"The doc's in surgery," one of the girls who helped out informed Sammy Jo. "Can I help you?"

Doc Carey performed minor operations at the clinic, usually on smaller pets like dogs and cats. Sammy Jo gazed thoughtfully at the closed door to the inner sanctuary.

"Where's the owner of the black truck outside?"

"Right here," Cooper's deep voice said from a side doorway.

"The doc let you into surgery?" Sammy Jo asked in surprise. "You really do get around."

"You're still mad about yesterday," he answered, unruffled.

The girl giggled, then held her hand to her mouth. Sammy Jo eyed her narrowly. "What do you mean?"

"About the marriage proposal."

The girl collapsed in a hysterical fit of laughter at Cooper's bald disclosure. "You told her?" Sammy Jo asked, too stunned to be upset.

"Oh, it's all over town," the girl said, exonerating Cooper. "I'm sorry, Miss Whalen, but I just can't picture you trying to . . . you know . . ."

"What?"

"Well . . ." She turned helpless eyes to Cooper who remained darkly silent.

"Sell myself to the highest bidder?" Sammy Jo asked in a tight, brittle voice.

The girl had the grace to look ashamed. Sammy Jo couldn't read Cooper's expression, but it didn't matter. She knew what he thought of her. And she didn't think much more of him.

She stood in utter silence for the space of five seconds, then marched through the door to Doc Carey's surgery, the girl squeaking out protests behind her.

"Doc?" Sammy Jo called through a tight throat, cracking open a door.

"Whoa, there, Sammy Jo," he called back. He was standing over an unconcious Irish setter, clearly getting ready to neuter the shaved animal.

"Sorry," Sammy Jo murmured. "Do you have a minute when you're finished?"

"I'll be right there, darlin'," the vet said, turning back to his task.

Nodding, Sammy Jo went the other way, down the hall to the back door and small wooden stairway that stood above a grass-choked alley. She was angry through and through. At herself mostly, but at the fates, too.

A hand settled on her shoulder. A strong, male hand. She prayed it was Doc Carey's.

"You all right?" Cooper asked quietly.

Do I look all right?

"Couldn't be better." She lifted her shoulder pointedly, but he didn't remove his palm. "What are you doing here?"

"The doc's going to inoculate my new cattle. I was just waiting to talk to him."

Sammy Jo nodded, her gaze straight ahead. "Me, too."

The heat from his hand penetrated through her cotton shirt to her skin. It seeped in and prickled, like an itch she wasn't able to scratch. Bothered, Sammy Jo moved away from his touch. Perversely, as soon as his hand was gone, she felt a pang of regret.

"I told him you were looking for him the other day," Cooper said easily.

"Pardon?"

"When you came to the Last Stand. You said you were looking for the vet."

Did he know it was a lie? Was that what he was really asking? Sammy Jo turned to eye him carefully, her gaze narrowed. "I was really looking for you that day."

"Ahhh . . ."

He *did* know, the bastard! The amusement deep in his blue eyes infuriated her. "I thought you might like to invest in the Triple R. I made a mistake, okay?"

"So, then you decided to dig up a husband."

"That's right," Sammy Jo said with a little less steam. Uncomfortable, she muttered, "What's it to you, anyway?"

"Nothing." He seemed to regret bringing it up, too. "Do whatever you want."

"I will. And next time, if it isn't too much to ask, maybe you could keep your nose out of my affairs instead of broadcasting them to the whole world."

She brushed past him. His hand shot out and grabbed her bare arm. The image of his hard fingers closed around her flesh burned in her brain and she barely heard his words.

"I'm sorry, okay?" he said. "I didn't know you'd be so sensitive."

"Just leave me alone."

"Why do you feel like exploding every time we have the simplest conversation?"

"An old habit of mine."

"I think it's something else."

She twisted her arm, attempting to ease it from his grip. Her emerald gaze met his: hers stormy, his determined. "I don't want to talk to you anymore."

"Well, you're damn well going to," Cooper said through his teeth. "You're the worst case of reverse misogyny I've ever encountered. Now, all I want to do is get along with you, but you're not making it easy."

"Reverse misogyny? I'm not even sure I know what that means."

"You're a man hater."

Sammy Jo's jaw dropped. "I'm a man hater? You have the lowest opinion of women I've ever seen! And…and you just want to *get along with me?*" She started laughing. "Oh, come on!"

Cooper finally released her, but the more she thought about that remark, the funnier it was. She doubled over with huge guffaws that echoed through the hot, quiet air and eddied outward like waves.

"You're hysterical," he stated flatly, which sent Sammy Jo into more gales of laughter. Stumbling backward, she grabbed the rail. And Cooper made the mistake of grabbing for her.

Sammy Jo froze instantly. "Let go of me."

"Look, I don't want to judge you. Lettie explained some things to me last night, and you're right. Your business is your business."

"What kind of things? What kind of things did Lettie tell you?"

Cooper realized he'd made a mistake again. "Nothing bad. She just explained about your family."

"My family," Sammy Jo repeated, her voice deadly.

"I already knew your dad ran that ranch into the ground. She just told me why." When Sammy Jo didn't respond, he added softly, "But that's still the worst reason to get married."

"You just said you'd stay out of my business," she stated flatly. "Now get your hands off me."

"What in God's name is the matter with you?"

"You. You're the matter with me!"

Suddenly, it wasn't funny anymore. She didn't want him touching her and she damned well didn't want to have to explain her roller-coaster emotions.

"I don't get you," he said, staring down at her.

Sammy Jo didn't like the expression on his face. If he were a scientist, she believed he might take a scalpel to her and rip her from stem to stern, determined to find out what strange internal makeup caused her to react the way she did. It was just a fury at the world as a whole and at him in particular, for reasons she didn't care to explore.

"I don't get you, either," she snapped.

"You've got attitude written all over you."

"Look who's talking!"

His lips tightened and her gaze fastened unwillingly on his mouth. A sensual mouth, she thought, bracketed by lines of disillusionment. From a woman? Sammy Jo never usually stopped long enough to psychoanalyze her fellow man, but now, just for an instant, she read deep pain in his face and she was surprised by the surge of understanding that swept through her.

"I . . ." She stopped, unable to complete her thought because, truthfully, there was no thought. No idea. No plan. Instead, to her intense amazement, the knowledge that they might have something in common other than a joint fence line, that there might be some emotional level at which they could touch stilled her tongue, leaving her speechless.

If Cooper felt the same, she couldn't tell. The feeling was primal and deep, from some secret core of herself she hadn't known existed until this moment. She tried to step backward again but there was nowhere to go. The rail stopped her on one side; Cooper filled up the other.

For the first time in her life, she called on her temper to rescue her and it wouldn't respond. Instead, she waited, lips parted, breath coming in fits and starts, throat dry, for Cooper's next move.

"Someone ought to take you in hand," he muttered, as if the very idea infuriated him.

"I think it's way too late for that." She stared at the hard tan line of his throat.

"What do you mean?"

"I'm a lost cause." Her words were meant to be flip, but they came out sounding pathetic. She shook her head, embarrassed.

"Sammy Jo," he hissed.

She waited, expectation like a living thing inside her, writhing, desperate, anxious to be free. Cooper hesitated. Did he understand they were on the threshold of something dangerous? She did. Something dangerous and intoxicating. Something she wasn't certain she wanted.

One moment the hard angles of his face swam above her, the next he swooped down to kiss her. But this was not some doting lover's kiss. She felt frustration in the way his lips crushed hers. She couldn't even tell if he *liked* her!

And that, finally, resurrected her temper. She jerked backward, clamping her lips together. Instead of releasing her, Cooper held her closer still, his mouth hot and commanding.

Sammy Jo paused. She didn't mean to. It just happened. She'd been about to fight with all her strength, but her muscles weakened, destroyed by some inner elixir that swept upward from her most feminine area, a sweet pathogen that dissolved reason in its path.

His mouth softened, sensing the change. That softening was her undoing. Her knees turned to water. Her fingers clamped around the rail but her hands itched to reach upward and wind themselves around his neck.

What is this? a distant, worried voice inside her head asked. She'd kissed men before. Boys, really. And it had always left her feeling mildly impatient and sure there was some great myth about the joys of melding one's lips to another's. She'd merely tolerated kisses. But Cooper's mouth brought out a hunger deep inside that made her limbs tremble with fear and her body shudder with untapped passion.

Tearing her mouth from his, she gasped when his lips pressed hard kisses against her jawline. "Stop it," she breathed, hearing the quaver in her voice.

"Make me."

A challenge. Delivered in a husky voice that robbed Sammy Jo of the power to meet it. Her eyelids fluttered closed. A pulse throbbed in her temple. Damn, but his lovemaking felt *good!*

A whoosh of air. "Sammy Jo?" Doc Carey called in a worried voice.

She choked, pushing at Cooper's shoulders.

"Oh, sorry." Doc's eyes twinkled mischievously. "I didn't mean to interrupt."

"No, no!" Sammy Jo struggled furiously. She punched at Cooper's chest with one tight fist, but he'd already released her, the look on his face saying he was as shocked as she was. "I—I wanted to know—about the bill."

"You can take your time. How's Tick-Tock doing?"

"Fine . . . fine."

Doc Carey glanced at Cooper who was remarkably quiet, his expression grim. "I'm just about finished here. I'll be heading out to Serenity soon."

"I'll be there," Cooper said.

The smile on the gossipy vet's face made Sammy Jo groan inwardly. She knew this little scene with Cooper would soon be all over town. She would have to work fast to make certain everyone knew she and Cooper were just neighbors, period.

The door swung shut behind Doc Carey. Utter silence prevailed.

"Well," Cooper said, his deep blue eyes cloudy with thought.

"Well," Sammy Jo answered.

He stuck out his hand, inviting her to shake it. Sammy Jo lifted one blond eyebrow, drawing a reluctant smile from Cooper.

"I'd like to start over," he said. "I'm sorry. I wish I could help you, but I really can't. Let's try to get along."

Sammy Jo nodded, not trusting herself to say the right thing. Cooper left moments later, apparently deciding it was safer to leave things as they were.

Sammy Jo looked down at her hand. She could still feel the hot pressure of his mouth against hers. With a snort of self-deprecation, she yanked open the door and hurried into the antiseptic-smelling hallway, drawing in huge breaths in an effort to clear away the musky, masculine scent of Cooper Ryan that seemed to fill her every pore and drug her senses.

Chapter Five

She was the laughingstock of the whole town!

Staring down at the *Corral,* the weekly that served as Coldwater Flats's local paper, Sammy Jo's eyes picked out the words in the sneaky little article that popped out at her like pointing fingers.

"...what feisty blond-haired rancher is looking for a man? No one without a healthy bank balance need apply...."

Sammy Jo crumpled the paper up into a tight ball. "Damn that Cooper Ryan!" she cried, even though she knew Ginny, or Josh, or Sam or anyone passing through the doors of Doc Carey's clinic could have gotten an earful about her. Plus, Lorna never knew when to keep her mouth shut.

Touching a finger to her trembling lips, she swallowed hard. She could still recall every moment of Cooper's kiss even though she'd done her darnedest to forget.

Sammy Jo stomped through the rest of her chores, squinting at the distant copse of trees where she knew the beaver dam stood. She was going to have to talk to Cooper again, but for the past few days, ever since that kiss, she'd been hiding out, unwilling to face him.

Which was a coward's way out, and totally unlike herself.

"Everything I do is unlike me these days," Sammy Jo muttered, washing her hands at the outdoor faucet beside the house.

She heard the distant report of a firecracker and made a face. Today was the Fourth of July. Before all this other mess, she'd planned to go see the local rodeo and avail herself of the cotton candy, caramel apples and curly fries at the carnival, which was always a part of the festivities. But she hadn't had the energy to ask Brent if he wanted to join her, and she just didn't feel like going alone.

She finished washing up and threw on her jeans and a white, pearl-buttoned shirt, rolling the sleeves up her forearms. It wasn't as though she'd be totally alone if she attended the celebration. She knew everybody in town. But for some strange reason, she felt melancholy.

Searching her feelings, she realized it was because Gil was gone. Her father had always been her companion. As a teenager, she'd tried to ditch him, favoring instead the wild times with Tommy Weatherwood and some of the girls in her class like Bev Hawkins who'd been Bev Jones then. But she'd slowly lost those friendships and ties, and as an adult, she'd been happy to be with Gil.

"Stop feeling sorry for yourself," she chided herself. "You could stay here and do chores until sunup and still not be done."

A depressing thought. A *really* depressing thought!

Sammy Jo made it until six o'clock that evening before she could stand it no longer. Jumping into her pickup, she drove into town, becoming part of the snarl of traffic as soon as she got within a half mile. The Coldwater Flats rodeo was small potatoes but extremely popular nonetheless. She could hear the announcer on the loudspeaker reminding people that the next show started at eight.

The sky was a dusty blue haze bent over hot streets and the smells of horses, popcorn and exhaust. Sammy Jo pulled into a spot next to the horse barns. Climbing from the pickup, she turned her gaze to the weathered bleachers that sat on the south end of the rodeo arena.

She'd spent a lot of years hanging around with cowboys and cowgirls. She'd even learned to chew tobacco before her father found out and nearly forced her out of rodeo right then and there.

Instead of heading to the rodeo grounds, she moved into the throngs walking along the streambed, which was little more than a swampy trickle during this hot summer. Kids were staring down at the names of the rodeo queens imprinted in the metal stars imbedded in the baked dirt. Sammy Jo's name was there twice. Unheard of. She'd won two years in a row, and after that, the rodeo council had changed the rules amid a flurry of complaints from the likes of Ginny Martin. Sammy Jo hadn't cared. And she'd been more annoyed than proud that her name was perennially nominated for princess of every court. The truth was, there weren't that many women around with her skills. She was a true daredevil, or at least had been, and though her temperament had never won her any awards, her expertise had.

But it was all nonsense, anyway. And her nickname, the Princess, was enough to shoot her temper into the danger zone.

Sammy Jo walked toward the center of town. The giant cowboy hat sat atop the clock tower and this year a humongous red bandanna was tied jauntily beneath it. Grinning, Sammy Jo deliberately threw off her self-pitying mood.

"Hey, Princess!" someone yelled.

Sammy Jo looked around. It was Josh Johnson, his red beard unmistakable. She waved at the same moment she realized he was with Tommy Weatherwood. With a groan, she steeled herself for the grief she was undoubtedly about to get.

"Hello, Sammy Jo," Tommy greeted her, kissing her smack on the lips, much to her dismay. "You oughta be in there." He jerked his head in the direction of the rodeo grounds.

"Those days are over," Sammy Jo told him, searching for a way to escape. She didn't want these two "adopting" her for the evening.

"Ah, yes. Josh here says you're tryin' hard to hang on to the Triple R."

"That's hardly a headline," Sammy Jo answered dryly.

"He also says you're lookin' for a husband. Ain't that right, Josh?" Tommy glanced at Josh for confirmation.

"Whoa, now. Uh-uh." Josh's complexion turned as red as his beard. "We were all just kiddin' around the other day, right, Sammy Jo?"

"Just kidding around," she agreed soberly.

Tommy looked down casually at his fingernails. "That ain't what I read in the *Corral.*"

"If you believe everything you read in the paper, especially that paper," Sammy Jo said with forced calm, "you're more gullible than I thought."

"It's common knowledge, Sammy Jo, babe." Tommy grinned like a lecher. Then again, he *was* a lecher.

"Get lost," she told him, smothering a smile. What a juvenile. She couldn't take him seriously.

A couple separated from the crowd that was milling around, and walked along the split-rail fence that surrounded Granger's Shopping Center. Sammy Jo swept in a surprised breath. Immediately, Josh and Tommy turned to follow her gaze.

Cooper Ryan was strolling toward them, Bev Hawkins hanging on his arm.

"I heard she and Roy broke up," Josh said, stunned, "but I didn't know she was out huntin' already."

Sammy Jo's heart beat so hard it threatened to suffocate her. She couldn't tear her eyes away from Cooper and Bev. *Bev Hawkins!* She should have known. Men couldn't help falling under Bev's spell, and Sammy Jo never had rightly believed that Bev was as happily married as she'd let on. Roy Hawkins was one of the wealthiest men in the area, but he was nothing compared to Cooper Ryan.

"How come the *Corral* hasn't reported on this yet?" Sammy Jo asked, forcing a lightness she didn't feel.

"Next week's edition," Tommy predicted. He seemed completely amused by the whole thing, but then he and Bev had shared some wilder times when she was younger.

Cooper and Bev spied their group just as Sammy Jo was trying to escape. They came over, arm in arm. Bev was delicately sucking on a gossamer strand of a lethal-looking blue cotton candy.

Be polite, Sammy Jo warned herself a trifle desperately. "Hi, Cooper. Hi, Bev."

"Hello, Sammy Jo," Bev said, smiling happily. "Cooper was just telling me how you and he are neighbors."

"Really?"

Cooper was eyeing Tommy. Sammy Jo glanced at Tommy, too, trying to see him as a stranger might. Tall, lean, looking appealingly worn-out, Tommy was really just an overgrown boy.

But the look Cooper gave him could have melted steel. Sammy Jo's heart lifted. Could he be just the tiniest bit jealous?

"I'm bringing Emmy over on Saturday," Bev said. "And she's got a couple of friends. Ginny's daughter, Vanessa, and of course, Lorna's daughter, Karen." Sammy Jo stared at her. "For the riding lesson? Lorna did tell you, didn't she?" Bev asked anxiously. "She promised she would!"

"Oh, yeah . . . I think she did mention it."

In truth, Sammy Jo wasn't completely sure. She and Lorna had talked about riding lessons, but either they'd never settled on a date, or Sammy Jo had been too unfocused to write it down. The lessons Sammy Jo gave had to be worked in around her schedule and with all her other problems, Sammy Jo hadn't been thinking about them at all.

"Emmy would be so disappointed," Bev babbled on, clearly picking up the correct vibes no matter what Sammy Jo said.

"Saturday, ten o'clock?" Sammy Jo asked.

"Lorna said noon, but ten o'clock would be fine if it's more convenient. I can call the girls—"

"Noon's perfect," Sammy Jo interjected. She glanced at Cooper, but couldn't read his thoughts. What did she care, anyway?

"We're headin' over to the Last Stand before the rodeo," Josh said. "Want to join us?"

Sammy Jo wasn't certain if he meant her or Bev and Cooper. Apparently, his invitation was for all and sundry because when Bev and Cooper demurred, he turned to her. "Sure," she said with a forced smile.

It took all her willpower not to watch them walk away, arm in arm, Bev's laughter husky and sensual, mingling with the powerful scents and calliope music of the carnival and the glow of the multicolored lights that circled, kaleidoscope-like, from the Ferris wheel.

An hour's worth of raucous Last Stand patrons and the shot of tequila Tommy had practically poured down her throat and Sammy Jo was about fed up. She wished she'd called Brent. Tommy Weatherwood was no answer to her problems. In fact, he *was* a problem. If he'd really inherited money, he was bound to drink it all away before the new year.

"Hey, where ya goin'?" Tommy demanded, clamping a hand on her shoulder.

"To the rodeo." She slipped away. Easy enough, since Tommy swayed uncertainly on his feet.

Josh, who was a man who could hold his liquor, asked, "Can I take you?"

"Thanks, Josh, but I'm feeling like being alone."

"Suit yourself." He shrugged, happy enough to keep his bar stool warm.

Sammy Jo drew a deep breath as she stepped onto the wooden sidewalk. She strode toward the carnival and rodeo grounds, the sky a deep purple bowl overhead, sprinkled with a dusting of stars.

She stood in line and bought herself a ticket to the grandstand, then sat down beside a jolly potbellied older man and his equally jolly wife. Calf-roping, wild cow milking, the tense acrobatics of the rodeo clown...it was always the same and its familiarity was soothing. Sammy Jo tensed during the barrel-racing, critically watching the latest contenders. They were good, and more important, the horses were good. Cheers rose in the crowd.

The couple next to her bought a bucket of beer. Out of the corner of her eye, Sammy Jo watched them balance the oversize container as they passed it back and forth, giggling. Beer sloshed over the rim several times but they didn't seem to notice.

Through it all, the loudspeaker rang over the noise, the announcer's voice a corny blend of homespun jokes and fast-talking patter guaranteed to whip the most lethargic spectator into a frenzy of excitement.

Sammy Jo slipped out halfway through, feeling disappointed somehow. No Gil to laugh with. No one to enjoy the sheer silliness with. No one.

Mad at herself over her doldrums, Sammy Jo set her jaw. Maybe marrying Brent had other possibilities. He could be here with her.

"I've been getting an earful about your rodeo history," Cooper's voice said, somewhere behind her.

She turned swiftly. He was balancing two colas and a tray of curly fries. "From Bev?"

"She thinks you're going to turn her daughter into a rodeo queen."

Sammy Jo snorted. "Only if she can stay on a horse. Bev's daughter? Sorry, I can't picture it."

"Snob." He grinned.

"I guess I am," Sammy Jo admitted. "So, what do you think of the rodeo?"

"I'm getting a charge out of it. I like Coldwater Flats." He slid a look to the stands. "Your friends waiting for you?"

"You mean Josh and Tommy? No. I left them drinking tequila at the Last Stand Saloon."

He absorbed that in silence, and then Sammy Jo thought of Bev waiting for him in the stands. "See ya," she said.

* * *

Cooper walked back to his date. Bev took her drink and chattered about the rodeo, her daughter, and how she wished her soon-to-be ex-husband would stop bothering her. She'd practically invited herself to be his date, and Cooper, feeling oddly lonely, hadn't turned her away.

Besides, he needed a reason to forget about Sammy Jo. He'd been cold and ruthless and it was eating away at his insides like acid.

"Happy Fourth of July," Bev suddenly said, leaning upward, eyes shining. Her lips were bare millimeters from his, a deep, luscious rose-pink.

But Cooper couldn't bring himself to do it. With a smile, he murmured, "Happy Fourth of July," then turned back to the action of the rodeo.

Saturday, promptly at noon, a car pulled up to the front of the house. Groaning, Sammy Jo met them on the gravel strewn front driveway. Emmy Hawkins jumped out, dressed in white jeans and a pink cowboy shirt with long, silvery fringe that jiggled and danced as the five-year-old rodeo-queen wanna-be ran to Sammy Jo.

"Hello," Sammy Jo drawled, shaking Emmy's hand.

"I want a white horse with blue eyes!" she cried.

"Emmy, you take whatever Sammy Jo has," Bev chided her. Bev wore black slacks and a white blouse. She carefully shook Sammy Jo's hand, wrist limp as a noodle.

"Emmy knows how to ride with a saddle. I don't know about this," she fussed.

Bev clearly was getting cold feet. Sammy Jo could just picture it. Emmy's father, Roy, probably suggested riding lessons to the little tomboy. Emmy had whooped and hollered and generally annoyed her mother until Bev, pleading a headache, had thrown up her hands and agreed. But clearly, Bev had dressed Emmy. No one who really rode horses wore white.

"You won't do anything dangerous, now?" Bev asked anxiously.

"Emmy will do only what she's capable of."

Bev glanced at her daughter and paled. "Oh, Lord! Look at her!"

The little girl was doing cartwheels on the dusty gravel driveway. Even Sammy Jo was impressed that Emmy seemed to feel no pain in her palms.

Emmy disregarded her mother entirely until Bev was screeching at the top of her lungs. Another car appeared as Bev sought vainly to corral her daughter. Emmy ran and squealed as the newcomer stopped. Sammy Jo felt like groaning again when she recognized Ginny. Ginny climbed from the driver's side and another little girl, this one as stone-faced and stubborn-looking as Emmy was animated, reluctantly slid across the seat to stand in the hot sun.

"Did Bev tell you I was bringing Van?" Ginny asked by way of greeting.

"She mentioned it." Ginny had suffered through one abortive marriage. It had been full of turmoil, fights and brawling—or so Sammy Jo had heard—and just when it was ending, Ginny had learned she was pregnant. The father left before the child's birth and, as they say in the movies, had never been seen or heard from again.

"Van wants to learn trick-riding," Ginny explained.

Sammy Jo smiled at the little girl who hid behind her mother's leg and watched Sammy Jo with somber, suspicious eyes. "Van" did not appear to want to learn anything. Sammy Jo had the feeling this trick-riding lesson, as a means to further their daughters' chances at the rodeo court, was more a popularity contest between the mothers than anything else.

Lorna's smoke-belching compact drove up next. "Hi there," Lorna greeted Sammy Jo with a big smile as she helped her daughter, Karen, from the car. "Y'all ready?"

"Raring to go," Sammy Jo told her dryly. "How about you?" she asked Karen.

Karen's thumb was firmly stuffed in her mouth. Since this was the child's usual state of affairs, Sammy Jo grabbed her other hand and led all three girls to the fenced paddock where Pokey, her Shetland, whose irascible temperament could be tamed by a succession of sugar cubes, waited under a solitary pine while flicking flies away with his tail.

"Okay, who wants to be first?" Sammy Jo asked, keenly aware of the group of mothers waiting by the fence. Lorna would be no problem, but anything could happen with Bev and Ginny. Bev stood apart from Ginny and Lorna, brushing dust off her blouse. Sammy Jo and Ginny definitely had their differences, but Bev was in a class by herself.

"I do! I do!" Emmy yelled.

"I do," Karen echoed in a subdued voice.

Van said nothing. Sammy Jo smiled at her. "Don't you want to ride?"

"No." Van was perfectly clear on that.

"Okay, Emmy, let's set you on Pokey." Sammy Jo picked up the little girl and plumped her onto the bareback saddle, a thick foam pad covered with heavy-duty yellow cotton. It saved the uninitiated from the soreness of real bareback riding and got the saddle out of the way.

Sammy Jo led Emmy around in a circle. The little girl squirmed and kicked and begged Pokey to speed up, but

Pokey listened only to Sammy Jo—and the call of the sugar cubes.

"I want to stand up!" Emmy cried. "Stand up!"

She struggled to her feet and Sammy Jo grabbed hold of her as Bev screeched from the sidelines. "Not yet. You're not ready."

"Yes, I am! Yes, I am! You meany!"

"Well, I may be a meany, but you're not ready to stand on top of a horse while it's moving. Look at your mom. Does she look happy with the idea?"

Bev's hand covered her mouth in horror.

"Don't care!" Emmy shrieked, kicking wildly. Sammy Jo hauled her off the horse and she ran screaming to Bev. Sighing, Sammy Jo looked at the other two. "Who's next?"

Van shrank back against the rails. If she could have melted into invisibility, it seemed she would have. Lorna threw Sammy Jo an amused look as Karen sucked her thumb vigorously and frowned down at her toes.

"We can just walk around in a circle," Sammy Jo encouraged. Karen scuffed her shoe in the dirt and nodded. Sammy Jo grabbed the little girl's free hand and pulled her to Pokey. Plunking her onto the bareback saddle, Sammy Jo said, "Okay?"

"'Kay," the little girl mumbled around her thumb.

Walking Pokey around in a circle, Sammy Jo hazarded a glance at the mothers. Ginny was clearly annoyed that Van wasn't joining in. Lorna beamed with delight. Bev couldn't decide whether to hug Emmy to her breast or save her silk blouse.

By the time they left, Sammy Jo wondered if it was worth the few dollars her lessons earned her. But then, money was money. And she needed every penny.

"See ya later," Lorna told her as she put the car into gear. "We need to talk."

"I'm afraid to ask about what." Sammy Jo waved to the other departing cars.

Lorna hooked her thumb in the direction of Cooper's ranch. "The rumors I've heard."

"He was with Bev on the Fourth of July."

"Did he really kiss you at the vet's?" Lorna shook her head in amazement.

"I thought it was a strange place, too," Sammy Jo answered, deliberately ignoring her friend's meaning.

"We do need to talk!" she repeated fervently.

"Goodbye, Lorna. 'Bye, Karen."

Sammy Jo stepped away from the car and waved as Lorna headed down the long driveway. A breeze ruffled Sammy Jo's hair, lifting it off her neck.

As she swatted dust from her jeans, Sammy Jo saw dark storm clouds gather along the horizon. Squinting, she calculated how long she had before the thunderstorm hit the ranch. Not long.

She considered a bath, but there was one more task she didn't want to put off any longer. Grimacing, she put a hand on the telephone. She needed to get that beaver dam taken care of, she reasoned, and therefore she needed to talk to Cooper.

She dialed swiftly, then glared down at her suddenly trembling fingers, infuriated by the hard, uneven beats of her heart. She cleared her throat several times, listening to the line ring at his end. What in God's name was wrong with her? He was just one solitary, chauvinistic, hardheaded, impossible man and—

"Hello?" The deep timbre of Cooper's voice sent a shiver down her spine.

She had to force herself not to slam down the receiver. Uncharacteristically tongue-tied, she said, "Cooper? It's Sammy Jo. I want to talk about the dam."

"Oh, right."

"Can you meet me there? We need to work together on this."

"When?"

"How about in an hour?"

She didn't have much faith that he would really drop everything and join her, but hey, it was time to make some decisions.

"We might get wet," Cooper observed.

With a quick glance to the thick, slate clouds settled over the mountains, she said, "Not if we hurry."

To her surprise, Cooper agreed to meet her there, so she described exactly where the dam was located, postponing her bath until later and hurrying to the barn. By the time she had her favorite quarter horse, Patty Cake, following the near-dry creek bed, the storm clouds had drawn closer and she could see the jagged flash of lightning forks.

"We'll make this quick." She patted Patty Cake's neck. By now she'd gotten herself in control and was amazed by her silly reaction to making that phone call. Good grief. She'd handled more than her share of men. She'd even wrestled some to the ground when they'd bugged her. Of course, that was in grade school, but as far as she was concerned, it still counted.

Just because some corporate-rancher-type had confused her with his good looks and tough attitude didn't mean she was whipped, either. She just hadn't expected him to kiss like that.

Like what? her ever present, impish conscience asked.

"Like *that,*" she answered aloud, feeling ridiculous. And so what that she'd liked his kiss? She was female, after all, and maybe the slumbering feminine side of her was finally waking up. It had been one long, deep sleep, she had to admit, but now it was over. And it was kind of nice to think maybe she could be interested in a man. Really interested. Interested in having one kiss her and touch her and maybe even make love to her...

"Oh, God," she murmured, then laughed aloud. Birds flew from the trees, squawking in protest at her ringing laughter. "Let's not get ahead of ourself, Sammy Jo!"

Catching a glimpse of red through the trees, she realized Cooper was already at the beaver dam. His red-and-black plaid shirt moved between the branches, looking hot as the dickens.

"Trying to bake yourself?" Sammy Jo asked, dropping lithely to the ground and winding Patty Cake's reins around a scrub bush.

He glanced down at his shirt. "Should I have come bare-chested?"

"I just meant, it's flannel and it looks...hot." His eyes said he read more into her comment than was there. Suddenly all business, Sammy Jo asked crisply, "What do you think?"

She gestured to the dam which, if possible, looked even sturdier and more formidable than before, branches woven tightly with mud and twigs, the felled tree limbs, some at least ten inches in diameter, tough girders indeed.

"This is going to take some serious work," Cooper said. He tested one of the branches with his foot. It didn't move an inch. "Where are the occupants?"

"Hiding," Sammy Jo said, smiling.

"Did you call the forest service?"

"We can relocate them to forest service land if we trap them and move them ourselves."

"And then after that, we'll pull this thing down." He looked at the dam.

"Kind of a shame, isn't it?" Sammy Jo said. "All that work."

Cooper shook his head. "It's going to be hell to break this up. It needs dynamite."

"Can't we dig it out?"

He gave her slim frame a long look. "We?"

"I'm stronger than I look."

"I don't doubt it. But this would be backbreaking."

He grinned and Sammy Jo's breath caught. He was handsome all right, but that smile was a killer. It took ten years off his age and sent her pulse rocketing into the ionosphere. Clearing her throat, Sammy Jo prayed that she appeared outwardly calm.

"Carl will help. When do you want to take it out?"

Thunder growled. Cooper glanced skyward and shrugged. "Some other time. This storm's going to catch us."

"You think?" Sammy Jo shook her head. "We'll make it back." At that moment, a fat raindrop plopped on the back of her neck and slid down her spine. Gasping, she added, "Or maybe not!"

Cooper laughed as raindrops spattered all around. He slapped his cowboy hat onto his head. Raindrops fell in a silver sheet. Sammy Jo ducked under a blanket of pine branches and Cooper joined her, his sleeve brushing her shoulder.

The rain ran over the sunbaked ground, turning to dusty rivulets that squiggled wildly in all directions. Sammy Jo inhaled and smelled more of Cooper's musky scent. She watched rain run off the brim of his hat and felt it trickle down her own temple.

They stood in silence for several moments while steam rose like wisps of smoke from the thirsty ground. Thunder rumbled threateningly after each split of lightning. Rain splattered and chattered like a frenzied conversation as it hit the still water of the pond. A beaver head appeared, then ducked back under the surface. Sammy Jo looked at Cooper, whose eyes crinkled with amusement.

"They're too cute for words, the little devils," she said. "Yes."

They stared at each other. Sammy Jo couldn't help remembering that last kiss. From the way his gaze traveled to her lips, he seemed to be thinking of it, too.

Thunder growled again. Sammy Jo stepped back, her boot slipping slightly. Cooper's hand automatically grasped her arm, but in the process, his fingers accidentally grazed her breast.

Sammy Jo swooped in a breath. She felt his fingers tighten, saw the change in his expression. Passion grew in the dense, warm privacy of the rain.

"Sammy Jo," he said softly, so softly she wasn't certain he'd really said anything.

"Maybe we should go back."

"Maybe," he agreed, pulling her close, too close. She shook her head as his mouth came down on hers, gently this time, completely shattering her resistance.

His hat slid down to the wet ground. He ignored it as his lips molded hers. Sammy Jo's breath escaped on a sigh of pleasure. His mouth drove conscious, sane thought from her mind. All she felt was moist heat from that kiss. Shivers down her back. Goose bumps on her arms.

His hand slid down her back to the base of her spine, drawing her forward until she was pressed so close she could scarcely breathe. Rain poured around them, dampening her hair, her skin, sticking her shirt to her back and chest. She felt his heart pounding sure and strong against breasts that felt oddly full and tight.

And then his lips parted hers, and he thrust his tongue inside her mouth. Sammy Jo jerked, mewed out a sound of protest, then was flooded with the most strange, liquid sensation. Her head reeled. The smell of moisture and damp leaves and some musky, primal scent she wasn't certain existed outside of herself blended into an exotic concoction; the scent of desire, she thought faintly, distantly.

She wound her arms around his neck. Heat emanated from his skin. Her fingers explored his hairline, and his own hands tangled in her mane, ripping the ponytail loose, luxuriating in the silken fullness of heavy blond strands.

BOOM! The crack of thunder was loud enough to wake the dead. Sammy Jo jumped, and even Cooper jerked in surprise. They broke apart, staring at each other. Sammy Jo's chest heaved.

"Just thunder," he said.

"Uh huh." His eyes were slumberous, yet flamed with pulsing excitement.

"And electricity," he added quietly.

"Yup." Sammy Jo couldn't speak. She watched his gaze drop to her still-trembling breasts, and her cheeks burned. "I don't understand," she admitted with pure honesty.

Cooper shook his head, the black strands of his hair sensuously wet. "Have you never kissed a man?"

"Of course I have!" she responded instantly. "Why? Did I do something wrong?"

"You know you didn't." He smiled, but passion lurked, waiting to be reignited.

"Well, I've kissed a man. Or two."

"Not like this."

His arrogance set her teeth on edge and her blood on fire. She fought against his compelling attraction. "No, not like this. This was—" she could feel his tension though he sought hard to disguise it "—better," Sammy Jo admitted, wrinkling her nose at her own honesty.

His lashes swept his cheek. "Better?"

Her heart slammed into her chest. "Yes, better."

Sammy Jo felt silly. Her fertile mind was already spinning pleasant scenarios. She couldn't help herself. Maybe Cooper wasn't so bad, after all.

"We could test the waters again," he suggested, his gaze frankly appreciative as it swept over her rain-soaked body.

"No," she demurred. This was dangerous. In an undefined way. Her feminine instincts were on overload, crying out for fulfillment. Fulfillment with Cooper. But this was tricky. Complicated. Downright reckless. "I've—I've got to think about things."

"What things?" His hand tugged on her arm, pulling her near once again. She concentrated on his top button, but above it, where his shirt gaped, she could see dark chest hair. Without conscious consent, her fingers touched that bare skin. He drew a sharp breath. "Sammy Jo," he warned huskily.

"This is nice, but I can't...."

"Can't?" he encouraged.

"Get sidetracked. I've got the Triple R to think about, and this won't work."

The words were ripped from that logical part of her mind that had led her throughout her life. It was a part that had served her well, all things considered. She never questioned its dominance over her emotions. Its logic was clear, where feelings and desires were murky and dangerous.

But it was the wrong thing to say to Cooper Ryan.

"Because I'm not husband material?" he asked in a quiet, ominous voice.

"Because you won't help me."

"What do you want me to do? Invest in the damn thing with you?"

"Why is that so terrible an idea?" Sammy Jo yanked her arm back, growing annoyed, in spite of her attraction to the man.

"You'd do anything to save this ranch, wouldn't you? You really *would* buy a husband!" He snatched up his hat, rain pouring off the brim unheeded. "Or maybe, just an investor," he added silkily.

His meaning wasn't lost on Sammy Jo. "You think I *kissed* you because I thought that might change your mind?"

"Well?"

Passion dissolved into fury. She wanted to kick him! "Actually, I hadn't thought of it until you put the idea in my head. Tell me, did it work?" she demanded coldly.

"No." His voice was frigid.

"Too damn bad. Looks like I'll have to marry Brent or Tommy or whoever decides to pop the question first!"

"You do that!"

"I sure will!"

"You wouldn't know the first thing about how to be a wife."

"Oh, wouldn't I? I'm sure as hell getting some great lessons on kissing, aren't I?"

His arm shot out. Sammy Jo jerked back, fists clenched. "Don't touch me."

"You can't see a damn thing beyond this ranch," he declared. "You hate the idea of marriage, but you'd get married just for the Triple R."

"I don't hate the idea of marriage."

"You're the worst liar I've ever met!" he snarled, his own temper igniting, and from the looks of it, it was a bear.

"Okay! I don't want to be married. I just want my ranch. Is that what you want to hear?"

"At least it's the truth!" He threw her a look of pure disgust.

"The hell it is," Sammy Jo snarled. "Your opinion of women is even lower than I thought!"

"I had a good teacher."

"Yeah?" Sammy Jo wasn't buying it. "Who?"

"My ex-wife."

Shaking her head, Sammy Jo said recklessly, "I feel for her. She must have been out of her head to ever marry you in the first place." Shoving at Cooper's chest, she surprised him into stepping backward. She unwound Patty Cake's reins, then led the horse away from the dam and Cooper, throwing him a last, disdainful look. His own expression had turned to stone. "I was nuts to think I could marry someone to save the ranch," she raged. "I was even nuttier to say so aloud. All it did was give chauvinists like you extra fodder. But the biggest mistake I ever made was thinking you might actually help me out of the kindness of your heart!"

With that, she slapped the reins against Patty Cake's neck and the mare trotted away from the pine grove.

Cooper balanced his glass of scotch and soda on his chest as he lounged deeply in the back-porch chair. He'd pulled his hat low over his eyes, effectively hiding his cold glare. He'd snarled at Jack and Lettie for no good reason, and now they were keeping their distance. Good. He wanted to be alone. He deserved to be alone. And he sure as hell was going to *be* alone, even if he had to bite someone's head off to do it!

What had he been thinking of? How could he have indulged in that spate of kissing with mule-stubborn Sammy Jo Whalen? Chauvinist? Hah! He was a *masochist!*

Swearing softly and succinctly under his breath, he poured a huge gulp of scotch and soda into his mouth, letting it burn his tongue and mouth for several seconds before swallowing.

Okay, she was attractive. And okay, there really hadn't been another woman since Pamela. The divorce had temporarily cooled his lust, dulled his sex drive. He'd been celibate ever since, though he'd never much thought about it, such had been his disinterest. But, hell. Sammy Jo Whalen had cured that temporary state. Being near her was like being burned alive.

He didn't even *like* her!

Cooper shifted position, uncomfortable with his thoughts. Sexual attraction knew no reason. Although he supposed he should be horrified that he was in lust with a woman he found repellent, he accepted it as the male curse. What he couldn't let himself do was act on it. That was a fact.

Okay, okay, for a moment there, he'd found her kind of charming. But it was the rain and the storm and the relaxing of that prickly wall she surrounded herself with. And then as soon as she showed her true colors again, he'd wanted to shake her until her teeth rattled and she showed some sign of . . . what? Remorse? Guilt for being who she was? Oh, *hell!* he thought. After he shook the living daylights out of her, he wanted to throw her on the ground and kiss her senseless.

Cooper growled in frustration, tossed back the rest of his drink and jumped to his feet. Stretching his shoulders, he prowled the space of the porch, his gaze involuntarily turning again and again to the Whalen property.

He needed a woman. A willing woman who could cure him of this self-destructive interest in Sammy Jo. It had been far too long, anyway. He snorted a laugh. Ninety percent of the world would think he was downright unnatural! They wouldn't understand that Pamela's wickedly avaricious ways had almost cured him of women altogether. But one sharp-tongued, headstrong, long-legged woman had reawakened his desire into an ache that couldn't be ignored. Or assuaged by anything less than a wild, sexual ride.

"Damn it," he said softly, annoyed right down to his boots.

The trouble was, he wanted only Sammy Jo.

Only Sammy Jo.

With fist-clenching resolve, he reached for the phone and called Bev Hawkins. Maybe she could save him.

"Hello, there! Anybody home?" Brent Rollins called from the barn door.

Sammy Jo slipped Tick-Tock an apple quarter and peeked around the end of the stall door. Brent was framed in the doorway.

"We're here," Doc Carey said before Sammy Jo could answer. He waved at Brent to come in.

Tick-Tock crunched the apple and blew against Sammy Jo's shirt. She rubbed the mare's nose absently.

"How's the mare?" Brent asked as he gingerly stepped across the hay-strewn barn floor. Sammy Jo could have told him there wasn't anything noxious he would step into, but she held her tongue and hid her annoyance.

"Needs to be shod," Doc Carey stated in his critical way.

"Barefoot and pregnant," Sammy Jo agreed with a smile.

Brent laughed, and Sammy Jo's mood improved. Anyone who appreciated her humor couldn't be all bad. He just wasn't a rancher.

"She looks good." Brent eyed the mare from a safe distance. Sammy Jo knew he'd be lucky to know which end was the front and which was the back.

"Healthy as a horse," Sammy Jo said with a smile.

"You take good care of her." Doc Carey scowled, as if Sammy Jo's levity were a sign of irresponsibility.

"I'll do my best."

"You just pay when you can."

The vet left the barn, and Sammy Jo couldn't prevent herself from heaving a sigh. She heard the engine of Doc Carey's truck sputter and cough before catching. Moments later, gravel crunched as the truck left.

Brent leaned against an empty stall door. "Ouch," he said, reading her thoughts. "Big bill?"

"Big enough. But I couldn't let Tick-Tock and her unborn foal die."

Brent nodded, looked around uncomfortably, then finally said what was on his mind, "There're a lot of rumors going around."

"About me?"

He nodded.

Sammy Jo could imagine. "What kind of rumors?" she asked tiredly.

"Oh, you know...." He shifted uneasily.

"Would the rumor you're referring to be the one about me wanting a husband to help save the Triple R? That one's true."

"Is that why you came to see me the other day?"

Her throat hurt. "Yup. Sorry if I've spoiled your illusions, Brent."

"I didn't have any illusions to spoil. You know how I feel about you."

His admission made her feel worse.

"I'm just afraid that you'd change your mind down the road," he said.

"If and when I get married, it's for keeps," she said with raw determination.

Brent's face relaxed. "I'd love to marry you. I'd just like to think you'd want to marry me, too. For me. Not just to save the ranch."

He'd said the words. He'd all but got down on one knee and proposed. But all Sammy Jo felt was utter numbness.

"I don't know what to say, Brent."

"Do I have a chance, Sammy Jo? I mean, there's nobody else in your life," he went on conversationally. "You've never shown interest in any other man. My biggest fear has always been that you didn't like us at all, if you know what I mean."

"I know what you mean," Sammy Jo said dryly.

"So, I've come to the conclusion that my biggest competition is the ranch."

"The ranch?" Sammy Jo repeated, somewhat surprised. She'd half expected him to name Cooper as his competition, as if he somehow knew about that hot kiss in the rain and her own reckless response. Obviously, he hadn't heard about the kiss at the veterinary clinic.

"The ranch. Ridge Range Ranch. The Triple R," he clarified. "Your only suitor. The only one you'll have."

"Don't be ridiculous," she snapped.

"But now there's a way that you can have your suitor, and maybe I can have a little bit of you, too," he added quietly. "What do you think?"

"About what?" she asked, half-hysterically.

"About you and I getting engaged. It's not such a bad idea, is it?"

She was about to tell him it was a terrible idea when she saw the anxious look on his face. Remembering Lorna's warning about being careful, she murmured painfully, "Brent..."

"It's the answer to your problems. And I think—I think I'd be good for you."

Sammy Jo turned away, hiding her face. It hurt because she knew it wasn't right. She could never be what he wanted, what he needed. She didn't feel that way about him, and she would never feel that way about him. Some things you just *knew*.

"Sammy Jo, I love you," Brent said awkwardly.

"No, Brent. No, you don't."

"Yes, I do!" he argued, belligerent as a child.

"Can I think it over?" she asked, wanting to end the conversation before she hurt him irrevocably.

"You don't have much time, though, right?"

"I'll think fast."

"Do that. Please."

She fought not to react when he kissed her lightly on the cheek before leaving. She heard him cross the barn floor, his steps careful as he negotiated his way through what might be lurking in the hay. She felt like laughing and crying at the same time.

She stayed beside Tick-Tock a long, long time after that, one hand stroking the mare's silken neck. She thought about Brent Rollins. Thought about his proposal.

But all she could really see was Cooper Ryan's strong face, and all she could think about was the touch of his hard fingers, his unique woodsy masculine scent, the sound of ragged breathing, the taste of rain on his lips. And the mesmerizing gaze of passion-filled blue eyes.

"Put *that* in the *Corral,* why don't you?" she murmured despondently, sinking onto a hay bale.

Tick-Tock nuzzled Sammy Jo's hair and ignored her problems completely.

Chapter Six

"Did ya hear the news?" Aggie chortled, ringing up bags of feed for Sammy Jo at Bentley Feed and Grain. "That handsome neighbor of yours is seeing Bev Hawkins!"

"I heard," Sammy Jo answered, her gaze fixed on the half a dozen thirty-pound bags. If Aggie didn't give her credit, she'd be in a heck of a pickle.

Aggie shook her head and swiped at the gray hair that had escaped her bandanna. "Ever since she and Roy split up, she's been actin' like a city gal. But I think that Mr. Cooper's just the man to keep her in town. Mmmm-hmmm!"

"Mr. Ryan."

"Huh?"

"His name's *Cooper* Ryan. Why can't anyone remember that?"

Aggie's shaggy eyebrows lifted at Sammy Jo's testiness. "I bet Bev remembers it." Sammy Jo clamped her jaw shut, her face blushing furiously. Aggie went right on, "Oh, that dark-haired fellow's got a sexy drawl. My, my. Supposedly from the city, but he ain't got any of them silly ways."

"He's got some silly ways," Sammy Jo argued darkly.

Aggie shot Sammy Jo an amused look. "Got your cap set for him, Sammy Jo?"

Sammy Jo snorted. "He'd be the last man I'd be interested in."

"And why is that?"

Realizing Aggie was digging for information, Sammy Jo wished she'd never allowed herself to be drawn into this conversation. "Because he's domineering, argumentative and judgmental, and I just don't like him."

"Oh." Aggie's look was knowing.

"And Brent Rollins asked me to marry him," Sammy Jo announced.

Instantly she regretted her rash words. Aggie's face lit up with delight. "Why, that's wonderful! Brent's a heck of a fellow."

"Yeah . . . I know." Her voice lacked enthusiasm.

"He'll be a good husband. Congratulations, Sammy Jo."

Sammy Jo smiled faintly. Since Brent's "sort-of" proposal in the barn, she'd seen him twice. Once for coffee, once for a picnic in the small park off Main Street. There'd been no more talk of marriage—thank God!—but Sammy Jo knew Brent was waiting for an answer.

This morning, Matt Durning had called and talked long and hard about Sammy Jo's plans. He was clearly feeling guilty about the bank's hard-line position, but his guilt didn't mean Valley Federal was changing its mind about foreclosure. Nosirree. Still, no one had come to kick her out the door just yet, so maybe she had a little time left.

But marriage? To Brent?

"So, when's the big date?" Aggie grinned broadly.

Sammy Jo was saved from answering by the arrival of Jack Babbitt.

"Well, hello there," Jack greeted her. "Long time no see."

"I know. I've been meaning to stop by," Sammy Jo apologized. Like she really would with Cooper there.

"Well, y'know the strawberries are lookin' peaked, but peaches are turnin' gold. And Lettie makes a fine peach cobbler."

"Oh, it's gonna be a few weeks 'til them peaches get good enough for a cobbler," Aggie argued. "Don't get Sammy Jo's mouth waterin' just yet."

"I promise to drop by as soon as I can," Sammy Jo said, ending the argument.

The cash register bell dinged loudly as Aggie pressed the button for the cash drawer. "Well, let's see now. How're you payin' for the feed?" Aggie asked Sammy Jo.

"Can you put it on my bill?" Sammy Jo asked, swallowing.

Aggie gave her a piercing look.

"Put it on Mr. Ryan's bill," Jack suggested. "The man said he owed Sammy Jo for what she and Carl did on that beaver dam that was stoppin' up Cotton Creek."

"No, put it on *my* bill," Sammy Jo reiterated sternly. She and Carl hadn't taken out the dam. They'd managed to move a few sticks around, but that was the extent of it. The beaver dam was still standing sturdy and strong. Luckily, the trapper they'd hired had managed to move the beaver family to forest service land without mishap—paid for courtesy of Cooper Ryan—so now she and Cooper were just left with one heck of an architectural wonder.

Aggie twiddled a pen in her fingers, clearly undecided. "Well, honey, you got a pretty big bill already," she murmured uneasily. "I don't know if I can give out any more credit."

"When'd you become such a stickler, Aggie?" Jack complained. "Give the girl the feed!"

"I gotta be careful, that's all."

"No, it's okay," Sammy Jo interrupted. "I'll—pick up the feed later."

"Damn it, Aggie!"

"Sammy Jo, honey, I'll put it on your bill," Aggie said, giving in. "I know you're good for it."

A hot lump swelled in Sammy Jo's throat as she watched Bentley employees load the feed into the back of her pickup. It had been difficult to thank Aggie properly for her kindness, so Sammy Jo had just nodded her appreciation. Now, her eyes stung and she had to clamp her jaw and blink rapidly several times to bring herself under control.

At the ranch, she hauled the feed to the storage bins in the barn, then headed dejectedly for the house. She had a date with Brent tonight. This was when she was supposed to give him her answer. He was waiting.

Sighing, she took a long, hot bath, then with extra care, she fixed her hair and pulled out a white dress with long, droopy lace around its elastic neckline. She pulled the neckline over her shoulders, and stared at her reflection. Slightly Spanish-looking, the dress had been one she'd bought on a lark, then had shoved to the back of her closet. Now, she stared at it grimly, aware she was about to make the most momentous decision of her life.

"Well, it isn't San Francisco. Not even close," Bev Hawkins giggled, "but it's nice, isn't it?"

Cooper glanced around The Riverside's slate patio. It was more like a deli, really, though in the evenings the place did serve one mouth-watering special. The best part about it was the view. Drought-bleached grass rolled down to the clearwater stream, which wound its way through downtown. During less dry seasons, the grass was green and lush, but Cooper still appreciated the prettiness of the setting. Around the patio's perimeter hung Japanese lanterns, creating an almost romantic atmosphere, and he could make out the outline of one or two of those metal stars that studded the bank.

Bev apparently felt the romance. She leaned her elbows on the table and gazed rapturously at Cooper. She was a beautiful woman in a well-tended way. Her skirt was short above shapely legs; her taupe silk blouse hugged her breasts. Her skin was smooth, and he suspected she helped keep it that way by buying products from those half-hour Info-mercials that clogged every cable channel on Sunday mornings.

She was definitely an expensive woman.

He could have told her he'd paid the price for her type once before—and the price was too damn high. But she was lonely and miserable. Contrary to popular belief, her husband had left *her,* and she was trying to pick up the pieces.

"Beautiful night, isn't it?" Bev remarked softly.

On that he could agree. The air had cooled down to a comfortable seventy-five degrees, and the night was still, warm and sparkling with countless stars. Cooper leaned back and took a deep breath, the director's chair creaking slightly under his weight. He'd left his hat at the house and traded his blue jeans for a pair of brushed chinos, as much a concession to fashion and proper attire as he cared to make.

"I guess that little thunderstorm the other day was a taste of what's to come," Bev went on with small talk. "Weatherman's predicting more later on this week."

"Hmm," Cooper answered.

"You're quite the conversationalist, aren't you?"

"Sorry." He made an effort. "I was thinking about the ranch."

"You've really gotten attached to Serenity, haven't you?"

"I like Coldwater Flats."

"This little burg?" She laughed. "I've spent my whole life here and the only time I've been happy is when I've taken trips to Los Angeles. But Roy would never move, and now..."

"You could leave," he suggested.

"Roy would move heaven and earth to keep Emmy, and I don't want the fight. But we were talking about you. You really like this place?" She gestured disbelievingly to her surroundings.

"I'm a small-town boy at heart," Cooper said with a smile.

"I don't believe that. This is just a diversion for you. It's not the real you."

Who was she trying to convince, him, or herself? It was clear Bev wanted to ship out. And she wanted to use him as the vessel.

Cooper was searching around for a way to make his feelings clear when musical, feminine laughter met his ears. Familiar laughter. Sammy Jo's laughter.

He turned, but apart from the ponderosa pines, aspens and scattering of wildflowers, there was no one in sight. Amazing, how someone with such a lemon-sour disposition could have such a beautiful laugh, Cooper reflected in irritation. Sammy Jo Whalen was the testiest, orneriest, most unfeminine woman he'd ever had the misfortune to run across, and woe to the unsuspecting male who—

She appeared at that moment, long tanned legs swinging around the corner of the slate patio. Her hair was down, loose, straight and full; her dress white, glowing softly in the dim light of dusk; her feet, delicately arched and small, enclosed in white strappy sandals; her mouth a soft smile, the kind of smile that could melt steel. A surge of possessive desire swept through him. Her long-lashed eyes crinkled at the corners with real humor, and they were focused on . . .

The man she was with.

Cooper couldn't help staring. The man was about Sammy Jo's age. Dark hair. Uncalloused hands. Wearing a suit. A business-type. Could even have been any number of the young men who'd buzzed into corporate ranching with big dreams and bigger mouths and who'd buzzed out again as soon as they realized they had to work for a living.

Unfair, his rational mind told him, but he didn't feel like being fair.

"Do you know Brent?" Bev asked.

"Brent?"

"Brent Rollins. He's Coldwater Flats's local real estate agent. There are others in the area, of course, but Brent's the only one who really matters. There isn't that much buying and selling going on here. You didn't use him when you bought Serenity?"

"I don't think so." The truth was, he hadn't paid a lot of attention. He'd seen the place, called the agency and signed papers within one week.

"I know you know Sammy Jo," she stated carefully.

He forced himself to drag his gaze from one of Sammy Jo's shapely legs. That ruffled dress had hiked up her thigh, giving him a good, long look before she tugged it down.

Cooper's mouth was cotton.

The waitress stopped by their table. "Tonight's picnic night," she said. "You'd be a fool not to order our special—the Riverside's own fried chicken, 'To Die For' potato salad and watermelon."

"God forbid I should be a fool," Cooper drawled. "I'll take the special." Glancing at Bev, he caught her nod of agreement, but past her, Sammy Jo's real estate friend was seating her at a table. "Make that two," he said just as his gaze collided with Sammy Jo's. "And I'd like another beer. Quick."

"White wine," Bev told the waitress, pointing to her empty glass.

Sammy Jo's animated face darkened, and she turned away quickly. Perversely, Cooper was glad to note that he affected her. Negatively, maybe, but at least it was something.

"You haven't had any run-ins with her, then?"

"Who?" he asked automatically.

"Sammy Jo," Bev stressed, fighting annoyance.

"What do you mean, run-ins?"

"Well, she's got this god-awful temper. Anybody who knows her will tell you the same. She's prickly as a porcupine and stubborn as a mule."

And pretty as a picture, his fertile mind couldn't help adding. "Honest as the day is long?" he asked, amused.

Bev stared at him uncomprehendingly. "I guess. At least I never heard anyone complain about her cheating them. Not yet, anyway."

"I'll keep my guard up."

Bev smiled faintly. Sammy Jo laughed again, and the sound seemed to envelop them, like the scent of expensive perfume. Irritated by his susceptibility to a self-proclaimed shrew, Cooper practically grabbed his beer off the waitress's tray and proceeded to gulp half of it down.

". . . you don't know how to take a compliment," Brent accused her, smiling. "I tell you how beautiful you look, and you laugh."

"You'd better believe it." Sammy Jo buried her nose in a glass of red wine. She preferred white, but seeing perfect Bev drawing her index finger around the rim of a glass of white wine, then slowly lifting the glass to her luscious red lips had changed Sammy Jo's mind on the spot. Juvenile, perhaps, but hey, who said she had to grow up all at once?

"You *are* beautiful," Brent insisted.

"Okay, I'm beautiful," Sammy Jo returned flippantly. For reasons probably buried deep in her psyche, she could never handle anyone commenting on her looks. Her personality, yes. The moment some bozo complained about her, she was ready to battle it out. But a compliment on her looks, something you were basically born with and could only alter so much—even with plastic surgery—made her uneasy. It almost compelled her to show the nasty side of her temper, though she'd told herself specifically to be on her best behavior with Brent.

She was going to accept his proposal of marriage. It was the prudent—the only—thing to do. Half the people in the world married for love and were miserable. She would marry for *like* and maybe be happy.

"What do you want to order?"

Feeling the weight of someone's gaze, she glanced up. Cooper flicked her a look, then turned back to Bev. Sammy Jo stared pointedly, then became conscious of Brent waiting.

She cleared her throat. "What's the special?"

"Fried chicken and picnic stuff."

"I'll take it." Spying his frown, she asked, "What about you?"

"I think I'll have the vegetarian sandwich."

"Do you like animals in any form, Brent?" Sammy Jo couldn't help making the barb. "You don't raise them, and you don't eat them."

"Do I detect a criticism?"

"Just curiosity."

"Does my answer matter?"

In her peripheral vision she saw Cooper lean forward to listen to something Bev was saying. Something about Emmy. Sammy Jo caught a glimpse of his strong jaw and dark lashes before she snapped her attention back to Brent. "No," she answered shortly, then could have kicked herself for the flash of hurt that crossed his face. "I mean, nobody has to love animals, and hey, I wish I could give up meat, but it just isn't in me."

"You're one in a million, Sammy Jo."

She couldn't tell from that remark whether that was good or bad. "Well, you know me," she deflected, gulping more wine.

She was too conscious of Cooper and Bev. It was as if the very air thrummed with their vibes.

Brent said, "Have you come to any decision yet?"

"About?"

"Marriage."

The subject was rearing up again sooner than she wanted. But she needed to take the plunge, didn't she? Beneath the table, her hand fisted, her nails biting into the flesh of her palm. She forced herself not to glance at Cooper again. "I've been thinking about it."

"And?"

"It's an important decision. A really tough one. And I don't mean that to sound negative," she added hurriedly. "But, you know . . ." She trailed off.

"I do know." His sincerity made her feel worse.

"I'm kind of independent." She half laughed.

"I like that about you."

"I'm a pain in the you-know-what. Everyone says so. And I'm going to run the Triple R the way I want to run it. Period."

"I have no interest in running the ranch."

She stared at him helplessly.

"I don't care how much trouble you are," he said, answering her look. "I love you. I've always loved you. I just thank my lucky stars that you need me!"

Sammy Jo couldn't disagree more, but she stilled her tongue. Brent reached across the table for her hand. The silence was eloquent as he waited for her answer.

Sammy Jo's heart thundered in her ears. She could feel Cooper's presence, overwhelmingly male and strong. It filled her senses, frighteningly so. She would be crushed by a man like him.

"I would like to marry you, Brent," she said in a clear voice, but to her ears it sounded as if it came from a long, long way away.

Cooper froze, unable to swallow the luscious bite of fried chicken. It lodged in his throat, as big as a whole watermelon. *Sammy Jo Whalen just agreed to marry that jackass!*

"Something wrong?" Bev's eyebrows drew together in concern.

He had to wash the bite down with beer. He couldn't breathe. His blood pounded, hot and throbbing.

Covertly, he watched the waiter serve Sammy Jo and Brent their meals. She shifted her weight, and he couldn't help but sneak another look at her slim legs.

Desire, dark and tempting, swept through him. He had to resist the urge to reach over and yank Sammy Jo from her chair, shake her and demand for her to think!

But that was just part of it. A small part. He really wanted to kiss her, bend her over his arm, or better yet, push her down on one of the red-and-white-checked table-cloths and cover her body with his.

The image was so hot, so tempting, so real, that he was momentarily blinded to anything but that desperate, swelling need.

"You look . . . stern," Bev said, glancing at Sammy Jo, though Cooper had purposely brought his attention back to the remains of his meal.

A pulse beat in his jaw. Images slashed across his mind. Images of a woman in the throes of passion. Sammy Jo. Head thrown back. Arms wrapped around his neck. Legs clamped tightly around his hips. Thrusting into her. Hot. Silky. Wet.

"Dessert?" the waiter asked.

Cooper nearly jumped from his skin. What the *hell* was the matter with him?

"No, thank you," Bev said primly.

"Check, please."

She arched penciled eyebrows. "We're leaving?"

"Did you want something else?"

His terseness didn't escape her notice. She hesitated. Almost as if she couldn't help herself, she looked over at Sammy Jo and Brent again. Brent was star-struck, gazing at Sammy Jo as if she'd given him the world. Sammy Jo was pale, and she ate slowly. Feeling Bev's gaze, she glanced up, but her eyes searched for Cooper.

His gut tightened. It hurt to look at her. Unsure why he was feeling so wildly protective and just plain randy, Cooper scratched out his name on the check and walked away, Bev trailing behind.

"Cooper..."

Sammy Jo's voice arrested him. With an effort, he turned her way, purposely keeping his features under control.

"Since the beavers are settling into their new, and hopefully happy, home, when do you want to take out the dam?"

Her green eyes were luminous. A whirl of color from the Japanese lanterns slashed across her bare shoulders, turning her white dress and skin into soft shades of peach, aquamarine and mint green.

"Tomorrow?" he suggested.

"D-day. Dam day," she added for clarification. "What time?"

"Let's make it early. I've got things to do."

His brusqueness wasn't lost on Sammy Jo. Her thick lashes drew together, a tiny line forming between her eyebrows. Cooper forced his gaze to remain on her face, though the dusky hollow between her breasts beckoned.

"I'll be there at six," she told him, then turned back to Brent.

"I'll bring the tractor."

They had already decided on their plan to remove the dam; Jack had told him he'd explained it all to Sammy Jo earlier. Now, she nodded dismissively and Cooper left.

Bev followed him to the car. He held the door for her, but didn't react to the whisper of nylon and silk as she slid inside. Sammy Jo's legs had been bare. He could have reached out and touched them. Smooth. Sleek. Muscular.

"Emmy's at her father's," Bev said by way of letting him know she was free until all hours.

"Sorry. I've got a lot of work to do tomorrow."

She nodded.

He felt like a horse's ass. He'd used her. He hadn't meant to, but it still wasn't fair. Maybe it was for the best. Bev wasn't his type. Neither, by God, was Sammy Jo.

He needed a woman. He still needed a woman. But maybe one not as high-profile as Bev Hawkins would fill the bill.

His house was dark when he got home. Lettie and Jack had trundled off to their bedroom at the south end of the house. Cooper was virtually alone. Standing on the back porch, he watched a moth fling itself at the porch light in what looked like ritualistic suicide. Finally, the insect sat next to the lamp while other moths joined it, circling and battering themselves senseless.

He felt in tune with them. Nothing he would like more than battering himself senseless. So thinking, he went in search of a bottle of Jack Daniel's, prepared for a long, lonely night.

Sammy Jo awakened with the birds. A dull heaviness hung over her, a vague dread. She had to search carefully through her mind to find its source, like picking through cold embers to find that still throbbing, hot coal.

She'd told Brent she'd marry him.

Groaning, she pressed her face into her pillow. Trigger jumped up and licked her cheek, and the next instant, Sammy Jo leaped to her feet and threw on her clothes. No shower today. She was heading straight for the beaver dam.

She drove the pickup, leaving a whining Trigger behind. Bumping across the field, the truck bounced and jarred along at a fast clip until the terrain grew too rocky and studded with trees, and she was forced to stop. She could hear the engine of Cooper's tractor. He'd come through the section of fence she'd jerry-rigged. It was at a point where Cotton Creek was fully on her property with about an acre of land between it and the dividing fence.

Cooper had squeezed the tractor down the field to where the creek cut off the acreage, near the fence. The growling vehicle now stood on a peninsula of land upstream from the dam on the opposite side of the creek from Sammy Jo.

Jack was there, too, yelling something to Cooper, who sat at the wheel of the tractor. Sammy Jo couldn't make out the words over the deafening thunder of the engine and the crack of wood as the hook attached to the tractor hitch bit into a sturdy timber, the backbone of the dam.

She got out of the pickup and waved, hoping the two men would see her. They were lost in their own conversation. Cooper shifted gears. The tractor jerked forward. Timber screamed, broke and threw particles of wood in all directions. Sammy Jo hit the ground, covering her face from the flying shrapnel.

The engine cut. Silence. "Sammy Jo!" Cooper called, aghast.

"I'm okay. Really." Slowly picking herself up, she brushed off bits of dirt, sticks and wet wood.

"I didn't know you were there."

"That's comforting," she said with a smile. "I'm glad to know it wasn't on purpose."

His look was inscrutable beneath the brim of his hat.

"We're gonna pull this baby down, sure enough," Jack said, hacking at the nearest logs with an ax.

"I can't help feeling a little bad," Sammy Jo remarked.

It had taken hours of labor for the beavers to build such a remarkable structure. Now, the poor beasts had to start from scratch. Yet, without Cotton Creek's sustaining water, the ground would dry up completely to the south and the vegetation that thrived at both the Triple R and Serenity Ranch would suffer.

Not to mention the ripple effect on the animals. No water, no feed, no nothing.

Cooper didn't answer her, just went about his business. It bugged her. Was he really so impervious to nature and its balance? Yes, the dam had to be taken down, but couldn't they at least mourn the wasted effort and feel pain in their hearts?

Knowing she was being overly sentimental, Sammy Jo fought her own feelings and helped drag dirt and debris out of the stream as Cooper's tractor yanked out the more massive logs. Soon water was trickling through a small V, then it was streaming, then it was rushing wildly, like a pack of racers fighting to be first over the finish line. The three of them pulled the last of the major branches to the shore.

"All done," Cooper called to her across the creek. Jack leaned on his ax, watching with satisfaction. Water poured over the thick mud, digging grooves through the sluggish silt, pushing it south. Soon Cotton Creek would be flowing smoothly and the mushy earth around the manufactured pond would dry out and revert to its normal state.

Cooper and Jack conferred for a moment, then Jack jumped on the tractor and drove it back toward the hole in the fence. To Sammy Jo's surprise, Cooper splashed through the creek and came up on her side.

"Hey," she murmured, stepping back.

"Well, that's one problem resolved."

"Yeah, right." Sammy Jo folded her arms over her chest and glanced in the direction of the house. "I'd better get to my chores."

"Wait a minute."

Sammy Jo gave him a cautious look. He hadn't shaved this morning, and it gave him a rakish appearance she found terribly appealing. *No, no, no!* This was no time to notice the way his strong brown hands swept off his cowboy hat and brushed through his hair. Nor should she realize that within his blue eyes were darker striations, deeper color that added to their mystery.

Nor should her pulse thud until it hurt.

"I heard you agree to marry Brent last night."

Her breath caught. "Oh?"

"So you're really going through with it?"

"I—guess so."

"You don't sound too sure."

"What's it to you?" she demanded, more angry at herself than him.

"Nothing. Not a damn thing," he stated with suppressed frustration.

"Good."

He seemed to want to say a heck of a lot more, but Sammy Jo gave him her coldest glare. If he wanted a fight, fine. She felt like a fight.

"You disappoint me," he said quietly, then turned back to the water, as if he'd said all he was going to say.

That did it. He'd scraped her nerves raw with her own guilt, a trick her father had been a master at, and now planned to run away! "How was Bev?" Sammy Jo asked tightly.

"Bev was fine."

"Just *fine?*" She didn't know what spurred her on, some basic masochistic need.

Cooper turned to her, his lips curved into a nasty smile Sammy Jo felt she'd somehow earned. "I took her home after dinner."

"Oh?" Sammy Jo's eyebrow arched. She believed that, all right!

"Are you asking about my sex life?" he demanded calmly. She snorted, but he went right on, "You are. You want to know if Bev and I got down to making love."

"Oh, come on!"

He gazed down at her coolly. "Actually, we did. In fact, I decided to show her the beaver dam. We came back to the ranch, crossed over the fence and stood right about here." He gestured to the trampled ground beneath their feet. Sammy Jo didn't believe him. He was doing this on purpose! But her heart started beating a hard, hurting tattoo. "Then we started kissing," he said, "kind of like you and I did earlier."

"Stop it!"

"And then . . ."

"You say one more word and I'll kill you!"

"I unbuttoned her blouse," Cooper went on relentlessly. "Each button through the hole, one by one. Then she was standing there, just skin and lace and I—"

Sammy Jo slugged him, with everything she had. The microsecond before she connected with his stomach, he twisted protectively, one arm slamming down on hers, deflecting the blow. She cried out as Cooper pushed her backward, against the hard trunk of a tree. Her breath came out in a whoosh, and she was left gasping for air.

"I didn't do a damn thing with Bev and if you had any sense in that rock-hard head of yours, you'd know it!"

"You bastard!" she snapped in fury.

"You asked for it!" he retorted, just as furious.

"Get your hands off me!"

"There you go again, pulling at me, pushing at me, then mad when I react. Well, you've got a lot to learn, lady rancher. A lot to learn!"

"Let go of me or I'll scream."

"Scream," he ordered. "As loud as you can."

Nothing could have clamped her lips closed faster and tighter. Sammy Jo glared at him mutinously, daring him to further manhandle her.

Cooper shook his head, as if he couldn't believe her at all. "Don't marry Rollins. It's a mistake."

"I'll marry whomever I damn well please."

"I thought you were better than this. Smarter."

"I like Brent, okay. Really like him. This isn't all about the Triple R."

"The hell it isn't." His mouth twisted. "You're marrying him to save the ranch. You're marrying him for money."

Sammy Jo squirmed, infuriated beyond reason. Cooper wasn't expecting her strength, and she was free before he could grab her again.

"Get off my property! Leave me alone, and just go away!"

"Gladly," he said through gritted teeth. He twisted on one heel, heading toward the creek. So furious she could scarcely see straight, Sammy Jo lifted one small booted foot and gave him a little helpful heave-ho in the derriere. Cooper stumbled and then to Sammy Jo's consternation, fell into the water, his hat floating on the surface.

"Oh, God!" Sammy Jo's eyes widened in horror. Clapping a hand to her mouth, she jumped forward, shocked at herself, ready to bolt as soon as his head reappeared. He would be furious! Oh, Lord, he would *kill* her!

He surfaced slowly, water streaming from his hair, his blue shirt sticking to his chest, his expression grim. He scooped up his hat and glared coldly at Sammy Jo. If Sammy Jo had ever seen murder in another person's eyes, it was burning in Cooper's at that moment.

Steepling her fingers, she rested them against her lips. "Sorry," she murmured. "I'm really sorry. Really."

Silently, he stalked up the muddy bank, slipping several times. Sammy Jo fought back a hysterical laugh. His eyes skewered hers and her own danced with mirth mingled with fear.

Cooper continued forward and Sammy Jo couldn't help staggering backward. Pine branches tangled in her hair, holding her captive. She couldn't break her gaze from his. There was no mercy in his eyes, just unrelenting, frigid fury.

"Cooper . . . really . . . I wasn't thinking."

"Do you ever?" he growled.

"You just made me so mad. I'm not proud of my tactics, but I'll . . . I'll make Brent a good wife. I will. It'll work out."

"Someone ought to teach you a lesson."

She frowned, not liking the sound of that at all.

"You've got a mean temper."

"You know, you're right. I do. And you do, too, sort of," she rattled on desperately, her fingers yanking on the pine branches to free herself.

"That's true." He loomed in front of her, bristling with male fury. "Someone ought to pound some sense into that hard head of yours."

"Well, it's not going to be you." She ripped her hair free. "Ow!"

He grabbed her arm, his hand shooting out with the speed of a striking rattler. Sammy Jo automatically resisted, glaring at him. She wasn't really afraid. She'd never been afraid of any man. But then, she'd never antagonized one quite so much before. At least not since she was a kid.

"Whatever you plan to do, don't," she advised. Her heart thundered, fear suddenly shooting through her veins like poison.

He pulled her forward. Intuitively, Sammy Jo knew he couldn't decide whether to bend her over his knee to tan her hide or to kiss her. How silly! How ironic! It was enough to make her laugh aloud.

Her lips curved, drawing his gaze. "Cooper, I—"

His mouth swept down on hers, hard and crushing. Her blood rose with the demand, surging wildly in response, singing. She gasped and his tongue followed as she bent over his arm like a willow branch.

His hand was in the small of her back, fingers hard against her skin. Her shoulders touched the bark of the pine. He pressed her backward, his hips hard against hers. His mouth promised pleasures she'd never dreamed of. Sammy Jo twisted away, but he was insistent, pulling her back, staring at her in such a way that her resistance melted like snowflakes under a hot sun.

"I don't . . ."

"Shh," he warned her, and instead of an angry, pursuing male, she was suddenly faced with a man trying to gain control of his emotions. He closed his eyes, fighting some inner demon, and Sammy Jo, fascinated, didn't use the opportunity to escape. Instead, she waited for him to open his eyes, waited breathlessly.

She wanted . . . something. Something he could give her. Reason fled beneath true sexual desire. When his lashes lifted, he gazed into pure, innocent eyes of crystal green.

"God," he whispered, kissing her again, insistently. This time, Sammy Jo didn't think of resistance. A small moan escaped her lips. The weight of his body was an intoxicant. She wanted to drag him closer, as close as possible, and he seemed intent on the same.

His hand slid up her back, around the front to cup her breast. He squeezed it hard and Sammy Jo panted, shocked. The buttons of her shirt miraculously fell free and then his thumb traveled the edge of her bra.

Heaviness infused her breasts. They felt hard and liquid at the same time. Her knees were water. His mouth kept hers prisoner while one hand cupped her breast and his hips thrust against hers.

"Cooper," Sammy Jo breathed, choking the name out.

The sound of her voice only spurred him onward. Now, his hand moved downward to the curve of her hip. Sammy Jo swept in a breath, alarmed, yet when his hand found the juncture of her thighs, rubbing through her jeans, she was too surprised and distracted by his boldness and the feel of it to do more than whisper a faint protest, which even to her ears sounded more like a moan of pleasure.

His fingers went to her belt. Above her head, the shriek of a blue jay nearly shattered her eardrum. Sammy Jo jumped. Her eyes flickered open. The jay scolded again and was joined by an irritated squirrel.

Reality struck, hard and painful. "What the hell do you think you're doing?" she demanded, thrusting him away, her fists balling.

Passion swam in those blue eyes. The glazed look he swept over her was almost her undoing, but horror had replaced desire, constricting her chest all over again.

"Kissing you," he admitted frankly. "And more."

"You forced yourself on me."

His mouth formed a silent, *"What?"*, as incredulity filled his expression.

"You did," Sammy Jo insisted. "I didn't ask to be manhandled. You...threatened me."

"You loved it!"

"I did not!" Sammy Jo shook with belated reaction. "I hate being touched, and I especially hate being touched by you!"

"Oh, yeah?"

"Yeah!"

The childishness of their conversation wasn't lost on either of them. Sammy Jo's chin was thrust forward, daring him to refute her. Cooper examined her face emotionlessly. A sound rumbled faintly. It took Sammy Jo a moment to realize it was laughter, low in his throat.

"You're too much," he said, his amusement spilling into a roar of mirth. The man actually tipped back his head and howled.

"I don't see what's so funny."

"Yes, you do." He brought himself under control with difficulty, passion dissipating with the release of emotion. "You're the biggest liar, and you do most of your lying to yourself."

That ticked her off royally. "I want the Triple R, and I'm going to make Brent Rollins a good wife!"

"I could have had you right now."

Slapping his hat onto his head, he splashed back through the creek. Sammy Jo didn't have time to do much, but she managed to scoop up some mud and fling it at him. It hit his shoulder, splattering like chocolate pudding to mark his entire shirt.

His deep chuckle was her only indication that he'd even noticed.

Chapter Seven

"**O**rnery, black-hearted, miserable, son-of-mongrel-dirt-chewing dog...doesn't deserve to live on the planet...hope he chokes on his own self-importance and dies a horrible, screaming death..."

The litany had gone on for hours. Days, actually. Any time Sammy Jo was alone, she vented her feelings about Cooper Ryan. At the house. In the barn. In the fields. It didn't matter that Ridge Range Ranch's livestock didn't seem to care. While the horses stared at her in gentle bewilderment, Sammy Jo kept up a stream of consciousness liberally sprinkled with words that would scorch the ears of the good, churchgoing people of Coldwater Flats, had they but heard them.

Sweating, Sammy Jo grabbed a bale by its twine and thumped it atop another at the crest of the hayloft. Her hands hurt, and she gasped for air. The air was dense as soup and almost as hot. Her eyes burned from floating bits of straw and dust.

She'd been called a lot of names over the years, some of them well and truly earned, but she'd never been treated so downright nastily by a member of the male sex. Who in God's name did he think he was, anyway? Telling her she would have lain down and *done it* with *him!*

"Bastard," Sammy Jo muttered fiercely. She hated him. All the way down to the tips of her boots.

Men like Cooper Ryan gave the whole male population a bad name.

Gazing out the open hayloft door, she focused on the dots of cattle and horses in the field. As if of their own volition, her eyes turned toward Cooper's property. Someone was standing by the fence about a quarter of a mile off. Cooper?

Sammy Jo aimed an imaginary rifle, pulled the trigger and blew him away. "Take that!"

Immediately, she felt like an idiot. She was smarter than this. Above it. So he'd been crude and superior and completely wrong. No reason to act like a child. She was going to marry Brent and she didn't give a rat's patootie what Cooper Ryan or the rest of Coldwater Flats thought about it.

You're the biggest liar. And you do most of your lying to yourself.

Through her anger, Sammy Jo could still feel the stab of that remark. It hadn't been as pointed as some of his other comments, but it had been the one that hit vital tissue. She knew he meant she was lying about Brent in particular.

Uneasy, she went back to yanking hay bales around until exhaustion forced her back to the house. After pouring a glass of lemonade down her parched throat, she wiped her mouth with the back of her hand, then gazed at the living-room telephone. She'd avoided Brent since their date. She'd avoided everyone.

Wrinkling her nose, she placed the call she'd been dreading for days.

"Rollins Real Estate," Brent's sister, Connie, answered.

"Hi, this is Sammy Jo. Is Brent around?"

"Oh, hi, Sammy Jo. He's showing the Pendleton house to some couple from California."

"Think I can barge in?"

Sammy Jo could hear her chew on her pencil. "Gee, I don't know."

"Okay, fine. I'll wait for his call." She hung up, her hand staying on the receiver for long seconds afterward. It had been three days since her fight with Cooper. She touched her lips experimentally. Three days since he'd last kissed her.

Snorting, she flung herself onto the couch. Kissed her? *Kissed her?* Hah! He'd done a lot more than just press his lips to hers. He'd made one pretty heavy-duty pass, baby. Really heavy-duty.

. . . you do most of your lying to yourself. . . .

Covering her face with her hands, Sammy Jo groaned in anguish. He was right! Instead of kicking him where it counts, she'd practically tumbled to the ground and begged him to take her right then and there!

And, why? *Why?* Sammy Jo shook her head in consternation. Over and over again in the past, she'd ripped guys verbally up one side and down the other as soon as they made the slightest remark about her feminine attributes. She'd stopped them cold with drop-dead stares and "make my day" body language. And she'd kicked butt a few times, too, although that was mainly when she'd been horsing around.

Why had she reacted so differently to Cooper? Why had she wanted him? Why did she *still* want him?

Sammy Jo groaned again and closed her eyes. "Holey, moley," she muttered through her teeth.

The phone rang and she jumped, staring at the receiver as if it might suddenly sprout fangs. Gingerly she picked it up. "Hello?"

"Sammy Jo, honey, I heard you called," Brent said, his voice thick with relief. "I've been trying to reach you for days!"

"I've really been busy. And I've got this thing with my throat, too." Sammy Jo manufactured a cough, goose-flesh rising on her arms as she once again recalled Cooper's accusations about her lies.

"Are you okay?" he asked, concerned.

Sammy Jo felt like a fraud. "Fine. I just needed some time . . . to recover."

"Good, well, are you busy tonight? I'd like to show you some things."

"What kind of things?" she asked doubtfully.

"Some documents I had drawn up. Nothing big."

"A prenuptial agreement?" Sammy Jo was faintly amused.

"Oh, no! What's mine is yours. It's just a way for us to seal our plans in a meaningful way."

Sammy Jo wasn't certain she liked the sound of that. Sighing, she said, "Why don't you come for dinner? We'll have corn on the cob, salad and lemonade."

"I'll bring a bottle of champagne," he agreed happily and rang off.

Vaguely disquieted, Sammy Jo wandered back to the kitchen. Could she marry Brent? Really? Could she?

Of course she could.

Slopping together a tuna and sweet pickle sandwich with more speed than style, Sammy Jo munched noisily and stared out the window. It was high noon, hot as a pistol, the sky more white than blue. Far off she could see the dark gathering of thunderclouds. Good, she thought. She could use a good storm. For some reason, she felt as if she were going to explode.

Brent showed up at six and by then Sammy Jo had managed to shower, wash her hair, change into a pair of shorts and sandals and look marginally presentable. They ate at the kitchen table, making companionable small talk. Brent neglected to uncork the champagne until the meal was over, even though Sammy Jo had tried to serve it earlier.

"Wait," he'd said, taking the bottle from her. Now, he unwound the protective wire, smiling at Sammy Jo as he did so. He poured them each a glass—in coffee mugs, as Sammy Jo wasn't loaded down with expensive crystal. "Cheers!" Brent said, clinking his mug to hers.

"So, where's the legal-eagle stuff you were talking about?" Sammy Jo asked.

"Well . . ." Brent went to his coat and pulled out several sheafs of paper, looking slightly sheepish as he brought them over to the table.

"What?" Sammy Jo asked, her gaze riveted.

"I just thought we'd make things official, before we tell everyone."

Whatever it was, Brent had printed it on Rollins Real Estate letterhead. Sammy Jo skimmed the text, a line forming between her eyebrows. "I don't get it."

He shrugged lightly. "It's mainly for fun."

Fun? Good grief, if this was Brent's idea of fun, she'd better run for the hills! According to this "contract," he wanted her to affix her John Henry to a paper that would guarantee that she would absolutely, definitely, indisputably marry him, no matter what. Brent was obviously covering his bases. Did he believe she would humiliate him by backing out at the last minute? She had to admit it wasn't outside the realm of possibility.

"Do you want this signed in blood?" Sammy Jo asked dryly.

He laughed, coloring slightly. At least he had the decency to be embarrassed. "I don't mean to make you feel . . ."

"Strangled?"

He shook his head.

Sammy Jo stared down at the document. The language was light and airy, as if the whole thing were a joke, but she knew there was an undercurrent of desperation here. Brent seemed to feel that if he tied her up with some hocus-pocus legal-looking document that bore her signature, Sammy Jo Whalen wouldn't get cold feet.

I got news for you, buddy. I've already got 'em.

Her reaction to Cooper had been proof of that.

The memory of Cooper and the way he'd pinned her against the tree, kissing her, touching her, making all reason flee . . . that's what finally did it. She quickly scratched her name to the bottom of the document.

"You won't be sorry," Brent said on a pent-up sigh of relief at the same moment thunder rumbled ominously somewhere to the north.

A bright flash of lightning spider-webbed downward, illuminating the sky like fireworks. Cooper stared out his back door. No rain. No moisture. No culmination. Just dry heat and frustration.

Cooper drank lustily from his long-necked bottle of beer. Another burst of lightning, white and blinding, was followed by an instant growl of thunder.

"Damn close," Cooper muttered, surprised. The storm was moving rapidly, black clouds boiling across the dark blue sky.

Jack and Lettie were out. Cooper had practically needed a crowbar to pry them from the ranch house. Apart from the fact that they both deserved time away, he wanted to be truly alone. Their living situation was fast becoming uncomfortable. He couldn't handle cohabitating with people, no matter how nice they were. He wanted his own space without the fear that someone would inadvertently invade it.

He was going to have to ask them to move out, and it made him feel like Simon Legree.

Simon Legree . . .

He grimaced. Remorse seemed to have made a permanent home inside his chest. What a terrible emotion. Made people recognize their own faults.

Cooper shook his head, clamping his jaw. He'd been hard on Sammy Jo. Cruel, really. He'd wanted to hurt her, which amazed him because he couldn't remember ever wanting to hurt anyone.

He'd wanted to force her to realize she couldn't marry Brent. He'd wanted to give her something to think about. He'd wanted to—hell! He'd wanted to make love to her and damn the consequences.

"Get hold of yourself," he admonished, tossing back the rest of his beer and slamming the empty bottle on the rail. A jab of lightning burst in front of his eyes. Thunder blasted, vibrating through him.

The air smelled of ozone, and the hair on his arms lifted with electricity. Cooper closed his eyes and swallowed. He saw Sammy Jo's face, the stubborn tilt of her chin, the quirk of her smile even while she acted like a shrew. And it *was* an act, Cooper conceded, realizing her very demeanor was part of the attraction. This was no woman trying to win his favors. Hell, no! She'd just as soon spit on him as talk to him.

He thought of her neck, the soft sheen of her skin, the curve of her breasts. It was enough to make him go hard on the spot.

The whole sky brightened; lightning jabbed somewhere to his left, toward the Triple R. Sammy Jo, Sammy Jo, Sammy Jo. With a growl of frustration, he pushed his fingers through his hair, wishing something, anything, would get her out of his mind.

A moment later, hot acrid smoke filled his nostrils. *Fire!* At a dead run he circled the house and saw an angry orange blaze throbbing past his screen of aspens and pines. Not Sammy Jo's house, he realized, his heart rate slowing a few beats. But something else on her property.

Slamming his hat on his head, he jumped into the truck, and bounced up the lane so hard he could feel his tailbone thunk all the way up to his neck. But he had to hurry. He kept one eye turned to that ominous fiery glow.

Lightning fire. Given the dryness of the grass, it could spread real fast. Too fast.

Sammy Jo sniffed the air. Smoke?

She was alone on the back porch, arms surrounding her chest, glad that Brent had gone home after an awkward kiss goodbye, telling herself over and over again that his silly pact was nothing to worry about. She was free to do as she liked. She was marrying him because she had to—to save the ranch. And because he loved her and given time, she could love him, too.

Liar. Her conscience wouldn't let up. Angry, Sammy Jo had headed outside to watch the storm at closer range. She loved storms, but it was an experience she generally enjoyed alone. If Brent were still here, she didn't know what she'd do.

Now, her skin prickled at the dense air. She glanced around anxiously. The lightning storm was a real doozy. Thunder rumbled, sounding like an underground train. Smoke drifted toward her again, and she ran off the porch to the dry ground.

A lightning fire? Where?

Her gaze flitted over the grounds: the barn, the paddocks, the fields beyond. Striding hurriedly to the front of the house, she gasped at the black funnel of smoke billowing from somewhere up the lane.

"Oh, God..."

What was it? What had caught fire?

The oak tree!

"No!" Sammy Jo ran for the pickup, jerking hard three times on the door, swearing and kicking and still the damn thing wouldn't budge. Panicked, she whirled, watching that distant haze of red.

The fire department.

She ran for the house, yanking open the screen door, sliding on dust-oiled boots across the smooth wooden floor, catching the receiver on the fly.

"Hello? Hello?" she cried as soon as she heard the connection completed. "This is Sammy Jo Whalen. We've got a fire here!"

"Sammy Jo? It's Tommy."

Tommy Weatherwood. God's gift to women. Sammy Jo didn't know whether to laugh or cry. "My oak tree's on fire. Up the lane. What the hell are you doing answering the phones?"

"Need all the volunteers we can. We got a real problem around here, Sammy Jo. Couple of barns aflame. Some houses. It's one helluva mess!"

Sammy Jo blinked. "Where are the fire trucks?" Coldwater Flats had a volunteer fire department. She knew the whole town only possessed a couple of fire trucks.

"Out doing what they gotta do! Is the tree close to the house?"

She could hear more lines ringing, could almost feel the panic of those unseen callers. "No, it's the one in the lane."

"Then we'll get to ya when we can. Call back if it starts gobblin' up your property. Need an ambulance?" he asked as an afterthought.

"No. Thanks, Tommy."

She hung up, distracted, scared, feeling seconds count. A fist banged on her door, pounding so loudly she jumped a foot and stifled a scream.

"Sammy Jo?" Cooper Ryan's voice demanded.

"Cooper!"

Her relief nearly blinded her as she ran to the front door.

"Call the fire department. The oak tree's on fire," reported tersely.

"I called. They'll get to us when they can."

Her voice nearly broke. He heard. Reaching out, he pulled her close. She listened to the strong beat of his heart.

"Any way to pump water out there?" he asked.

She shook her head. "Not fast enough."

"Maybe it'll burn itself out without catching anything else on fire."

She hurt inside. How could she explain her feelings about that tree? It was the symbol of everything she cared about. But if she cried, she would sound hysterical, and above all else, she couldn't be hysterical now.

"We need shovels. Tarps. Barrels of water." He pushed her back gently and looked in her eyes. "Can you find those things?"

"I've got some empty barrels in the garage. You get the water. I'll find the shovels and tarp."

"Good girl."

A calm settled over Sammy Jo. There was nothing she could do but help Cooper try to contain the fire. She found the tools and tarp and tossed them in the back of his truck. She could feel flashes of heat from the inferno.

Cooper hauled two barrels of water into the back of the truck, and then they were heading for the fire. Rounding the bend, Sammy Jo's mouth opened in horror. The oak tree was split in two, limbs surrounded by dancing orange and yellow and black flames, liquid, gleeful and twisting.

Sammy Jo jumped out before the truck came to a full stop. She ran forward, blasted by heat, lungs burning for air, thighs shaking. Smoke and the smell of bubbling sap filled her nostrils.

"My God!" Cooper expelled, dragging her back a foot or two.

The fire raged all around the tree, engulfing it, searing the wood to black. An ominous cracking sounded, reverberating over the angry roar of the flames. In a furious blaze, a limb crashed to the ground, scarlet and gold sparks spiraling into the black sky. Smoke fanned out like beckoning hands, inviting one and all to enjoy the spectacle.

Sammy Jo's eyes burned. Her friend. Her oldest friend.

"Get back," Cooper urged.

In sudden fury, she shook off his hands. Momentarily disoriented, she stumbled, choking on a sob. Cooper grabbed her again and pulled to the truck. He held her for a moment until the fight went out of her. Then, systematically, he hauled out the water barrels from the back, rolling them on the ground. Darting tongues of flame fell like rain all around him. Opening a barrel, he poured a stream of water on the hot, licking tendrils, deadly offspring of the mother fire. The ground hissed.

Sammy Jo grabbed the tarp. She smothered other fiery upstarts. Tears fought for release, but she clamped her jaw and fought them back.

She and Cooper worked in silence. All they could do was destroy the fire's attempts at escape. But it was torture to watch the tree burn on and on, a ghastly funeral pyre.

Cooper shoveled a trench, muscles gleaming with blackened sweat as he fought to keep the fire from spreading in the direction of the Triple R. His shirt was streaked with dirt and smoke. The effort seemed futile to Sammy Jo. She stood by limply, hurting all over. Then, realizing she was being useless, she grabbed a shovel and joined him.

They threw hard, sunbaked dirt over their shoulders and beat at escaping flames. Sammy Jo swore and raged and kept working, furious at the fates, at everything.

"The wind!" Cooper yelled.

She'd felt it. A cool breeze against her arms. But she'd thought it was borne of the fire. Looking up, she saw the flames lash eastward, flung by the wind that had erupted in the wake of the storm.

"Where's the rain?" she screeched. "Where's the goddamn rain?"

Sirens blared faintly, far away. Was it her imagination? She listened hard, straining. No, she wasn't imagining it! They were coming. They were coming!

The fire truck arrived in a wail of sirens and spiraling flashes of red and white lights. Tommy Weatherwood jumped down and barked orders to two other men Sammy Jo didn't recognize. Cooper grabbed one of the snaking hoses without being asked.

The team poured a stream of water on the oak tree. Water sprayed and sparkled, hissing and sputtering as it slapped against the flaming oak.

Sammy Jo stood back, hot and aching. It was over in a matter of minutes, water pumped from the tanks aboard the truck.

But it didn't matter. Soon the tree was a charred, miserable creature, broken in two, puffing up clouds of steam.

"You okay?" Tommy asked her, wiping his forehead. A slash of white cut his blackened face as he smiled at her.

"Couldn't be better," Sammy Jo managed to say.

"Heard you're marryin' Brent. If you change your mind, come on down to Shady Glen and look me up."

He jumped back on the truck, barking to his fellow volunteers. Sammy Jo was too tired to scream, but that's exactly what she wanted to do. She wanted to yell at him for his insensitivity, his lack of caring. It was all an adventure to Tommy.

Cooper was leaning against his truck, his expression unfathomable as he gazed at the ugly hulk left behind. Sammy Jo stared at him, her fury transferred to him. She knew she was being irrational. It wasn't his fault the tree was gone. It wasn't Tommy's, either.

Mutely, she turned her attention to the oak. Lord, it was awful. Hearing faint mewing sounds, she glanced around, then realized they were coming from her own throat. Miserable little sobs, fighting their way out.

She pressed her lips together and fought the shaking misery that consumed her. Turning in the direction of the house, she closed her eyes and tried to swallow, though her throat felt permanently closed.

"Get in the truck. I'll drive you."

She wheeled on him, shivering in the heat. "Thanks for helping, but I want to be left alone now."

"You're going to fall over halfway down the lane. You're done in."

She was. She'd worked until her muscles screamed and her head throbbed dully. But she ignored him and kept walking.

She wasn't ready when he scooped her up and carried her to the truck. She wanted to give in. To just let this man carry her, but it wasn't in her nature. Coming alive, she wriggled desperately to free herself, but Cooper half threw her inside.

"Stop it!" he ordered.

She scrabbled for the door handle. He clamped his hand over her wrist, and she clawed at his strong fingers. It was at that moment the rain finally arrived, pouring so hard, so fast, and so furiously it was a drenching silver sheet in mere moments, enclosing them in the hot cab of his truck, thickening the air.

"I'm sorry, okay?" he said, teeth grinding. "About the other day."

Sammy Jo didn't answer.

"And I'm sorry about the tree."

Clamping her arms around her waist, Sammy Jo stared out the steamy side window and listened to the cacophony of the rain. She wasn't going to cry. She wasn't.

Cooper drove her to her house. They both stepped out into the downpour. Soaked, they walked to the door, and Sammy Jo didn't have the energy to tell him to get lost.

He seemed reluctant to leave her, and truthfully, she didn't want to be alone. Not completely.

She washed her face and neck in the bathroom. When she returned to the living room, Cooper was examining her trophies.

"I heard you were a rodeo princess," he said.

"A lifetime ago," she answered expressionlessly. She had no feelings left whatsoever. The fire had drained her completely. Totally. She'd lost her closest friend.

Cooper's dark blue eyes swept over her. It was hot in the room. Too hot. She brushed past him to the back porch.

The rain stopped just as suddenly as it began, as if someone turned off the tap. Water dripped musically from the eaves, warm, soft. The hoarse croak of frogs suddenly exploded. Sammy Jo listened, swallowing, enveloped by moist heat. Soon the puddles would dry and that would be it. Back to the everyday.

Except her beloved oak tree was gone.

She heard the screen door squeak open behind her. Cooper. She could smell his scent mixed in with the heat and smoke and thick odor of wet vegetation.

"You've got a whole army of suitors in this town," he remarked.

"You mean Tommy Weatherwood? He was just kidding."

"Maybe he wasn't."

"What's it to you, anyway?"

"Sammy Jo, relax. At least for tonight. I know you're hurting."

She turned away from him, lifting a shoulder to further block out his maleness. "Go away. I can't deal with this." She stalked to the porch swing and fell into it, refusing to meet his penetrating eyes. She felt near collapse.

"I could help you."

"Help me?"

"Financially. I could buy the ranch."

The glare she sent him could have sliced through metal. "If I wanted to sell, Mr. Ryan, I'd sell."

"What do you think your real estate lover's going to do? As soon as you're married, he's going to sell this place so fast it'll make your head spin. And he'll sell it to me."

She didn't need this abuse. Not now. "You don't know anything about it!"

"Don't I?"

"I'd rather eat snails than sell this ranch to you!"

"Snails aren't so bad," Cooper answered reasonably.

"They're slimy and make me sick!"

"Don't marry Rollins," Cooper said again, tersely.

"I'll do what I darned well please."

He hesitated and she hugged her arms around her waist, still unwilling to look his way. But she could sense his every move. The creak of his leather belt, the smell of his skin. It was maddening.

"You always do what you please," he said quietly. "Everybody knows that. But for once in your life, *think,* before you fly into a rage."

Sammy Jo was nearly suffocated by the hurt and misery choking her. She didn't want to talk. She just wanted to be alone to lick her wounds. "I'd really like . . . some privacy now."

"I can't leave you like this, Sammy Jo." He sounded almost annoyed with himself.

"Oh, why not?" she demanded in exasperation. "Just go!"

"You want to pick a fight, don't you?"

He was right. Dead right. She wanted to pick a fight with him. She wanted to scream and wail and stomp her feet and throw herself on the ground and bawl her eyes out.

"Don't," he said when she opened her mouth.

"Don't what?" she asked bitterly.

"Fight."

He sank onto the swing beside her. It was a wide, cushioned affair that barely rocked unless you really threw some body English into it. Curled in the corner, arms protectively wrapped around her chest, elbows and knees drawn up, Sammy Jo gazed at him uneasily.

Seeing her dirt-crusted knee, he brushed absently at it, feeling her tense muscles through her jeans.

"Don't touch me," she whispered.

Growing irritated in spite of himself, Cooper kept his hand where it was. "You bring half of this on yourself, you know."

"Half of what?"

"Everyone's frustration with you. *My* frustration. I'm sorry about the tree and your finances and everything. But you won't let anyone get close to you. You're like a snapping dog. Bite, bite, bite."

"I didn't invite you over here."

"Good point." Cooper got to his feet, snatching up his hat from where he'd laid it on the porch rail. He slapped it against his thigh several times.

"Wait," Sammy Jo murmured.

He looked down at her. To his surprise, he saw crystal tears glimmering in her eyes. She fought hard to pretend they weren't there, but she couldn't quite succeed.

"Sammy Jo . . . !" he said in surprise.

Her hands covered her face and he saw the silent tremor that shook her as she struggled with her emotions. Unable to stop himself, he leaned down and brushed her hands away, capturing one silvery tear with his thumb. A shudder went through her. "I hate being helpless," she said, voice trembling. "Absolutely hate it."

He didn't answer. He wanted to be close to her, as close as humanly possible, and if she didn't let her guard down a bit, just a fraction, he would never get past the barbs and self-protective barrier she enforced at all times.

Her lashes were wet with tears. She swiped at them. Cupping her chin in one hand, he forced her to look at him. No defiance in her eyes. Just weariness and sorrow and faint distrust.

"Sammy Jo," he said softly.

"Don't make me cry."

"I don't want to make you cry."

"Well, you are."

"No. You're just hurting."

Cooper enfolded her in his arms. In some distant part of his brain, he reminded himself that she needed comfort, only comfort. But she was sweet, warm, living heat in his arms, and he couldn't resist just one kiss.

Her lips were salty with tears. She kissed him back. Tentatively. Emboldened, he kissed her again, conscious of her rapidly thudding heart, response to the danger signals his embrace was creating.

"No..." She pushed at him gently. He stared down at her. Sammy Jo's eyes were wide and darkly shadowed. "I can't do this."

"I shouldn't." But his lips brushed hers again, lightly.

That caught her attention. "*You* shouldn't?"

"We don't like each other very much."

A faint smile crossed her lips. Cooper smiled back, knowing he was an out-and-out liar.

"You really ticked me off the other day."

He nodded.

Time passed. His watch clicked softly, counterpoint to the water dripping slowly off the eaves. Her breathing was quiet, but her heart was still beating fast, a rapid galloping thud that said more about her state of mind than words.

He kissed her cheek, then let his tongue touch that downy skin. Half expecting to be rejected, he was gratified at her shaky sigh.

Sammy Jo slid lower in the swing. She was melting. She could feel it. His kisses were like wine, dark and intoxicating. A distant voice reminded her of obligations, but she shushed it angrily. She ached all over, and she wanted some relief.

Her mouth sought his, carefully, tentatively, as her arms slowly wound around his neck. She felt him hesitate, as if questioning the wisdom of this, but then he buried his hands in her hair. A choking sob erupted from her throat, shocking her.

"Sammy Jo," he murmured, his mouth searching the curve of her jaw, her neck.

She was a virgin and as such, she reminded herself, she shouldn't be doing this. But why not? another voice demanded. Why not? She wanted to be reckless. She wanted pure emotion. She was so incredibly sane all the time! Couldn't she have this? This one moment of insanity and pleasure?

No!

Her ruthless conscience smote her. Suddenly struggling, she gasped when she saw her shirt was already undone, the lacy top of her bra white in the dark night. In that moment of suspended reality, Cooper deftly unhooked her bra, her breasts tumbling into his warm palms.

"Sammy Jo," he whispered, and the worshipful tone of his voice was her undoing. She watched as his thumb rubbed over one crest, felt a deep, primal pull, as if invisible strings tied her nipple to some secret part of herself.

His head bent to her breast. She sucked in a breath, lips parting in wonder at the hot wetness and shooting desire. So, this is what it's about! she realized, jolted.

She tensed. Her fingers clenched, frozen. Cooper sucked hard, and Sammy Jo relaxed, liquid, boneless, weightless.

She suddenly wanted to know more. Closing her eyes, she held his head to her breast, moaning faintly. Her legs moved, shifting restlessly. He responded, one heavy leg pinning her down to the cushions. She could feel *him*, that part of him that was totally male, and another shock wave rocked through her.

Sammy Jo's mouth opened in surprise. Cooper moved downward, his fingers working a strange, seductive magic along the curve of her hip, then between her legs.

"Sammy Jo," he gasped suddenly.

She knew the question. How far could he go? For an answer, she pulled his mouth to hers, plundering it with her tongue. His hips pressed tensely to hers. She wanted more!

His fingers tore at her clothes; she helped him. Eagerly she fumbled with the buckle of his jeans, aiding him in his efforts to fling off his clothes. *Hurry, hurry, hurry.* Before sense comes back. Before reason returns.

Then they were naked together on the swing, which swayed ever so gently, rhythmic, mesmerizing. With wonder Sammy Jo felt the weight of his body on hers.

He pulled back to look at her, to brush her sweat-dampened hair away from her face. But looking straight at him brought doubts to mind, and she couldn't bear it. She dragged him close, stealing more of his drugging kisses, her hands tentatively searching the sinewy strength of his back muscles.

Magic. He was making magic with his tongue as it searched the shell of her ear, the downy curve of her jaw-line, her breasts, the nipples.... She arched upward with a moan, and he shifted until there was nothing between them but themselves.

A pulse beat hard in her throat. She swallowed, scared, feeling the tip of his manhood probe that liquid part of herself that seemed to have a heartbeat of its own.

Latent conscience assailed her. "Cooper," she breathed.

But it was too late. He moved against her, slowly, achingly slowly, and in such a way that sensation superseded reality. His kisses grew harder, his arms taut as they surrounded her.

Her legs felt disembodied, parting, opening for him. She sensed his movements, knew what was happening, wouldn't stop if she'd been able. . . .

Then he thrust inside her, and she cried out. He stiffened, shocked. "Sammy Jo!"

Her lips quivered. She couldn't speak. His palms held her face. His expression was grim as he stared at her.

"I didn't mean to hurt you."

"You didn't." She moved inadvertently, and he sucked air between his teeth, his body shuddering.

A sense of power enveloped her. She did that! She could do that to him. She moved her hips, and he closed his eyes and groaned. No more pain, just a delicious feeling of excitement and oh, Lord, a thrusting jab of desire.

"I can't stop," he groaned through gritted teeth.

"Don't," she whispered, then gasped as he thrust full-length into her, filling her up in a thrilling, thrilling way.

He began to move, rhythmically, hard, driving into her so that her fingers clutched at the skin of his shoulders, her head tossed back, her lips trembling with passion. She writhed like a wild thing and suddenly he cried out, spilling himself into her at the same moment her own climax enveloped her, her own mouth gasped with pleasure, her own body shuddered and trembled.

She couldn't speak. Couldn't move. It felt as if an eternity passed while she drifted in some nameless cocoon of sweet sensation. Surfacing, she heard his breathing, his heartbeat, felt his mouth pressed against the side of her neck, his weight a welcome blanket.

"Sammy Jo," he murmured, shifting, thick-tongued with his own pleasure, kissing her possessively, so that she wound herself around him tighter still, loving this moment, this feeling, this man.

"Don't leave me," she begged.

"I won't. I promise."

Sammy Jo shivered and he hugged her closer, cradling her against his chest. Way, way back in her mind, she already knew she would hate herself for revealing her vulnerability, but she didn't care. Not now. She wanted this moment to last forever.

Forever.

Chapter Eight

The lusty song of the frogs ended with the last of the drying puddles. Silence filled the hot air. Silence except for the rhythm of Cooper's breathing. Sammy Jo inhaled deeply, enjoying his scent, the sight of his well-muscled back, the crisp curliness of his chest hair.

Her conscience was screaming now, but she blocked it out. Later. Much later, she would face it. Not now. Not when her emotions were raw and untamed and rollicking with the speed of a roller coaster, too close to the surface to conceal.

He stirred, his breath warm against her temple. She closed her eyes, unwilling to meet his gaze, afraid she might see, what? Censure? Conquest? An unspoken I-told-you-so?

He lifted his head, gazing at her lazily, a smile curving his lips as he stretched like a sated jungle cat. Sammy Jo snuggled close. Distantly she heard the whine and scratching of

Trigger, and she realized she'd inadvertently locked the dog inside her bedroom.

"That's Trigger," she murmured.

Cooper's answer was a kiss, slow as molasses and just as sweet. "I don't want to move."

Neither did Sammy Jo. She wanted this moment to spin out endlessly. Nagging recriminations banged on the door of her conscience, but she refused to listen.

"You are so beautiful," he commented, one hand sliding down her rib cage to the curve of her hip.

"Yeah, beautiful."

"You are."

She opened her eyes fully, shivering slightly even though there was heat everywhere. She thought of the oak tree and sadness enveloped her. Her one, true desire was to bury herself in the warmth of his embrace and just shut out everything.

Brent.

She actually jerked at the thought of her "husband-to-be." Searching her feelings, she realized she didn't feel as if she'd betrayed him. Agreeing to marry him had been the betrayal. Betrayal of herself. She knew now she couldn't go through with the wedding, document or no document. If she'd been honest with herself, she'd known it when she signed the silly thing....

As if reading her thoughts, Cooper said huskily, "You can't marry Rollins now."

Sammy Jo made a face that he couldn't see. "I suppose you're right."

"You suppose?" His thumb lifted her chin until she was forced to meet his blue eyes dead on.

"This would be difficult to explain," she admitted.

"You can't still be thinking about marriage!"

"I'm not. Not...really."

He jerked, his expression tightening. Sammy Jo wasn't quite certain what she'd said that was so repellent, but he went on to make his feelings clear. "You would actually still consider marrying Brent Rollins after we made love, just so you could save this ranch?"

He practically shouted at her. Unnerved, Sammy Jo pulled back. "I didn't say that."

"Yes, you did." He was coldly positive.

She didn't like the way this was going. Reaching for her clothes, she jammed her arms through the sleeves of her shirt. No, she didn't like the way this was going at all.

"What's the matter with you?" she demanded, wriggling completely away from him. On her feet, she snatched up the rest of her clothes, turning her back to him as she dragged on her pants, her fingers fumbling with growing panic.

"Nothing. Not a damn thing."

"Then stop barking at me."

"I'm not barking," he said through his teeth.

Sammy Jo glanced back in time to see Cooper snap up his jeans and shirt, and dress with surprising speed. His jaw was a rock.

Nope, she didn't like this at all.

"I'm not going to marry Brent," she told him.

"Good."

The events of the evening crowded inside Sammy Jo's head. She fought back the pain and concentrated on Cooper's sudden, pigheaded attitude. As if he owned her, for Pete's sake! And he was mad that *she* wasn't behaving properly.

They'd just made love, for crying out loud. Shouldn't he be a little more tender? More caring? Less...*annoying?* Raw emotion and a perverse sense of self-destruction spurred Sammy Jo on.

"Well, maybe I will marry Brent, after all. Why not, now that I've had some experience? What's the problem? After all, all Sammy Jo Whalen really wants is to save her ranch and she'll go about it any way that works."

Cooper gazed at her coldly. Clearly, he heard her mockery, but for some reason, he couldn't quite see how ridiculous he was being. Sammy Jo ached inside. More than anything, she wanted to throw herself in his arms and beg him to stop fighting with her and make love to her all over again.

But she couldn't. He wouldn't let her. She wouldn't let herself....

"How far would you go to get what you want?" he asked.

"I didn't ask you to make love to me!" she declared, appalled. "You came to me and acted like you felt sorry for me and then one thing led to another and..."

"And?"

"And we made love!" she finished. "So don't act like I set this whole thing up! You were a part of this, too, remember?"

Her words found their mark. She saw the way he winced, as if he'd taken a direct hit. Good, she thought, furious. He was taking away her good feelings over what had just occurred and making her feel horrible and used.

"You were a virgin," he murmured.

That stopped her cold. He had to have suspected. He'd accused her of never being properly kissed before. Was he feeling regrets? She didn't think she could take that. "Don't make a big deal over it."

"Isn't it a big deal?"

Sammy Jo shrugged, not trusting herself to talk. She didn't want to think about what had transpired between them, or she might fall apart.

"You didn't ever intend to marry Rollins?" he asked neutrally.

"No. I don't think so. Maybe." Sammy Jo struggled.

"You're not sure."

"Would you just leave me alone?" she demanded, her patience gone.

Cooper shook his head, clearly in the grips of an emotion as intense as her own. But unlike Sammy Jo, he didn't give voice to his feelings. To her amazement, all he said was, "I'm sorry about your tree. Glad nothing worse happened."

Didn't it? Sammy Jo thought. How could he do this? How could he act as if the most monumental moment of her life were just a walk in the park?

"Marrying Brent couldn't be any worse than giving myself to someone as coldhearted as you," she said aloud.

"As you pointed out before, it's not my business."

Having her words thrown back in her face, each syllable bitten off as if it tasted bad, reminded Sammy Jo why she couldn't tolerate this man. Never mind that making love with him had been wonderful, bordering on fantastic. There had to be other men who were just as able lovers.

"I don't know what possessed me. I was just so . . . so . . . *miserable* about the oak tree, and there you were. If I'd had any sense, I'd have called up Brent. He should have been the one here tonight. Not you!"

"It wouldn't have happened if you'd been with Brent." Sammy Jo's mouth dropped open. "You wouldn't have let it happen," he said with pure arrogance.

"You think just because you're the . . . that I was a . . ." She drew a swift breath. "Sorry to disillusion you, but it was timing, pure and simple. And next time, it will be Brent!"

Cooper's expression blackened. "Tell him about what happened tonight and see if there is a next time!"

"There'll be a next time and a next time and a next time, because, by God, I'm going to marry him if it's the last thing I do!"

Sammy Jo took a step backward when he suddenly advanced on her. He snatched up his hat and strode around the side of the house. Moments later, she heard the roar of his truck's engine and the spin of tires in gravel as he disappeared in a seething rage.

Sammy Jo collapsed onto the swing, spent and filled with so many feelings, she could scarcely breathe. She hadn't wanted him to go. She hadn't meant to fight.

Wrapping her arms around herself, she bent her head, mentally reviewing every wrong thing she'd said, flinching at her own scorching tongue, but infuriated right down to her socks over his absolute certainty that, no matter what, she would do anything to save the ranch. Even if it was sell her soul.

If there was ever a woman he needed to stay away from it was that conniving, calculating, irresponsible, self-serving Sammy Jo Whalen! God, what a woman! She ought to be locked up and only let out under armed guard!

Cooper slammed into the house, fists clenched, jaw hard as iron, too enraged to even speak. With a growl of frustration, he strode into his bedroom, torn between the desire to pick up the desk and throw it across the room and the equally primal urge to turn right around, drive back to the Triple R, drag Sammy Jo to the bedroom and prove she was wrong. So damned wrong!

But how much could one man take? She'd proven over and over again that she wouldn't listen to reason or her very own instincts. Couldn't she tell that what they'd shared was special? How could she not know, when he could still feel the silken spell of her quivering flesh surrounding him?

"Damn," he groaned.

He had to get out of here. Had to get some air. Had to get Sammy Jo Whalen out of his system.

As soon as he was outside, however, he could smell the scorched air, a remnant of tonight's fire. The memory of Sammy Jo's aching sadness over the loss of the oak stopped him cold. He'd wanted to comfort her. Hell, he'd wanted to make love to her. He'd done both, but now he felt empty and angry and dissatisfied.

At least she wouldn't marry Brent Rollins now, he consoled himself. For all her talk, she was too smart a lady for that.

Wasn't she?

"Damn it all to hell!" he muttered, scraping his fingers through his hair. He hadn't believed her. Not really. But way down deep…well, way down deep he knew better than to credit her with honorable intentions she'd never claimed to possess. He'd made that mistake before; he wasn't going to make it again. And Sammy Jo had come right out and told everyone she wanted a husband to save the ranch! Just because she'd made love to him in a moment of vulnerability didn't mean her philosophy had changed.

But oh, he'd wanted her to tell him it had. He'd wanted her to make him believe it. Instead, she'd gotten mad, and though he sympathized somewhat—he hadn't exactly been the doting lover spouting words of "forever-ness"—he'd been dying inside to hear her say how much their lovemaking meant to her, how marrying Brent Rollins was laughable, a joke, how she never wanted Cooper to let her go.

And yet he, himself, hadn't been able to say the same….

The evening had been a complete and total disaster from beginning to end.

Would she marry Rollins? Would she?

Cooper tortured himself with scenarios of Sammy Jo coming down the aisle, a smile on her face, dollar signs in her eyes. *Would she?*

"No!"

Pamela would have—but she had been cagey enough to keep that information to herself. Sammy Jo was right out in the open, and that was a thousand times worse because she almost made him believe it was her only option!

For a wild moment, he considered stepping in as Sammy Jo's prospective bridegroom, marching her down the aisle by her hair, if necessary, and demanding that she say, "I do!" He could have the Triple R *and* Sammy Jo.

And a whole pack of trouble.

Muttering imprecations, Cooper rejected that idea outright. He'd made the "marrying mistake" once. He'd be damned if he'd do it again. Even if it meant lusting after Sammy Jo Whalen from afar.

But maybe there was another way, he realized as a thought came to him. Maybe there was.

Sammy Jo slowed the pickup to a throbbing rumble and threw it into park. Outside her window, the oak tree lay twisted, ravaged and helpless. She stared at its charred remains. Blackened embers. Skeleton branches. Gray ash.

If she were superstitious, she would believe it was a sign to give up. There was nothing left for her here. She might as well move out of town and start over.

Climbing from the cab of the truck, Sammy Jo wiped sweat from her forehead, then walked through the dust and debris, poking at a burned fragment with the toe of her boot. Swallowing, she tried hard not to mind.

And just as hard, she tried to forget the aftermath of the fire, those sweet, hot, melting moments in Cooper's arms where some passionate stranger inside her had reveled in his touch, smell and taste.

Groaning at the memory, Sammy Jo squeezed her eyes tightly shut. Her whole body tensed; her teeth clenched.

"No!" she shouted to the empty air and listless oak. She was not going to give in. Not to pain and despair, and not to Cooper Ryan ever again.

With that, she kicked at the rubble and stomped back to the pickup, yanking open the door in one try. A faint, self-deprecating smile crossed her lips. At least she'd won that small battle.

At the house, she rinsed the sweat from her face, then glanced at the table. The mail lay scattered across its scarred finish, one letter catching Sammy Jo's attention: Valley Federal's latest missive, this one with a deadline.

She couldn't marry Brent now. She never really could. But she knew if she went down to the bank today and told Matt Durning that she and Brent were getting married, and that Brent had told her he would put up part of his money to pay off part of her mortgage and trade mortgages on some of his other real estate for the rest, Matt would call off the hounds. She would still have the Triple R.

It was that simple.

And that hard.

The thought made her skin itch. Shaking her head, she walked to the barn, grabbed a bridle and a pan of oats before going into the fields in search of Pokey; Emmy, Van and Karen would soon be at the ranch to hone their rodeo skills on the Shetland.

She caught up with the horse fairly quickly and seduced him with ridiculous ease. Pokey's number-one concern was food. By the time she got back to the house, the little girls were already there, as were Bev, Ginny and Lorna.

Bev's greeting was noticeably chillier than it had been, but Sammy Jo didn't much care. She didn't want to even think about Cooper Ryan. The memory of their lovemaking made her shiver with guilt. Best to block it out entirely.

"Me first! Me first!" Emmy cried. Sammy Jo lifted the five-year-old onto the bareback saddle. Pokey dutifully began plodding around in a circle.

Emmy quickly grew impatient. Before Sammy Jo could stop her, she'd climbed to her feet and bent over, clutching the saddle's handle. "No!" she cried when Sammy Jo stopped Pokey. "Go! Go!"

"Sammy Jo Whalen, you get her down from there!" Bev screeched.

"Emmy, you aren't ready for that."

"Yes, I am!"

A part of Sammy Jo had to admire the little girl's stubbornness—a kindred spirit. But she wasn't about to let Emmy risk injury.

Realizing Pokey wasn't going to move unless she sat down, Emmy did the exact opposite, standing straight up on the horse and toppling onto the ground.

"Emmy!" Sammy Jo cried, rushing to the girl.

Bev was beside her in an instant, clawing Sammy Jo away, screaming to beat the band. Scared, Pokey jumped forward and raced to the other side of the paddock, reins flying. Emmy started crying as Bev scooped her up.

"You have no business teaching riding if you can't control your animals!" Bev shrieked.

"Is she all right?" Sammy Jo asked anxiously, reaching toward Emmy.

"She fell off!" Tears filled Bev's eyes.

"Let go of me!" Emmy demanded, squirming furiously. "I want to ride. I want to ride!"

It took all Sammy Jo's willpower not to smile. She could feel the smile growing, twitching the corners of her mouth, threatening to break into a shout of laughter.

Bev stared in horror at her dust-grimed daughter who was valiantly seeking escape. Reluctantly, Bev let her slip to the ground. Emmy tried to tear off toward Pokey, but Bev held on to her daughter's arm. "You're going to see a doctor!" Bev declared.

Emmy howled in frustration. "I want to ride Pokey. I want to ride!"

Bev's jaw tightened. Sammy Jo sucked in a breath, expecting Bev to shake the little girl's arm, she was so mad. But Bev released her, and Emmy ran for Pokey, who led Emmy on a merry chase around the corral, seeming to delight in keeping just out of reach.

"She won't be coming back for lessons," Bev said tightly.

"Bev, she just fell off. It happens in rodeo-riding." Sammy Jo was losing patience herself.

"It's dangerous. I won't have it. And I won't let Roy buy her any more lessons from you, either!"

"Fine. But you won't hear the end of this."

"Just what do you mean by that?" Bev demanded acidly.

Hooking a thumb in Emmy's direction, Sammy Jo said, "Your daughter wants to rodeo. She loves horses, and she's fearless. She won't give you a minute's peace. And yes, I'm speaking from experience."

The other two little girls watched Emmy with a mixture of delight and horror. Ginny sucked on a cigarette, squinting against the smoke. Van squeezed her mother's hand tightly. Sammy Jo didn't have to be told that Van was through with rodeo-riding. Conversely, Ginny seemed kind of reluctant to give it up.

"Emmy okay?" Ginny asked.

"No, she's not okay." Bev was frosty.

"She's tough," Sammy Jo answered in a sideways compliment as Emmy finally caught hold of Pokey's reins and then proceeded to stroke the Shetland's nose.

"I never thought this was a good idea. It's too dangerous. And it's . . . smelly!" Bev looked down at her grimy clothes in disgust.

Lorna snorted in amusement, and Bev sent her an icy look.

"I want to ride," Karen suddenly piped in, her thumb hovering just outside her mouth.

Everyone turned to look at her. Lorna grinned.

"You have to promise to stay seated," Sammy Jo told Karen.

"Promise," she mumbled, the thumb firmly implanted once more.

Emmy threw a fit when she realized Karen was going to get to ride. Bev tried reasoning with her, and when that didn't work, she grabbed Emmy's arm and dragged her around the house because Emmy refused to walk on her own power.

Karen rode docilely around the paddock. When she was finished, Sammy Jo brought Pokey over to the rail. Lorna swept Karen into her arms and held her tightly, filled with pride.

"You sure you don't want to ride?" Sammy Jo asked Van.

The little girl glared at Sammy Jo. Ginny's mouth was tight, and Sammy Jo realized she was angry because Van hadn't measured up to Ginny's expectations. At that moment, Sammy Jo vowed to herself that if she ever had children, she would never put her child in competition with anyone else's. It was a dangerous game.

Suddenly, Emmy came racing around the house, her face shining. "I get one more ride! One more ride!"

"Oh, honey, I don't think so. Your mom's kind of upset and she won't want you to—"

The words died in Sammy Jo's throat as Bev suddenly strolled toward her. Cooper Ryan was at her side.

Sammy Jo's heart banged in her chest. She had to look away. Anywhere. Just not at Cooper's broad chest and sinewy forearms. Not at his lean legs and hips.

What was he doing here? The bastard, she added purposely, determined to stay as angry at him as she'd been the night of the fire.

"Hello, Cooper." Ginny's voice thrummed with pleasure and grated against Sammy Jo's nerves.

"Hi, Ginny."

"This is my daughter, Vanessa. Van, say hi to Mr. Ryan." Van's suspicious gaze slid over him, and she remained ominously silent.

"Well, Mr. *Ryan,*" Lorna stressed, shooting Sammy Jo a glance of amusement. "It's a pleasure to meet you. I've heard a lot about you. I'm Lorna Miller, and this is my daughter, Karen."

Cooper shook her hand. Sammy Jo licked her lips and squinted at a faraway tree as if she were focusing on something important. She just couldn't look at Cooper. Cooper... At least Lorna had gotten his name right this time.

"You work at the bank, don't you?" Cooper asked, his voice sending a chill down Sammy Jo's back, in spite of the heat.

"I sure do," Lorna said, sounding gratified he'd remembered.

"Lorna's a teller," Bev revealed in an icy breath.

Emmy had climbed the fence. Sammy Jo helped her down and sent her scampering toward Pokey since Bev seemed to have swallowed her objections. Lorna held Karen's free hand while Karen smiled up at Sammy Jo, clearly pleased with her riding lesson.

"The girls were having a riding lesson until Emmy fell off," Bev told Cooper. "It's a miracle she wasn't seriously injured. Sammy Jo assured me it would be safe."

Sammy Jo shot Bev a glare. The woman's animosity had fast changed to something else. Jealousy? Female territorialism? Bev clearly wanted Cooper enough to risk another ride for Emmy on Pokey.

He deserves Bev, she told herself judiciously.

"She looks all right to me," Cooper drawled, his gaze following Emmy's progress before turning to Sammy Jo. Color heated Sammy Jo's cheeks and she turned away, heading for Emmy and the safety of the far end of the corral.

"Will you show me?" Emmy demanded. "Will you show me how to do it?"

"Do what?" Out of the corner of her eye, she could see Ginny and Bev hang on Cooper's every drawling syllable. Her blood boiled.

"How to stand up on a horse? Please, please, please!"

"Emmy, I can't stand up on Pokey. It's not good for him. I'm too big."

"Then another horse. I want to see!"

"I was a barrel-racer. Trick-riding wasn't something I did much."

"But you can do it, can't you?" she kept after Sammy Jo. "You can!"

"Yeah, I guess I can."

"Then do it!"

An infantile part of herself wanted to perform. Like in seventh grade, when she'd shown the prissy girls in her class how to slide underneath the belly of a running horse without getting hurt. Of course, that was after she'd been trampled once and broken her arm in two places, but she hadn't mentioned that to her impressed friends.

Nope. She wasn't going to pull that stunt again.

"Sorry," Sammy Jo told the little girl, hauling her onto Pokey's broad back.

Emmy stayed seated but she squirmed and jiggled and bopped as if to some music of her own. Sammy Jo circled around several times and came to a stop in front of Cooper and the other women.

"So you give rodeo-riding lessons," he said to Sammy Jo. His first direct conversation. Was he feeling as awkward as she was?

"Yup." Sammy Jo still couldn't meet his gaze.

"Maybe I should take a course."

He was baiting her, the monster. She glanced up, her green eyes cool. "Sure, why not? Anytime you feel like it."

"Now why does that sound like a challenge?"

'Cause maybe it is one.

It annoyed her that every remark she made fueled his amusement. Burning, Sammy Jo refused to say anything more, but Lorna had no such compunction.

"You know, you ought to take lessons. I think Sammy Jo could teach you a thing or two."

Sammy Jo stared at her friend in horror. She'd been debating on telling Lorna about what had happened between her and Cooper; she needed a confidante. But now she knew she couldn't. Lorna insisted on playing matchmaker between her and Cooper even though she knew Sammy Jo was still "sort-of" engaged to Brent.

"Is that right?" Cooper asked.

"I don't think Sammy Jo teaches adults," Bev said quickly.

It took every ounce of willpower Sammy Jo possessed, but she managed to keep from giving Bev the rough side of her tongue. Ginny looked as if she wanted to kill Bev, too. Good. Let the two of them duke it out.

"Could I talk to you up at the house?" Sammy Jo asked Lorna, forcing a sweet smile.

"Sure thing."

Lorna grabbed Karen's hand as Sammy Jo climbed the fence and dropped lithely to the ground beside Bev, Ginny and Cooper. With long strides, she put distance between herself and their little group. Lorna had to half run to catch up.

"Do you mind?" Sammy Jo demanded in a furious whisper when they reached the back porch. She shot a glance toward Cooper. Ginny and Bev had hung back, their faces turned up to Cooper, silently begging him to notice them.

"You like him," Lorna declared. "It's written all over you."

"I think I hate him."

Lorna laughed and Karen, hearing her mother, removed her thumb and laughed, too. "You can hardly stand them," Lorna said, jerking her head in Ginny and Bev's direction. "You're eaten up with jealousy."

"Oh, for God's sake! Just because I don't want to fawn over him like they do? Give me a break. By the way, I notice you finally got his name right."

"Sammy Jo, listen to yourself. You want some advice?"

"No."

"Tell Brent it's over. It was all a mistake. And then, let things happen with Cooper. He wants it, too."

"You don't know what you're talking about," Sammy Jo grumbled.

"Let me ask you this—who would you rather sleep with? Brent or Cooper?"

"Lorna!" Sammy Jo shot a meaningful look toward Karen who was sucking happily on her thumb, her gaze fixed on Pokey.

"Think about it." Lorna gave Sammy Jo a hug, then walked around the side of the house.

Sammy Jo stared after her. Shouting, she said to the remaining group, "I've got some work to do. You all can hang out as long as you like."

With that, she opened the creaking back door and walked into the house. They didn't take the hint. Long after she was inside, and peeking through the curtains, they were all still standing by the rail. She could see the way Ginny and Bev fought for Cooper's attention, even though she couldn't hear a word. And Cooper just ate it up. Just ate it up.

She eyed the width of his shoulders through his denim shirt, the sexy way his jeans hugged his hips, the way his hair curled against his neck beneath his hat. "How could I have ever slept with him?" she demanded in a whisper to the empty room.

The phone rang. Sammy Jo snatched it up in relief. Anything to get her mind off Cooper.

"Hi, there," Brent greeted her fondly.

Guilt pierced her soul. "Brent," she responded dully.

"I went down to the *Corral* offices today and put our marriage announcement in. It'll come out in next week's edition."

Sammy Jo drew in a breath. Her mind went blank.

"You still there?" Brent asked.

"Um . . . yeah."

"I hope you're not mad."

She laughed shakily. Mad? She was stark raving bonkers!

"I hate to push you, Sammy Jo. But when are we getting that marriage license? And truthfully, I'm going to need to see about your finances, so I can talk to Matt Durning myself and get him to halt the foreclosure."

"Brent, I'm not sure about this."

"About what?" he asked, his voice growing sober.

"About everything," she said guiltily.

"Sammy Jo!"

Her hand tightened around the receiver. She felt like a heel.

"I'll come by tonight," he said quickly. "We'll talk then. Don't back out on me now, darling. You signed a contract, remember?" he added, an attempt at humor that fell flat. "I love you, Sammy Jo."

She guessed he expected her to say the words back. She wanted to, if only to make him feel better. But no sound issued from her throat and Brent hung up. Brent, whom Cooper had accused of planning to sell the Triple R out from under her. About that, Cooper was horribly wrong. The situation was much worse. Brent wanted her for *her,* not for her property.

Replacing the receiver, she drew a deep, calming breath and closed her eyes, bitterness welling up inside her, a bitterness she had no right to feel. When she opened her eyes again, she realized Cooper was standing at the back door, watching her. Her heart jumped. Had he heard her conversation with Brent?

"Where're Ginny and Bev?" Sammy Jo asked.

"They left."

"Too bad."

He pulled open the screen door and strode in uninvited. Sammy Jo glared pointedly at him, silently demanding what he thought he was doing.

"Don't you even want to know why I stopped by?" he asked.

"To see Bev?" Sammy Jo guessed. "Or maybe you just want to harass me."

Clearly he didn't like her tone. "If I wanted to see Bev, I'd go to her place, not yours." A beat. "And, yes, I did come to harass you."

Sammy Jo turned away, making herself busy at the sink, washing some peaches for Lettie that really didn't need to be washed. She hated his tone. Its seductive lightness. A soft, bantering flattery she couldn't afford to succumb to. "Maybe I don't feel like being harassed tonight. Could you come back later in the week?"

"I've been thinking a lot about the other night," he said, ignoring her sarcasm.

"Really?"

He chuckled, and she bit her lip, wishing he didn't find everything she did so amusing. In a more sober tone, he said, "It shouldn't have happened."

Her breath caught. "On that, we agree completely."

"I guess there's a first time for everything," he said, and the self-deprecating humor in his voice made Sammy Jo's heart do strange little flips.

His next words chilled her blood. "Have you told Rollins about what happened yet?"

Sammy Jo fought back a telling gasp. She checked her watch. "Oops, time's up. No more harassing today."

"Don't want to talk about it, huh?"

"No, I don't," she admitted. "And now, I've got things to do. So, if you don't mind, why don't you vamoose, so I can do them?"

"You haven't told him."

"Okay, I haven't told him. Yet. But I will. And now I'm through talking." Sammy Jo pointed toward the door. "Why don't you go find Ginny or Bev or some other warm body?"

"Because I want you."

His bold confession stopped her cold. She blinked, not completely certain she'd heard him right. "Excuse me?"

"I want you," he repeated, mouth twisting. "I don't want to, but I do. I've been thinking about you all week. It's about all I do."

Her lips parted in amazement. He was telling the truth! Wasn't he? Or was this part of some elaborate plot? Sammy Jo wished she could trust her instincts, but ever since Cooper had come into her life, that particular internal compass seemed to be permanently out of whack.

"Cat got your tongue?" he asked to her silence.

"Well, this is all really interesting, not that I believe it for a minute," she added hurriedly, just in case he was setting her up. "But since I'm marrying Brent, it's not important."

"You're not marrying Brent."

Her heart beat heavily, darn near deafening her. "He's coming over here tonight."

"And you're telling him it's over."

Had he overheard her conversation with Brent? Or was he clairvoyant on top of everything else? Stubbornly, she clung to her lie, needing it for reasons she couldn't quite explain. "I have to marry Brent."

"Have to? Why?"

"You know why."

He crossed the room to her. Sammy Jo twisted to give him her back, her heart beating double time. Facing out the window, she inhaled as his arms suddenly surrounded her waist, warm and strong and strangely possessive. The thrill of it was electric.

"You want the Triple R. I'll give you the Triple R," he murmured in her ear.

Sammy Jo blinked, surprised. "How? What do you mean?"

Slowly he turned her around. She caught the sensual fire in his blue eyes and her body responded immediately. "I'll pay off your loan," he said, his gaze locking on her mouth.

"Why?"

"Because I want you," he repeated.

His mouth found hers, hard, his tongue thrusting deeply. Sammy Jo's eyes closed. She tried to fight the sensation, her hands gripping his arms for support, but it was impossible. His palms spanned her waist, fingers digging into her flesh as if he could scarcely contain himself. It shot thrills to her toes. Her heart pumped hard. A shiver went down her spine. All Sammy Jo's good intentions melted away like rivers to the ocean.

"Kiss me," he ordered roughly. "I want you to kiss me."

"I don't want to."

"Yes, you do."

She shook her head, the hair tumbling around her shoulders. His thumb rubbed her lips and she made the mistake of looking up. Yes, she wanted to kiss him, but she couldn't. She hated him. She hated him. Hated him . . .

Her mouth was oblivious to her thoughts. It tilted upward, ready, eager, responsive. His lips pressed against hers and Sammy Jo reveled in the taste of him, the texture. Her hands sought the warm skin at the back of his neck, curling around possessively, dragging him closer.

"You want me, too," he said hoarsely.

Sighing, she kissed him of her own volition, her mouth feather-light, drawing out the sensation. Then she kissed him harder. Cooper groaned, his hands sliding over her hips to cup her bottom, drawing her into direct contact with his hardness.

"Say it," he whispered.

Sammy Jo squeezed her eyes tightly closed.

"Say it."

"I want you."

His mouth curved into a smile of triumph. Bemused, Sammy Jo thought dimly that she should distrust that smile, but her senses were too swamped with desire. She craved his touch. And somewhere, distantly, she recognized that only Cooper could exact these feelings. Only Cooper.

"We can run this ranch together," he said. "We can make it what you've dreamed of."

"We?"

"We. Us. You and I." He buried his face in the silken tangle of her hair.

Sammy Jo surfaced dully from her sensual daze. "Are you talking about a partnership?"

"A partnership. I like that." He scooped her into his arms and Sammy Jo realized he intended to take her into the bedroom. Halfway there, at the hallway door, she clamped her fingers around the archway molding, stopping Cooper in his tracks. Reality was difficult to suspend for too long, even under Cooper's expert sensual attack. "What kind of partnership?"

"You ask too many questions," he teased, and the blue, sexual flame in his eyes almost drove the doubts from her mind.

Almost.

"Do I have to pry those fingers loose?" he asked, arching a seductive eyebrow.

"Cooper..."

"Shh. Whatever it is, it'll keep."

Sammy Jo's grip relaxed ever so slightly. Cooper's gaze held her captive. Her body ached. This was dangerous. Truly dangerous. Every instinct she possessed screamed against it. Except the most basic instinct. The one that wanted possession.

"I don't know...." Her voice sounded as unsure as she felt. "About what happened the other night...I just don't know."

Cooper gently tugged until her grip loosened completely. Slowly he carried her into her bedroom. Sammy Jo knew she could protest any time and he would stop, but she couldn't bring herself to.

He lay her down on the bed. Trigger growled low in her throat from her seat at the foot of the rocker in the corner. "It's okay," Sammy Jo warned the dog. "Go on, now."

With great reluctance, Trigger got to her feet. She eyed Cooper and Cooper eyed her right back, a smile playing at the corners of his mouth. "She's never minded me before."

"Maybe she feels what's happening."

"Think so?"

"No. I don't know."

Cooper slipped loose the top buttons of her shirt, his eyes watching hers so intently that something inside melted her into a warm pool of desire.

"Do you know they call you the Princess in town?" His lips twitched.

"Among other things."

"One of these days, you're going to have to show me how you ride."

The double entendre wasn't lost on Sammy Jo. She narrowed her eyes. "Keep talking, cowboy."

He laughed, pressing her onto the bed. She couldn't fight a smile, and Cooper, spying those dimples, kissed each one. Then he lay atop her and wriggled wildly until she was laughing hysterically.

"Stop!" she cried. Trigger bounded into the room and growled furiously. "No, you silly dog!" Sammy Jo laughed, shoving the Border collie's head away. "You know she's not going to leave us alone," she said to Cooper.

"Maybe we should lock her out."

"I don't know...." Sammy Jo was having definite second, third and fourth thoughts. As if reading her mind, Cooper got up to move the dog, but Sammy Jo rolled over to take Trigger from him.

He waited, leaning negligently against the bedstead as Sammy Jo scolded the dog even while she scratched Trigger's head, then led the collie into the kitchen to find her a biscuit to crunch down. When Sammy Jo came back to the room, her head was down. Then she looked up at him sexily from lowered eyes.

His breath caught. Did she know what she did to him? Did she guess her power? He wanted to drown inside her. She made him lose his head completely and forget sanity. Why? he wondered, lost. Why?

Perching on the bed beside him, she said, "This is a mistake."

"No, it isn't."

The glance she sent him was full of confusion. He understood. He felt confused himself.

Sammy Jo shook her head. "I think I've lost my mind."

"Good."

He reached for her, dragging her to him until her face was scant inches away, her long limbs tangling with his. Those lush, emerald eyes stared at him doubtfully.

"Partners?" she asked.

"Partners." He wanted to trace the line of her lips with his tongue.

"You're not expecting me to sell you part of the ranch, are you?" she asked suspiciously.

"I know you wouldn't do that. I'm not going to even ask."

"Then what do you want from me?"

She was completely serious. He kissed her mouth, tugging gently on her bottom lip with his teeth. "I like what's going on right now."

Sammy Jo pulled away slightly, a frown deepening her expression. "You already told me you don't want marriage."

"There're no strings attached to this arrangement."

"So you want a mistress?"

Her tension transmitted itself to him. "You really like labels, don't you?" he demanded, exasperated.

"Well, isn't that what you're saying? You want a mistress?"

"For God's sake, Sammy Jo. Stop being so literal!"

"You're going to buy off my mortgage just so you and I can be together like this?" Her eyes flashed dangerously.

Cooper felt just as dangerous. "Like *this?* Like about to make love?"

"You call it making love, but it sounds like something else to me."

"Oh, yeah?" The hairs on the back of his neck stood on end. Damn the woman! She always made everything so difficult. "Let me get this straight, it's okay to *buy* a husband, but making love to a business partner is out of line? Am I getting this right, Sammy Jo? I feel like I'm getting this right even though it doesn't make a damn bit of sense!"

"The hell it doesn't! At least Brent cares about me. He even told me he loved me. But you're not in love with me, are you? I'm just available and desperate and...and...you want sex!''

Cooper leaped to his feet. ''That's right! That's all this is! Can't you tell?''

Sammy Jo wanted to stomp her foot and scream. She threw him a look of pure venom that shot Cooper's simmering temper to a full-scale boil.

''You wanted a husband so you could keep the ranch. I'm offering you the ranch without a husband, and you spit on the idea. You should be thrilled.''

''To have you as my lord and master? Drop dead!''

Cooper growled. ''Only you could turn a good deed into total war.'' He swept up his hat and crammed it on his head.

''Good deed?'' Sammy Jo nearly screamed. ''So that's what you're calling it? Get out of my life, Cooper Ryan. And get the hell off my property! If I ever catch you coming around here again, I'll shoot first and ask questions later!''

His lips flattened. Sammy Jo braced herself, waiting for the next onslaught.

She wanted to strangle him!

''You're impossible,'' he snapped, then spun on his heel and stalked out the door.

Chapter Nine

Sammy Jo paced restlessly from one room of the house to another. Her mother's picture mocked her. Sammy Jo shoved it into a drawer. There was no one for her to trust; there never had been. Even her father had let her down.

Stepping outside, she was glad for the hot breeze that rustled the pines and aspens, bent the tall grasses and stirred the dry, red dirt. Brent would be here soon, and she would have to tell him to rip up that silly contract. What fun. She should have known better.

As the sun lowered, she waved at Carl as he came in from the fields, looking hot and tired. She was hot and tired, herself. What had ever possessed her to nearly make love to Cooper *again?*

"How ya farin'?" Carl asked, patting his pocket for a nonexistent cigarette package.

"Not so hot," Sammy Jo admitted. "Are you going home?"

"Yup. Tick-Tock's about due, y'know."

"I know."

"Read about yer engagement. Congratulations."

Carl peered at Sammy Jo through kind eyes, but Sammy Jo's expression changed from interested to horrified. "Oh, God."

"The *Corral* get it wrong?" he asked. "Had to go to town, so I picked up a copy hot off the presses."

"Um…no…not really…but…" She gave up. She had to talk to Brent before she said anything to anyone else. "The paper doesn't come 'til later."

"Brent Rollins is a fine man."

There was something missing in his tone, which Sammy Jo's sensitive ears picked up on instantly. "He's not a rancher," she said, guessing.

"No, he's not." Carl smiled at Sammy Jo before walking back to the barn where he'd parked his beat-up rig. He waved his hat at her as he left, cowboy-style. She waved back and returned to the house.

The *Corral* was on her front porch, rubber-banded into a roll. Sammy Jo unsnapped the band and smoothed the paper out. Her engagement announcement was on the second page. Brief and to the point, it alluded to an early fall wedding and mentioned the couple's long-standing relationship, harking back to the second grade at good old Harding Elementary. It also mentioned Gil Whalen and the Rollins family as long-time Coldwater Flats residents. Everything sounded hunky-dory. A match made in heaven.

Groaning, she crumpled the whole thing up, twisted it into a rope, then walked into the living room and tossed it into the cold ashes of the fireplace. She couldn't marry him for any reason.

And it isn't because of Cooper Ryan! she railed at her ever-vigilant conscience.

The drawer where she'd stashed her mother's picture gaped open, the frame's gilt edge stuck. Opening the drawer, Sammy Jo pulled out the photo and rearranged it on the table. Irene had run away from responsibility. She'd run away from Gil and her three-year-old daughter. Apparently there'd been a man waiting for her. Rumors had circled for years. But it didn't matter because Sammy Jo was nothing like Irene. No way. Gil had certainly told her enough times.

Marrying a man she didn't love would be totally irresponsible.

But you would have the ranch. And the ranch is everything.

"Not everything," Sammy Jo said aloud, remembering how she'd felt when Cooper Ryan had made love to her.

Everything, that voice in her head argued.

The doorbell rang and Sammy Jo ran out of the living room as if ghosts were chasing her.

"Hello, there," Brent greeted her, waving a handful of daisies at her like a peace offering.

"Hi, Brent." Sammy Jo opened the door and he stepped inside. She braced herself for a kiss on the cheek, but he must have sensed her mood because he simply walked into the living room and waited for her to follow.

"I know what you're going to say. You're going to give every reason from now until Sunday why you can't marry me."

Sammy Jo perched on an ottoman, her hands clasped together. "It's just not fair to either one of us."

"Is what Gil did to you fair?"

"This isn't about my father."

"Yes, it is, Sammy Jo. He set this whole thing up so you'd have to get married or lose the ranch. It's archaic and ridiculous, but there it is. I think we could make it work out between us. I really do. And so I'm willing to do whatever you want as long as you don't postpone the wedding past September. I'm ready to get married and have children. And I want a strong woman to share all that with me. Don't you want that, too?''

She stared at him. "Yes, I guess I do.''

"Is there any reason you can't marry me? I mean, are you carrying on some secret love affair with someone else?'' He grinned.

Sammy Jo looked down at her clenched hands, afraid what he might read in her face. "What if I was, Brent?''

"It doesn't matter, because you're not. What matters is our future, and the future of the Triple R. Without my help, you'll lose this place, and I know how much it means to you. It's your family.'' Sammy Jo shot him a surprised look, amazed by his insight. "But it doesn't have to be your only family.''

"I've made some mistakes. Recently. And I can't just pretend they haven't happened.'' Her throat was dust. She swallowed hard. "I was involved with another man.''

"Who?'' formed on his lips as his face registered shock. Sammy Jo smiled crookedly. Even Brent couldn't believe that Sammy Jo Whalen had actually fallen for some guy.

He simply sat there blinking for long moments, processing this new, disturbing information. "Well,'' he said. Then again, "Well.''

"So you may not want me now,'' Sammy Jo finished, deciding to put the matter in his hands and let him be the one to end this farce of an engagement.

To her disbelief, he said, "I want you, Sammy Jo.''

I want you. His echo of Cooper's words made her mentally squirm.

"Tomorrow we'll go to Valley Federal and get everything straight with Matt about the Triple R.''

"Brent, I can't marry you!"

"What else are you going to do?" he asked, and for once Sammy Jo was completely speechless.

It could have been the same day that Sammy Jo first walked in to Valley Federal and encountered Cooper Ryan. Matt sat at his desk, smiling with forced patience at her while Sammy Jo glowered back at him. Only, Cooper wasn't standing by the window. Instead, Brent was in the room, seated beside her, holding her hand while Matt and he discussed the fate of the Triple R.

Sammy Jo's ironic comments about Valley Federal's lack of faith in her had so irked Matt that he was all but ignoring her now. It was Brent he spoke to. Brent in command.

Which, in turn, irked the hell out of Sammy Jo.

What was she doing here, anyway? She had no intention of marrying someone she didn't love. Some silly, never-say-die part of herself had hoped this interview would proceed differently. Rather than fight Brent on the marriage issue, she'd thought she might be able to convince him and Matt Durning that the Triple R was hers and there was no reason to take it away from her.

Desperate hopes of a desperate woman.

Instead, Brent was practically picking out the colors for the wedding. She was leaning toward black and gray.

"...no need to foreclose," Matt was saying now, reaching across his desk to clasp Brent's hand. Brent was forced to release Sammy Jo's palm to do the honors. Surreptitiously, she wiped the hand on her jeans. Half an hour warmed by Brent's nervous palm had turned it into a sweat-fest.

"Glad you came to your senses, Sammy Jo," Matt added, extending his good humor and hand to include her.

She smiled tightly. Valley Federal's walls were closing in on her and she couldn't breathe. "Could I have a glass of water?" she asked in order to keep from screaming at him.

"Certainly. Glenda!" Matt called his secretary over. Glenda shot Sammy Jo a concerned look, which didn't bode well for Sammy Jo's appearance. Did she look as wrung-out as she felt?

As Glenda hurried away to get the water, Brent and Matt talked business. Brent kept reaching over to touch her hand, but Sammy Jo's arms were now folded protectively around her waist. Several times he threw her a worried glance, as if wondering why she'd barricaded herself inside an ice fortress.

"Here, honey," Glenda said, putting the paper cup in Sammy Jo's hands. "Carl says you've been working yourself to the bone."

"He's the one who's been working." Sammy Jo swallowed.

"I'll be paying him first thing," Brent spoke up.

"Oh, I never worried about that." Glenda waved him away. "I knew Sammy Jo was always good for it. Just mighta taken a little time, that's all, but friends help friends, now don't they?"

Matt frowned at his secretary, as if she'd said something objectionable. Brent got to his feet, inviting Sammy Jo to do the same. She stood up quickly. Nothing she wanted more than to shake the dust of Valley Federal off her boots.

"This isn't going to work, you know," Sammy Jo said as she walked with Brent to his red sports car convertible.

"You just want everything your own way."

Sammy Jo almost laughed. He was so right! But why did it feel like nothing was going her way, and that it was never going to go her way again?

Brent opened her door with a flourish. Sammy Jo felt as if she were sleepwalking. Dimly she heard birds twitter and the click-click-click of winged grasshoppers as they flew across the sunbaked asphalt path that circled the bank into the straw dry grasses of a neighboring field.

Brent climbed behind the wheel. "Sammy Jo, there's something we haven't talked about, and I think it's time we did." Sammy Jo waited as he cautiously negotiated the potholes in the road. "We never discussed our wedding night. Now, you know they're calling you the last virgin over twenty-five in the county." He laughed shortly. "Maybe we should talk about that."

Sammy Jo was momentarily speechless. "Who are *they?*" she finally sputtered.

"Oh, you know, people . . ."

"Look, Brent. I've wanted things to be different, but they're not. I can't marry you, even if it means losing the Triple R."

"You will lose it. That Cooper Ryan fellow will buy the ranch as soon as it's in foreclosure. He wants it, you know."

"Funny. He expects you to try to sell it out from under me when it's in *your* control."

Brent was affronted. "Is that what's holding you back?"

"No. I just can't marry someone I don't love."

"Is it this other man? The guy you told me about?"

"No!" Sammy Jo shrieked above the wind streaming past the windshield. "And Brent, for the record, I'm not a virgin, so you don't have to talk to me about sex."

Stupefaction filled Brent's face. Sammy Jo felt a moment of satisfaction. Clearly, that one had come out of left field. His expression was priceless. Just priceless!

"Really?" he huffed.

"Really. As if it's anybody's business but mine." Sammy Jo slid him a sideways glance. "Does it make a difference?"

What a question! Clearly it did. Brent was out-and-out shocked by her confession, and that made Sammy Jo mad all over again.

"No, of course not," he murmured, flustered. "I just assumed, from what everyone said...."

"If you mean what Tommy Weatherwood and the like say about me and everyone else in town, I'm surprised they thought I was a virgin at all! They'd be more likely to claim I was another notch on their belts. Oh, no, wait." Sammy Jo lifted a hand in understanding. "I get it. If I didn't have sex with them, I couldn't possibly have had sex with anyone else, right?"

"Now, Sammy Jo..."

"Don't patronize me, Brent."

"Well, I hope you were smart about it, that's all." He sniffed, nose in the air.

"As a matter of fact, I wasn't smart about it at all," she disagreed querulously. "I was downright stupid. In fact, I think I could win a medal in the Stupidest Person of the Year contest!"

"You don't have to yell."

"Don't I?" Sammy Jo shouted.

"Well, who was he? Assuming there was just the one incident?"

Her jaw dropped. "Stop the car, Brent. Stop it right now because I'm getting out!"

He ignored her and the convertible sped out of town to the twin driveways for Serenity and the Triple R. Sammy Jo had one hand on the door handle. It took every ounce of willpower she possessed not to throw herself out at thirty miles an hour.

He didn't even spare a glance for the burned oak. "We'll talk later," he told her as she slammed the car door on her way out.

"The hell we will!" she snapped, stomping into the house, nearly apoplectic with fury. What gave him the right to treat her like that? Good grief, how many ways did she have to say, "I can't marry you!" before he believed her.

No man owned her, and no man ever would. By God, if it cost her everything she owned, she would never sacrifice herself for some self-serving, arrogant, patronizing male!

Slamming out of the house, Trigger at her heels barking like she'd lost her head completely, Sammy Jo ran for the barn, needing something, *anything,* to get her mind off her troubles.

It had been a beastly day. Kicked by one of the cattle, wounded by a rusty strand of barbed wire that had forced him to get a tetanus-booster shot, losing his hat in Cotton Creek when he'd gone to inspect the remains of the beaver dam, and then finally, faced with Lettie's peach cobbler as the Babbitts had loaded up their belongings because he'd asked them several weeks ago if they would mind finding a place of their own since he, Cooper Ryan, needed his privacy.

Never mind that in the eleventh hour he'd done his damnedest to reverse that ultimatum. Not that Lettie and Jack seemed to care. They'd been planning to leave, even had a little place at the edge of town just right for the two of them. The ease with which they'd taken their dismissal made him feel all the worse.

But it was too late now.

The peach cobbler mocked him. Lettie had insisted he keep it. "Maybe it'll make you stop growlin' like a grumpy old bear," she said.

"I don't want you to leave. To be honest, I'm pretty damn sick and tired of my own company."

"I know." Lettie winked. "That's why we have to go."

He was still puzzling over that mysterious comment as he prowled around the ranch house. He stopped at the archway to the living room. Someone had turned down the lights to a dim yellow glow. Softly romantic, the illumination underscored the basic country style of the ranch house, highlighting the living room's chintz curtains and circular coffee table with its wagon-wheel base—old man Riggs's pride and joy.

He'd asked Lettie what she meant by that remark. "Oh, now, you know," she'd said, patting his arm as if they shared some mysterious secret. "We were gonna have to move out sooner or later. Don't worry yourself none. I'll keep cookin' your meals."

She'd chuckled as she'd met Jack at the truck, and they'd both waved and grinned as they departed. Cooper had stood at the door, wishing he'd handled things differently. Not only with Lettie and Jack, but with Sammy Jo, too. Hell, these were the people who mattered in his life now and all he'd done was trample their feelings and hurt them, all in the name of self-preservation.

A white card sat on the table. Cooper picked it up, frowning.

You won't have to wait too long.

He flipped the card over. Nothing on the back. Lettie and her cryptic comments made him feel as if he were missing something very important. But for the life of him, he couldn't imagine what.

Roaming around the room, Cooper found he wasn't comfortable with his own thoughts. A part of him couldn't help revisiting that last scene with Sammy Jo. He wanted to be with her now, regardless of how deep-down angry he was with her.

He stopped at the front window and reviewed their argument, but his thoughts kept slipping into dangerous territory. He could recall the satin softness of her skin. The sharp, passionate flare in her green eyes. Those dimples . . .

Groaning, he ran his fingers through his hair, then froze as headlights snaked their way down his driveway. Sammy Jo!

But the car that drove up to his front door wasn't a blue pickup. It was a small white compact that jogged Cooper's memory.

"Bev," he said with a sigh, turning on the light and watching as she shifted her sleek legs from the car, grinned and waved at him, then pulled a foil-wrapped package from the back seat.

Is this what Lettie had been winking about?

"Hi, there. Hope you don't mind." Bev lifted her shoulders sheepishly. "I made dinner. You haven't eaten yet, have you?"

"No."

"I heard Lettie saying she and Jack were moving out. Although it sounded kind of like you expected other company?"

Cooper shook his head. He realized suddenly, humorously, that Lettie had been expecting him to get with *Sammy Jo.*

"It's kind of a picnic," Bev babbled, clearly feeling a little presumptuous. "We could eat in the kitchen or dining room or . . . ?"

"Here." He took the tray from her and led her into the family room. Placing the food on the round table, he sat in a chair and Bev perched herself on the couch.

Looking at her well-manicured profile, Cooper told himself that this was what he needed to expunge Sammy Jo from his system. There was absolutely nothing wrong with Bev. On the contrary, she was beautiful, intelligent and clearly interested in him.

She removed the foil and revealed cold sandwiches and cucumber salad. "It's so hot," she murmured.

"It's great."

Cooper found himself a beer. There was no wine for Bev, so after a long, hard look at his beverages, she accepted a longneck herself. One sip and she was through, however. Cooper had to at least congratulate her on being a good sport.

As soon as they were finished eating, Bev settled deeper into the couch, her eyes silently inviting him to join her. With a heavy reluctance that made him irritated with himself, he sank onto the couch beside her, but he made no move to touch her.

What in God's name is wrong with me? he asked himself, scowling.

Bev read his expression. "Something wrong?"

"No. I was just . . . thinking."

"About what?" She smiled encouragingly.

Sammy Jo. "The ranch."

"You said you were going to change the name, but it's still Serenity, isn't it?"

Cooper grimaced. "I'd thought about trying to combine it with the Triple R. I even made a kind of suggestion to Sammy Jo."

Bev straightened abruptly. "You mean, buy it from her?"

"In a manner of speaking. Except she could still run the place. Then the name of the whole spread could be the Triple R."

"By your tone, I take it she turned you down."

"She wasn't too keen on the idea," he sidestepped, mouth quirking at the memory of Sammy Jo's raging fury.

"Well, I'm glad." Bev snuggled closer.

"Glad?"

"Sammy Jo is so one-way. You'd be fighting with her all the time and nothing you'd do would be good enough. Now, if she sold it to you outright, that would be different. But take it from me. I've known Sammy Jo Whalen most of my life and she's . . . well, she's tough and stubborn!"

Cooper heard the words but all he remembered was the way she'd moved in his arms, the way she'd tasted like warm honey, the sadness that had wrapped around his soul over the waste of the oak tree, her friend.

"She's going to marry Brent to save that ranch, but it won't last."

"The marriage?" The words tasted like ashes in Cooper's mouth.

"And the ranch. Brent will sell that place just like that." She snapped her fingers. "That's what he *does*. And though he may like Sammy Jo—I mean, he's always been infatuated with her, God knows why—he'll still dump the Triple R as soon as he can. He hates ranching."

"Sammy Jo will never give it up."

"She may be smart, but if he's putting up the money, she won't have much of a choice. I know her. She'll feel too guilty. And then when it becomes available, all you have to do is grab it. Trust me on this."

He did. He sensed that every word she spoke was the unvarnished truth, and Sammy Jo would come out the loser no matter what she did. But she couldn't marry Rollins. She couldn't!

"Did you see this afternoon's *Corral?*"

"The local rag?" Cooper smiled at her mock outrage. "No."

"Their engagement was announced."

"Whose?" he asked automatically, though dread filled up every spare space inside him as he waited for the expected answer.

"Why, Brent and Sammy Jo. That's who we're talking about, isn't it? The wedding's early this fall. Cooper, you could have the Triple R in your hands by the end of the year!"

Her eyes shone. She not only wanted him, he realized, she wanted a healthy bank balance. And she was a quick study when it came to cold hard cash.

Pamela had been, too.

She snuggled closer to him, clearly waiting to be kissed. Conversation had dwindled to nothing. A clock ticked gently. It could have been romantic, seductive and private, a perfect place for lovemaking, the perfect woman to erase the memory of Sammy Jo. But it wasn't. Something was wrong. And Cooper worried that what was wrong, wasn't going to be easily fixed.

"Bev..."

She placed manicured fingers on his lips. "Don't say anything."

With that, she kissed him lightly, invitingly. Detached, Cooper checked his own reactions and was both relieved and mildly disgusted to learn she had no effect on him whatsoever.

She drew back expectantly. He couldn't even fake an interest, and his feelings must have shown for she suddenly pulled back, stunned. "You don't want me here, do you?"

"I'm not sure what I want," he said honestly.

"Well, I guess I've made a fool of myself!"

"No."

Bev didn't listen. In a nyloned-whisper of righteous indignation, she got to her feet and quickly put some space between her and Cooper. He climbed to his feet more slowly.

"You know, they told me I was wasting my time. Told me to go back to Roy, as if he'd have me," she added on a bitter laugh. "But I didn't listen. I just wouldn't listen."

"Who told you?" Cooper asked as Bev snatched her purse and headed for the door.

"Everybody! Half the town thinks you're trying to steal Sammy Jo Whalen's ranch from her, the other half thinks you're in love with her."

"I'm not in love with her," Cooper denied quickly.

"In lust, then. We're not blind, you know. Not really." At the door, Bev hesitated, seemingly at a loss. Finally, she shrugged and added, "But she'll marry Brent Rollins to save that damn ranch before she'd even look at a man. That's the kind of woman she is. She's already married to the Triple R, and she doesn't want any other lover. Keep that in mind when you're in bed alone, Mr. Ryan, and remember what you threw away!"

Once Sammy Jo reached the barn, she threw a bridle over Patty Cake's tossing head and led the quarter horse into the corral, then proceeded to yank off her boots and socks. Mounting the bareback animal, she clucked to her with her tongue until Patty Cake was moving around the ring in a slow, rhythmic gallop.

Heart slamming against her ribs, Sammy Jo pulled her feet to the mare's withers, gathering her courage. Carefully, she transferred her weight to her feet until she was riding Patty Cake in a tense squat. She tied the reins and let them fall over the horse's neck.

"Keep going," she whispered. "Keep going."

Patty Cake's ears flicked back and forth. She tried to quicken her pace but Sammy Jo shushed her back to her gentle gallop. With painstaking care, Sammy Jo straightened her legs, then unbent until she was standing, arms straight, knees slightly bent, the wind provided by the running horse fanning through her hair.

What the hell are you trying to prove?

The pain inside her chest was a hard ball. She fought it even as she concentrated on Patty Cake's rhythmic movements.

I love him. I love Cooper.

Sammy Jo's foot moved. Her arms circled wildly. With a cry, she struggled to slide down but she was too late. Suddenly, she was flying through the air, the ground rushing up to meet her. Her cheek smashed down as she landed face-first in the hard dust.

She was out cold before Patty Cake had run another ten hoofbeats.

Chapter Ten

Cooper pounded his fist against Sammy Jo's front door. The noise echoed across the fields, but there was no answer from inside the house apart from Trigger's frantic barking.

Frowning, Cooper walked to where Sammy Jo's pickup stood. He touched the hood. Cold. Was she with Rollins? It was entirely possible. Probable, even. He just didn't want to believe it, yet they'd announced their wedding plans this afternoon, so clearly Sammy Jo had done nothing to call the marriage off.

"Damn." He kicked dust with his boot. Hearing the snort of a horse, he walked around the side of the house, feeling like a trespasser. The bay with the white blaze down its nose that she'd ridden to the beaver dam stared at him over the top rail of the fence.

"Hi there," Cooper greeted the horse. It shook its head and snorted, and he walked toward it, his mind elsewhere.

A jean-clad leg showed through the rails.

"Sammy Jo!"

Cooper ran the last few yards. She lay completely still, her cheek buried in dirt, her arms and legs flung wide. He vaulted the rail and was at her side in two ragged breaths, feeling for a pulse.

Her heart beat pure and strong. The wash of relief that engulfed him left him shaking. Groaning, Sammy Jo winced as her eyelids dragged open.

"Sammy Jo," Cooper said. "Are you all right? Please tell me you're all right."

She slowly turned over. Another groan, louder. Cooper tried to stop her from moving, his hands on her shoulders.

"Oh, my head," she moaned, squeezing her eyes closed.

"Did you fall? What happened?"

"I was riding Patty Cake and I..." Sammy Jo sucked in a breath. "Screwed up."

A strange feeling came over Cooper. He wanted to shout with laughter and drag her close to his chest at the same time. "This might ruin your reputation as an accomplished horsewoman."

"No more trick-riding," she murmured as she struggled upward.

"Whoa. Stay down a minute and let me do some checking."

Sammy Jo's eyes flew open and she inhaled sharply as Cooper's hands ran down her arms, chest, hips and legs. "What kind of trick-riding were you doing?" he asked, his hands lingering lightly on her shins.

"How am I?"

"No broken bones."

Cooper slid an arm around Sammy Jo's shoulders. She waited a moment, gathering strength, before climbing to her feet. Her knees wobbled, and she hung on to Cooper as if he were a lifeline.

"Maybe I should take you to a doctor."

"Oh, please. I just need to get into the house." Sammy Jo stepped forward, grabbed hard for Cooper and winced. Looking down at her hand, she muttered, "My wrist."

"It's starting to swell. You must have sprained it." He eyed her closely. "You're white as a sheet."

"I'm fine. Really."

"I'm not going to feel right unless you see a doctor. Come on."

Over her protests, he led her to his truck and drove her into the Coldwater Flats clinic. It was late, but the town's doctor was still at work and willing to check Sammy Jo out. Cooper marveled at the continual surprises this small town offered.

"If we were in L.A., you'd have to check into the emergency room and hope a doctor would see you before Monday," he told Sammy Jo as she headed for the clinic's back rooms.

She smiled wanly.

An hour later, she was returned to him, her wrist wrapped with an elastic bandage. Cooper liked it when the doctor told him the extent of Sammy Jo's injuries—which amounted to bruises, scrapes and a sprained wrist—as if she somehow belonged to him. Sammy Jo, however, was clearly not as appreciative of the situation, if Cooper correctly interpreted the looks she was giving both him and the doctor.

"She isn't concussed," the doctor finished. "But I think it would be a good idea to keep a watch on her."

"I'm fine," Sammy Jo insisted.

"I'll stay with her," Cooper told him.

Sammy Jo kept her silence as he drove her home, but when he tried to help her inside, she shook off his arm and walked to the couch on her own power. Once settled, she said clearly, "Thank you, Cooper, but I'm really okay. You don't have to stay."

"I want to stay."

His concern touched a corner of her heart, but she fought to ignore it. "And they say I'm stubborn," she mumbled, bringing a grin to his lips.

"What kind of trick-riding?" he asked again, plumping a pillow behind her head. He was gratified to see color had returned to her face.

"Nothing." She looked away, plucking at the tassel on a pillow, purposely avoiding his probing gaze.

"Don't tell me you were *standing* on that horse! Or worse!"

"Was there a purpose to your visit? Besides your rescue, that is, which I'm grateful for."

"Sammy Jo, for God's sake!" Cooper prowled around the room in frustration. "What are you trying to do, kill yourself?"

Her lips parted. Sweet pink lips. He steeled himself for the spurt of fury bound to be forthcoming, but instead of answering, she went suddenly silent. Her jaw snapped shut.

"That *is* what you were doing, wasn't it?"

"Of course not! I was just feeling reckless and out of sorts."

"So you stood on the back of a running horse when no one was around? That's perfect, Sammy Jo! Just perfect!"

"Well, it seemed like the last time I might be able to do it!"

"Why?"

"Because I can't marry Brent! And I'm going to lose the ranch. And there's not a damn thing I can do about it!" Sammy Jo's voice broke in spite of her resolve to control herself. Aching inside, she turned her face into the pillow, furious with herself and with Cooper for a whole passel of reasons.

The silence that followed stretched her nerves to breaking. "You and Brent have called it off?"

"I've been trying, believe me." Her voice was muffled.

Cooper perched beside her. She inhaled his familiar scent and silently berated herself for being so susceptible. "What about the ranch?"

"The ranch," she repeated bitterly. "It's what you want, isn't it?"

"I don't—" He cut himself off, gritting his teeth. "I don't want to see you unhappy."

"Too late. I'm miserable."

"What can I do to help?"

The words sounded torn from his soul. Sammy Jo risked a look into his blue eyes and saw only deep sincerity and concern. She licked her lips. "Is the offer still open?"

"Offer?"

"To be your mistress if you'd let me run the ranch. If your offer's still on the table, I'd like to accept."

"Sammy Jo..." Cooper automatically reached for her, but she fended him off.

"Answer me first. Please." Her voice shook with determination and pain.

"You don't have to make that deal." He felt sick with himself.

"Didn't you ask me what you could do to help? Well, I'm answering. Do we have a deal, or not?"

Cooper gazed down into her dirt-streaked, stubborn face. Her chin trembled, but she wouldn't cry. He was caught off guard by an intense wave of emotion as Sammy Jo inched her chin higher, waiting for his reply.

He'd backed this brave, feisty woman into a corner and he hated himself for it. His offer, which he'd fooled himself into believing would be good for both of them, was cheap and dirty. It was a back-room deal, and she'd only agreed out of desperation.

Yet he was jubilant that she'd given up Rollins.

"Can we talk about this later?"

"I don't have later, Mr. Ryan." The words were full of bitterness.

Cooper mentally kicked himself for creating a situation he couldn't get out of. If he tried to back out now, he'd destroy her pride entirely.

"Is it a deal?" she demanded again.

"It's a deal," he responded, and with that, Sammy Jo turned her back to him, falling into uneasy sleep after heaving one long, shuddering sigh that stabbed like a knife in Cooper's chest.

A knock on the back door brought Cooper out of a self-induced daze. He'd been watching Sammy Jo's breathing, determined to stay and make sure she was all right, no matter that she would undoubtedly chew his ear off for his concern as soon as she awakened.

Looking up, Cooper saw it was Carl, Sammy Jo's hired hand. Quietly he got to his feet, walked across the room, slowly opened the squeaking screen door and joined Carl on the back porch.

"I'm done for the day," the older man said, patting his pockets for the crumpled pack of cigarettes. Putting one to his lips, he mumbled, "But I think this might be my last day. Is Sammy Jo inside?"

"She's asleep. She had a fall off a horse."

"Really? Don't sound much like Sammy Jo. Is she all right?"

"I'm kind of keeping an eye on her."

Frowning, Carl said, "Wish I'd been here. I was up untanglin' one of the cows from some old barbed wire. A real mess. The animal bawlin' and jumpin'. But she's unhurt." Carl hesitated, his frown lines deepening into dark crevasses. "I got a job over in Prineville with a construction company. I know Sammy Jo'll pay me when she can, but I gotta take this job now."

"Sammy Jo and I have agreed to become business partners," Cooper said slowly. "If you come over to my place tomorrow, I'll bring your wages up-to-date."

"Are you sure?" His expression lightened. "I mean, I don't want to upset Sammy Jo. She don't like charity."

"It's not charity, believe me," Cooper said dryly.

"I sure could use the money."

Cooper walked to the barn with him to where the man's beat-up truck was parked next to an equally dilapidated tractor. As Carl climbed inside the truck, he seemed to develop second thoughts.

"I thought Sammy Jo was marryin' Brent Rollins. How come you're her business partner?"

"That marriage might not come off," Cooper revealed, stepping back so Carl could reverse. The truck's engine bumped and throbbed and missed. Carl had to give it some serious gas while throwing it into reverse. Cooper unlatched the gate, and the vehicle departed in a plume of dust.

He entered the house, looked down at his dust-covered boots and decided to take them off. In stocking feet, he returned to where Sammy Jo lay on the couch. Checking her breathing, he thought about waking her up to make sure she was okay. The doctor didn't think she had a concussion, but Cooper didn't want to take chances.

Sighing, he sank onto the couch beside her. The cushions depressed beneath his weight. A part of him wanted to just haul her into his arms, but, knowing Sammy Jo, the struggle was bound to be an out-and-out battle, and he wasn't certain she was up to it. That didn't mean she wouldn't fight like the devil, of course. The woman was too stubborn for her own good.

"Sammy Jo," he murmured, stroking hair away from her cheek. Her color was still improving. A good sign. "Sammy Jo?"

She heaved a deep sigh and pushed at him ineffectively to leave her alone. Cooper chuckled. An even better sign.

"I just want to make sure you're all right," he told her softly.

Long moments passed while he listened to her rhythmic breathing. He loved the sound of it. Glancing at her earlobe, he examined the way it lay against her neck. Pink and soft, it invited exploration, and Cooper, where Sammy Jo was concerned, had no resistance. He gently kissed her ear.

She swatted at him again. "Go 'way."

"Only if you open your eyes and let me look at you."

Slowly Sammy Jo lifted her gold-tipped lashes and stared at him through those beautiful emerald eyes.

"Pupils aren't dilated," he commented.

She arched an eyebrow. "What is this?"

"You seem okay. I'm glad."

Snorting, she glanced away. "You can go now." Her color heightened and Cooper was transfixed by the way the rosy glow climbed up her neck and flamed her cheeks.

Without thinking about it, he leaned over and kissed her lips, lightly. "To seal our bargain," he told her.

She wanted to be mad. Her lips pursed, and she turned away. But he heard her rapid breathing and knew her heart rate had increased. Fascinated, he kissed her again. This time, her lips parted, the tip of her tongue touching his.

"I think you should leave," she said, swallowing.

"Do you?"

"Immediately, if not sooner."

"I don't want to leave."

"I'm fine, Cooper. Really." She moved her arms and legs to show him. "I've just got a sore wrist and a bump on my head."

"Where?"

She pointed to the back of her head. His fingers delved into her luxurious mane, the strands silky smooth and slick. She sucked in a breath when he encountered a knot.

"Ouch," he agreed.

"Damn right!"

"Kiss me, Sammy Jo."

"Cooper, go away. I mean it." She struggled upward, but he held her shoulders down with gentle yet firm pressure.

"Relax. You've got a bruise forming on your left cheek, too." His thumb grazed the swelling, but instead of flinching, Sammy Jo looked down at his throat, as if unable to meet his gaze any longer. "What are we doing?" he asked huskily, then kissed her again, harder.

Her body tensed, then slowly, painstakingly, she lifted her arms, sliding her hands up his forearms and biceps, inviting his embrace.

It was sheer madness, the kind Sammy Jo couldn't afford to indulge in, but she couldn't seem to stop herself. Her mind was a jumble of impressions. His hair-roughened jaw, rock-hard muscles beneath a blue denim work shirt, surprisingly soft lips pressed against hers with driving pressure. She wanted him in a liquid, melting, demanding way that she couldn't control. As of their own volition, her legs shifted, her body turned, forming an unspoken invitation he couldn't help but understand.

And then he was lying atop her, balancing his weight on his forearms so that all she felt were his hips hot against hers and the lightest pressure as the tips of her breasts grazed his chest.

She groaned, low and needy. Cooper answered by gently rotating his hips in a slow-motion circle that had her throbbing and anxious so fast it was embarrassing.

"Cooper," she breathed, pulse pounding.

He kissed her throat, her cheek, the lobe of her ear, his breath ragged and hot. Shifting position, he pulled her on top of him, his fingers digging at the buttons of her shirt.

She slowly shook her head, fighting in spite of her body's raging need.

"Let me," he whispered.

With a sigh, she gave in, collapsing on his chest as he pulled off her shirt and deftly unhooked her bra. Then she lay against him, bare-chested, and suddenly the tiny buttons on his shirt were too much to bear. With a kind of studied determination, she undid the row of buttons down the front of his shirt, her almost clinical detachment too much for Cooper. His blue eyes flamed. His mouth reached up to hers. She kissed him and he dragged her breasts against his bare chest, his hips thrusting upward.

There was no time after that. In moments they were both naked. Cooper tried to go slowly, but Sammy Jo wouldn't let him. She demanded his possession. She rotated across his hips, in control of their lovemaking, yet unwilling to make it last too long.

She slid over him and his hands dug into her buttocks, pulling her down until she gasped with pleasure. Sammy Jo moved. Her eyes closed. A rush of feeling shot through her, so intense she was afraid she might be burned. Crying out, she collapsed against his chest, then was gratified moments later when his deep groan and shuddering release answered her passion.

They made love again. He wouldn't leave, and she stopped asking. The second time was more deliberate, and Sammy Jo learned things about herself that had her blushing and Cooper grinning like an idiot.

He stayed until dawn, and when Sammy Jo's stomach growled, he got up and dressed and made her some toast, which was burned and smothered in butter and which Sammy Jo ate as if it were the most delicious meal she'd ever had.

Wiping crumbs from the corner of her mouth, she dragged the afghan closer to her chest, vulnerable now that he was dressed and she was still nude. "Thanks. I should hire you to cook for me."

"That's the extent of my culinary skills, I'm afraid," he drawled, and she loved the sound of his voice.

Sammy Jo pulled the blanket up to her collarbone, gripping it tightly. "And thanks for finding me last night. I was feeling . . . kind of low. . . ."

"My pleasure."

The husky throb of amusement in his voice bothered her. Was he laughing at her? "Well, I should get dressed."

"Go ahead."

She flushed. "I don't want you to watch me."

"You watched me," he said.

It was true. When he'd gotten up from the couch, she'd feasted on the sight of his muscular back and legs and been almost sorry when he'd slipped into his jeans. Except those jeans rode low on his hips and were damn sexy-looking.

"I don't want you to watch me. So, go in the kitchen, or something. Carl will be here soon and I want to have some clothes on, if you don't mind."

He rubbed his unshaven jaw. Sammy Jo followed the slow action, shocked at the feeling even his simplest movement seemed to stir up inside her. "Actually, Carl won't be here today."

"Why?"

"He got offered a construction job and decided to take it."

"Oh. He wanted to be paid," she said, an attempt at humor that fell flat. She could hear her bitterness.

"Don't worry about it. We'll get somebody else."

We. That's right. Last night they'd agreed on a partnership in which she was his mistress. Her heart sank. She'd forgotten. She'd made herself forget last night in the heat of passion. She'd wanted him too much, and she'd sacrificed her pride. Sick. She felt physically sick.

"I need to pay Carl," she murmured dully.

"Taken care of."

His proprietary tone scraped her nerves. He was so miserably sure of himself. "You paid him?"

"He's stopping by my place today for the entire amount."

"You told him about our...arrangement?"

Cooper's eyes narrowed thoughtfully. Could he hear the throb of rebellion and anger in her voice? Undoubtedly. She made no attempt to hide it.

"I told him we were business partners."

"Nice title! Kind of makes it sound legitimate, doesn't it?"

"What the hell's eating you?"

Sammy Jo ground her teeth together, dragging her gaze from the dark chest hair and lean-hipped male in front of her. She wanted to scream. She hated herself for wanting him so much. What was she, crazy?

The answer came again, with the speed and force and unexpectancy of a bullet: she loved him. *Loved him!* She, Sammy Jo Whalen, the cold, the proud, the Princess . . . had fallen in love. Fallen in love with a man who could hurt her. No! Worse! Fallen in love with a man to whom she'd *handed over* the power to hurt her.

A vision of her writhing beneath him, begging him to make love to her, consumed her with visceral disgust and horror. She couldn't hold on to the thought; it was too terrible. She shied away, seeking some other explanation, but it was plain in its horror and simplicity. Love had reduced her to this. The type of woman she most abhorred.

He made a move toward her, a bare shift in her direction, and she jumped back, arms clamped around the blanket as if expecting him to yank it off her. Cooper frowned.

"What is going through your head?"

"I have to talk to Brent," she babbled. "Right away. I've got to be clear on this. You understand."

"No, I don't," he said tersely. "What do you mean?"

"I just . . . I need to be alone. Please. I just need to be alone."

"You're acting like I'm going to . . . I don't know . . . attack you, or something." He smiled, in Sammy Jo's mind looking as if he was clear in his knowledge that she was his for the taking.

And she was, she thought miserably. If he came too close to her, she didn't know what she'd do. She didn't trust herself anymore. She'd never been in love before, and she didn't like it one bit. She felt vulnerable, anxious, totally unlike herself.

"I've got some things I've got to do, too," Cooper said, staring at her thoughtfully. "I'll be back later. You sure you're okay?"

"I'm fine." With an effort, she pasted on a crooked smile.

"I don't see a dimple," Cooper stated flatly, confusing Sammy Jo, but he snatched up his shirt and hat, and she didn't ask any further questions.

He stopped, looked at her hard, then shook his head. "We'll hammer out the details later. You won't be sorry, Sammy Jo. This is going to work out for both of us."

The rumble of his truck's engine filled the room and reached into Sammy Jo's bones. She couldn't breathe. She couldn't see. She was completely immersed in inner turmoil that made her feel weak, breathless and soul-sick.

"I've sold out," she said in a small voice to the empty room, and tears burned so hot in her eyes that she bit hard into her lip until it bled.

Chapter Eleven

"He's out selling the Granger place," Connie revealed when Sammy Jo walked into the real estate office and inquired about her soon-to-be-ex-fiancé. "You know the Grangers. Ever since they built that shopping center, ranching hasn't been on their minds at all."

Granger Ranch was a small one on the opposite edge of town from the Triple R. Sammy Jo had never been too impressed with it, but that was due more to a function of the owners' upkeep and interest than the parcel of land itself.

"I'll catch up with him there," Sammy Jo told her.

"He's real excited about the wedding!" Connie grinned.

"Oh?"

"He's been as cheerful as a canary."

Sammy Jo shook off her bad feelings as she strode to her pickup. Kicking the door hard several times, she yanked it open and vowed to herself one more time to get it fixed.

She drove straight to Granger Ranch, practicing in her mind all the things she would say to Brent. But her head felt stuffed with cotton and by the time she was walking up the concrete stairs to the front stoop, a nagging headache had developed.

"Hello, there, Sammy Jo," Mrs. Granger greeted her. She was a heavyset woman with iron-gray hair and a sweet smile. "You looking for Brent?"

"Is he here?"

"Sure is."

She held open the door, and Sammy Jo stepped inside. The whole place seemed sort of forlorn and forgotten. With a sinking feeling, Sammy Jo realized the Triple R wasn't far behind in that.

Brent was outside, talking to "Eagle-Eye" Granger, as Tommy Weatherwood and friends had dubbed him after Granger had caught them sneaking beer from the grocery store's back loading ramp when they were still underage. Spying Sammy Jo, Brent waved and broke away.

"Hi, there," he said, his smile of greeting fading when he saw Sammy Jo's sober expression.

"Can we talk?"

"Sounds serious," he said.

"It is," Sammy Jo admitted.

Brent extricated himself with speed and walked Sammy Jo out to the front of the house where sunlight glinted blindingly off his red sports car. "It's over, isn't it?" he said before Sammy Jo could even begin. She was too taken aback to answer immediately, but her silence was answer enough. Brent's expression darkened. "Why am I not surprised?"

Sammy Jo lifted her shoulders, feeling terrible. "I wanted it to work. I really did."

"What changed your mind?"

"I got cold feet. I—"

"Sure it wasn't Cooper Ryan?"

Sammy Jo stared into Brent's eyes, knowing he could see way too much on her face. "I'm not selling him the ranch. And no matter what you might hear, I'm not in partnership with him."

"So it's just me, huh?" Brent looked away, upset. She could tell he was fighting for control.

"Actually, I think it's me. I've always been a pain in the rear, you know that." She laughed shortly. "And lately I've been making some mistakes that were doozies. I didn't mean to lead you on."

"Well, Sammy Jo, I wish I could say good luck and all that, but I can't right now."

"I'm sorry, Brent."

"Yeah. Me, too."

He climbed into his car and drove away, carefully, probably to keep the dust from ruining the sports car's bright-red finish. Or maybe just to keep his temper in check.

Rubbing her temple, Sammy Jo grimaced as she yanked on the pickup's door handle. She drove straight to the bank, deciding to take all her bitter pills at once.

"Matt's with a customer," Donna told her quickly, half rising from her chair as if expecting Sammy Jo to charge past her again. Truth to tell, Sammy Jo just didn't have the energy today.

"I'll wait." Sinking into a chair, she snatched up the latest edition of the *Corral*. No headlines about her today. A nice surprise, she thought ironically.

It took the better part of an hour, but for once Sammy Jo wasn't squirming with anxiety and annoyance. She just wanted to be left alone.

Lorna signaled at Sammy Jo to come over to tellers' row. Sammy Jo shook her head and mouthed, "Later".

Finally, Matt strode out with his client, a tiny, white-haired woman with a silver cane and a bulldog expression. Matt looked slightly worse for wear, as if the woman had come out the victor instead of Valley Federal.

Not good, Sammy Jo thought grimly. He wasn't going to be in any mood for her news.

Spying her, he said, "Sammy Jo," with absolutely zero enthusiasm. Did he already know? She didn't think Brent had had time to tell him, buy maybe he'd beelined to the bank to cut her out of his life.

"Hi, Matt. I'm afraid I've got some bad news."

He snorted and gestured for her to follow him to his desk. She sank into one of the chairs, holding on to the last shreds of her composure.

"You look terrible, Sammy Jo," he said.

"Thanks."

"Who gave you that bruise?"

Sammy Jo's hand flew to her cheek. For the first time that day, she actually smiled. "Patty Cake. My horse. No, that's not fair. I gave this little trophy to myself."

"And the wrist, too?" At Sammy Jo's nod, he asked, "So what's the bad news?"

"I guess you haven't seen Brent yet, then. He and I called off our engagement. Looks like the Triple R's not going to be rescued."

Matt looked nonplussed. He smoothed back his hair. "I thought you were in partnership with Cooper Ryan."

"What?" Sammy Jo froze.

"He stopped by here today and said you and he are in business together. Naturally, I asked him about Brent, but he said this deal was between him and you."

Sammy Jo stared at him, her hands balled into fists. "Cooper Ryan came by to tell you that he and I had made a deal?"

The words sounded far away. The voice wasn't her own. Sammy Jo couldn't believe what a fool she'd been! And she'd let him. No! Begged him! She could hear the little sounds of pleasure and begging moans she'd uttered in the name of passion and love.

"Sammy Jo, are you okay?" Matt asked anxiously.

"Perfect."

The coldness of her tone didn't invite further conversation. She got to her feet, head pounding, and twisted on her heel. Then she turned back. "Cooper Ryan and I have no deal, you understand? *No deal!* As far as I'm concerned, Valley Federal owns the Triple R now. I'll start packing."

Matt Durning's executive mouth dropped open as Sammy Jo stomped out of the bank, the sound of her determined voice still ringing throughout the room.

Cooper whistled as he went about his chores. He was going to have to hire more help. With his place and the Triple R as one working ranch, it was going to be a whole lot more than either he or Sammy Jo could handle.

When he thought about Sammy Jo's defeat, his heart twisted a little. But she'd forgiven him for the position he'd put her in. She'd never have been able to make love to him otherwise.

Ignoring the tiny doubt that he couldn't seem to kill, he hurried into the house, running into Lettie who was at the oven, shoving in a pan of berry cobbler, even though the outside temperature was sky-high and the kitchen felt like an oven itself.

"I'm going over to the Triple R," he told her, to which Lettie smirked with delight.

"Good idea, Mr. Ryan."

Sammy Jo's pickup stood in front of the house but when he knocked on the door, he got no response. Circling the house, he ran into Trigger who barked happily upon seeing him. At least he'd won over one female completely, he thought with some amusement.

Sammy Jo was in the barn, he realized, hearing a storm of swearing coming from somewhere inside. Grinning, he hurried to catch up to her. He couldn't recall ever being so excited about the future. It was insane, really, but hell, it was great.

"Hi, there," he greeted her, his boots echoing on the weathered plank boards.

She was feeding the pregnant mare. Tick-Tock, he recalled. When she glanced his way, Cooper was taken aback at the expression on her face. Her emerald eyes were miniature glaciers. His gaze immediately fell on the purpling mark on her cheek. "That's one nasty bruise," he remarked.

Her lashes fluttered; he'd distracted her. Encouraged, he moved toward her, then stopped short when she backed against the wall of the stall, suddenly spitting-mad.

"I've rethought our arrangement," she announced frigidly. "No deal. No partnership. No sex for payment."

"Sammy Jo!" Cooper half laughed.

"I'm through with you, Ryan. Go find the rock you crawled out from beneath, and get back under there."

"What are you talking about?"

"You know."

"Sammy Jo, what happened between us didn't have anything to do with the ranch."

"That's not how I remember it." She closed the stall and circled away from him. Perversely, her actions only increased his desire to drag her close. He wanted to grab her and hold on and make her realize that they were made for each other.

That struck like a bolt of lightning. Amazed, Cooper assessed his feelings, which were all tangled and deep and damn near incomprehensible when it came to Sammy Jo.

"I know the way it came off," he said, thinking back. He inwardly winced when he remembered how they'd struck their bargain. "But that's not how it is and you know it. I just didn't want you to think I'd fall into that marriage trap."

"That marriage trap?"

If he'd been listening closer, he would have heard the early warning signs: her careful tone; her body's frozen stillness; the expectancy, as if she were waiting for him to keep digging his own grave. Which, unfortunately, he did.

"I've been through one marriage, and it was hell. My ex-wife gave new meaning to the term 'avaricious.'"

"Oh..." She crossed her arms, still waiting.

"I know it works for some people, but it didn't work for me. And knowing you, I don't think it'd work for you, either."

"Uh-huh."

"I told you I wanted to buy this ranch, but you made it clear you weren't selling."

"So you fell back on your only other option."

A prickling along his nerves warned him. In a slower voice, he said cautiously, "If you mean the partnership, then yes."

"Do you do this often, Mr. Ryan?"

"What's this 'Mr. Ryan' stuff?" he growled, annoyed.

"Do you seduce your way into all business transactions? Or is it just gullible women who fall for it?"

Cooper's eyes held hers. She was fighting for control, her fury and hurt palpable in the still, dry air and slanting sunlight of the barn. "You agreed on our partnership. I didn't force you."

"You didn't have to." Raw bitterness roughened her voice. "I was desperate. But I'm not anymore."

"What does that mean?"

"I'm letting the bank take the ranch. I'd rather lose the Triple R than my self-respect. So get the hell off my property. It's the last time I'm asking."

Cooper slowly began to count inside his head, silently swearing all the way from one to ten. He'd about had it with Sammy Jo and her mercurial temperament. "Fine. Let the bank take your property! You don't know how to accept help when people are throwing it at you!"

"Help? Helping yourself, you mean!"

"Damn it, Sammy Jo. You liked making love as much as I did."

"This isn't about making love!" she snarled through gritted teeth.

"The hell it isn't," he growled. "You're mad because I haven't offered a lifetime commitment. Is that what you want? A marriage proposal? Want me to make an honest woman out of you?"

He hadn't meant to hurt so deeply. He truly didn't understand the depth of her insecurity. But as soon as the words were out, he regretted them. Deeply. The wounded look that crossed her face was like a blow to his stomach. He'd hurt her. Bruised her. Far worse than any fall off Patty Cake.

"Sammy Jo, I'm sorry." He reached forward. Her reaction was predictable. She kicked him in the shins. He tightened his grip on her wrists and she struggled for several seconds before tossing back her hair and glaring at him with all the strength of her personality, which was formidable to say the least.

"I must have been out of my mind," she told him in a shaking voice, "to give myself to such a slimeball. If I hadn't been so miserable, I would have never struck such a bargain. Never! I'm not interested in you. You can't have the ranch, and you can't have me. I'm leaving Coldwater Flats. And you, Mr. Ryan, can find some other easy prey. Hell, there's lots of women in this town who want you. Try Bev, or Ginny, or maybe both together! I don't care what you do, but you'd damned—well—better—keep your hands—off me!" she declared, twisting her arms with each sharply punctuated word in an effort to dislodge his fingers. Pain slashed across her face when she turned her injured wrist.

"Sammy Jo, for God's sake!"

"Let me go!"

He released his hands, automatically bracing himself, half expecting another attack. Breathing hard, she glared at him. Her mouth quivered. Self-loathing swept through him at how terribly he'd mishandled this. His own feelings about love and marriage had shattered Sammy Jo's illusions. It had been her first time, and he'd been insensitive.

And he realized, belatedly and with a hard jolt, that he cared for her deeply. More deeply than he'd imagined. More deeply than he'd seriously thought possible. He shied away from labeling it "love," but it was damn close. As close as Cooper Ryan was ever going to get.

"Don't give up the ranch. I'll pay off the mortgage and you can still—"

"You can't buy me off!" she shouted.

"Damn it, Sammy Jo," Cooper said, exasperated. "If you'd just listen for a moment instead of jumping in and screaming at me, you'd see I'm not trying to do that."

That did it. She shoved past him, pounding out of the barn, a booted whirlwind of repressed fury. Cooper charged after her, his ground-devouring strides catching up with her at the corral rail.

"Touch me again, and I'll kill you," she snarled.

He almost laughed. This blond spitfire couldn't engender fear no matter how hard she tried. But laughing would lose him more ground, something he couldn't afford.

"You're just mad because you still want me," he said instead, arrogantly. "And you know we're good together."

She swept in a shocked breath. "Well, you're certainly a smug bastard. I'll give you that."

"Name-calling will get you anything you want."

"I want you to leave."

"No, you don't."

"And I'm tired of your telling me what I want. What are you doing?" she demanded suspiciously when Cooper moved closer.

"I'm going to kiss you goodbye."

Her lips parted in pure disbelief. Then her gaze drifted to the pitchfork propped up against a post.

"Don't even think about it," he said, leaning down to fulfill his promise.

"I'll bite your lip," she stated flatly.

Grinning, Cooper delicately kissed her bruised cheek. She stiffened, but didn't make any untoward moves. "I'm not giving up," he told her.

With that, he left, unsettled but certain he could make things right. He didn't see the quick look she darted him, nor witness her resigned, bitter smile.

He forgot that Sammy Jo Whalen sometimes had more backbone than sense, more pride than reason. While Cooper drove away, she walked straight to the phone.

"Hi, Tommy," she greeted her old buddy. "The bank's foreclosing on the ranch and I've got a lot of livestock to sell cheap. Find me someone who's ready to make a quick deal. You can have first pick...."

* * *

"What?" Cooper demanded, three days later, his stunned gaze spearing both Lettie and Jack.

Jack shifted his weight from one foot to the other. "Sammy Jo went and sold every bit of livestock. Got Tommy to help her move it. Tommy's half thief, you know, but Sammy Jo don't seem to care."

Lettie banged a pan on the stove. "Maybe she shoulda married Brent," she fretted. "Namby-pamby, he is, but she'd still have the ranch."

She slid Cooper a glance of unspoken criticism that nevertheless spoke volumes. Cooper shoved his hands through his hair in exasperation. He'd been forced to take a quick trip to Los Angeles, one he'd been putting off because he knew he'd run into Pamela. But he'd needed her signature to sell off the last of his California property and she'd been there, cool as ice and as approachable as a distant planet.

The funny thing was, all his animosity had disappeared. One look at Pamela, and Cooper had expected his chest to tighten up with anger. Instead, he'd felt nothing. Just a kind of urgency to get the transaction over with, so he could get on with the rest of his life. Amazed, Cooper had smiled at his ex-wife, and that had earned him a dark scowl.

"What are you up to now?" she'd demanded in that husky voice of his memories.

"Just getting on with my life."

"In some godforsaken Oregon village? I'm so lucky we divorced!"

"Me, too," he agreed reflectively.

No hostility. No burning anger. Nothing.

He'd left L.A. feeling as if a heavy load had been lifted. As if a faith healer had worked his magic and renewed Cooper's soul. And he saw the future in a different light.

Except Sammy Jo was thwarting him again!

"She sold every bit of livestock?" Cooper repeated, disbelieving.

"Down to the last hoof," Jack admitted.

"What about the pregnant mare? Tick-Tock?"

"Doc Carey took her. Hardest thing he ever had to do. Sammy Jo standin' there with tears in her eyes and insistin' he take the reins." Jack shook his head. "But there's no talkin' to that girl when she's like that. You think Rollins threw her over, and that's why she's so upset?"

Lettie sniffed. "I think she got her heart broke," she stated coldly, meaningfully.

"All she's got left is her dog," Jack went on. "She's still at the house, I reckon, but not for long. Told Matt Durning she was leavin', and that was that. Made the banker feel like dirt."

"As well he should!" Lettie sniffed. "The poor thing!"

"Oh, Lettie, you know Sammy Jo'll come out all right. She's tough. Too tough, maybe."

Lettie stared her husband down. "You better start lookin' with more than your eyes. That girl's suffered a lot of pain and covers it all up with stubbornness and anger. Her mama left her when she was three. Her dad took away the only thing she loved. She's alone and she's got a pretty thin shell to fight off the world." She banged another pan. "So don't go actin' like Sammy Jo ain't hurtin', 'cause she is."

"She's still at the house?" Cooper grabbed on to the one piece of information that could help him.

"Far as I know." Lettie softened a bit. "You gonna try to help her?"

Grabbing his hat, Cooper growled, "She won't let me within fifty feet of her. But I'll die trying."

Lettie watched him leave, then glared at her husband who was sitting at the table, hands raised in surrender. "You got somethin' else to say about Sammy Jo?"

Jack Babbitt knew his wife better than himself. "A fine-lookin' woman," he said. "Make Cooper a good wife someday."

Lettie slowly lowered the frying pan in her right hand. "I believe you're right."

Sammy Jo walked along the stream path, eyeing the imbedded stars with disdain. What a legacy. Rodeo princess eternal; queen for several years. And not a dime to her name.

Oh, sure. She'd sold the livestock, but she'd made a point of being paid in cash and then dumping the bag of money on Matt Durning's desk. Childish. Not really Matt's fault. But it had felt good for the moment, and Sammy Jo needed to feel good about something, no matter how fleeting the sensation.

So, okay, she was done. Trigger awaited her at the house. And Patty Cake was still there, though Josh Johnson had purchased her and promised to take good care of her. Josh had told Sammy Jo she could keep the quarter horse until she was really good and ready to leave town.

"Hate to see you leave," he'd told her as they'd shaken hands to finalize their agreement. "What's Coldwater Flats without Sammy Jo Whalen?"

"I can't stay, Josh. You understand."

His eyes were full of sympathy. "Yeah."

Brent had stopped by, full of regret. "You should have made Durning toss you out by force."

She'd almost laughed at that. Brent? Suggesting she defy authority? Maybe there was more to him than she'd originally thought.

"It didn't have to come to this, Sammy Jo," he told her sadly.

"Yes, it did, Brent."

She hadn't thought of Cooper once. Well, okay, she'd thought of him, but she'd driven those unworthy memories from her mind each time they popped in. It wasn't really his fault any more than it was hers. She just hated making such serious mistakes. Hated admitting that she, Sammy Jo Whalen, was capable of mega-idiocy where men were concerned. She, who'd always been so in control.

Sighing, she kicked at one of the stars, scuffing it with her boot. She'd been living like a fairy-tale princess, believing in her own infallibility and innate ability to choose a prince when the time was right.

She groaned, ran her fingers through her loose hair, then drew a deep, cleansing breath. Okay. She'd made some major errors. But every ending was a beginning, right? Some sap had spouted that wisdom somewhere, and by God, she was going to make herself believe it if it killed her.

Checking her watch, she realized she was late in meeting Lorna. Lorna wanted to talk, and Sammy Jo had put her off and put her off. The conversation was bound to be about Cooper, and Sammy Jo wasn't in the mood.

But now there was no reason not to see her friend. She needed to say goodbye, anyway, so she'd called and left a message that she would meet Lorna for lunch.

The lobby of Valley Federal was a cool, blessed relief from the early-August heat. Sammy Jo strode inside, her booted footsteps echoing familiarly. For once, she didn't pound over to Matt Durning's desk but instead turned to tellers' row. Lorna waved, but she was helping a customer. Sammy Jo seated herself in a wooden chair and tried not to dwell on her predicament.

Cooper hadn't called. She'd tossed him out and apparently he'd actually listened this time.

Swinging her jean-clad leg, she sighed, ran her hands through her hair and tried to fight that depressing thought. *Did you think he'd come back for more?* her nagging conscience demanded. *How many times can you tell someone to get lost before they finally do it?*

"Hey!" Lorna appeared, slightly breathless, slinging her purse over her shoulder. "Let's head over to the Last Stand."

"It's a little early for beer," Sammy Jo said without much interest.

"They make great burgers, though."

The Last Stand was filled with a rough-looking lunch crowd. Sam smiled at Sammy Jo and Lorna as they grabbed a little table at the far end of the poolroom.

"I heard you sold everything just like that!" Lorna snapped her fingers. "I've been trying to reach you for days!"

"I didn't feel like answering the phone."

"Are you all right? Sammy Jo, this isn't like you."

Sammy Jo laughed without humor. "Cooper was right. I was out of options. I just didn't know it. Lorna, I didn't have a choice."

"I saw Cooper come into the bank and afterward Matt said you and he were in a partnership together. But then...?" Lorna waited for Sammy Jo to fill in the blanks.

Sammy Jo looked at her friend. Why not tell her? What did she have to lose now? "You want the whole story."

"Lay it on me," Lorna said, settling back in her chair.

It took Sammy Jo the better part of Lorna's hour lunch break to explain the events that had led up to her decision. It wasn't all that long a story, but Sammy Jo found it difficult to admit to her feelings for Cooper. It was even harder to tell about their lovemaking, but though she tried to gloss over it, Lorna pounced on what Sammy Jo "didn't" say.

"Oh-my-god! You made love!"

"Shh!"

"No wonder you're such a wreck!"

"What do you mean?" Sammy Jo demanded.

"Sammy Jo, you're in love with him and you don't even know it. Oh-my-god!" she gasped again. "This could be the answer!"

"You think I should have agreed to be his mistress to save the ranch?" Sammy Jo demanded.

Lorna rolled her eyes. "Oh, Sammy Jo, for goodness sakes. Get over that. Have you thought about his feelings? Don't you see what's happening?"

"He wants the Triple R. Period."

Lorna shook her head. "He's trying to tie you up all over the place. Making you his partner instead of waiting until you went under. If all he wanted was the ranch, he'd just sit pretty until Matt foreclosed on you."

There was a certain logic there, but Sammy Jo didn't want to believe it. She couldn't. Trusting in people's good natures had never worked in the past.

"There's something else I want to talk to you about, though," Lorna added, frowning.

"I can hardly wait," Sammy Jo murmured, responding to Lorna's serious tone.

"Matt got a call from Peter Whalen."

"Uncle Peter?" Sammy Jo's blood ran cold. "When?"

"I wasn't supposed to know, but when I heard your last name, well ..." She made a face. "I think he's hoping he can buy up the Triple R."

"Good old Uncle Peter," Sammy Jo said through her teeth, boiling inside.

"If you don't want him to have it, you'd better go find Cooper Ryan."

Sammy Jo didn't remember the rest of the conversation. She paid the check by rote and walked Lorna back to the bank. *I shouldn't care,* she told herself. *It's over.* But it wasn't over. Not with Uncle Peter.

She drove to Serenity and barged through the front door without knocking. Lettie looked up in surprise. "Hello there, Sammy Jo. Did Mr. Ryan find you?"

"Was he looking for me?"

"He went over to the Triple R."

Sammy Jo left without another word, wondering what Cooper could possibly have to say to her. But he wasn't at the house when she arrived, and though she strode outside and hollered his name, he was nowhere on her property.

Think, think, think!

Drawing a deep breath, Sammy Jo whistled to Trigger, then the two of them walked up the lane to the remains of the oak tree. Her mind raced. How could she live with herself if Uncle Peter ended up with her beloved ranch? It was bad enough she'd lost it. But to *him?*

"I'd rather let Cooper have the ranch," she said aloud. He'd offered to let her run it. He'd blamed her for overreacting to the mistress bit. Sammy Jo bit into her bottom lip. Maybe she had overreacted. Or maybe she'd acted that way because deep down inside she'd hoped...prayed...*dreamed* there might be a marriage proposal lurking around somewhere.

"Idiot," she muttered. But if she were willing to swallow her pride, she could work with Cooper.

It was time for some heavy decision-making.

Chapter Twelve

Tracking Sammy Jo Whalen all day had been easy; everyone remembered seeing her and they were quick to tell Cooper what she'd been wearing, what time it was they'd seen her and how sorry they were about her losing that ranch of hers. With scarcely a wrong turn, Cooper had ended up at the bank and talked to Lorna, who bent his ear for half an hour about Sammy Jo and the miserable state of her affairs and how he ought to pay attention to his heart and stop making so damn many mistakes.

And then Matt Durning had called him over for another enlightening conversation. Now, hours later, it was growing dark and he was standing at the rail that divided his property from Sammy Jo's, staring across at the soft yellow light beaming from the windows of her house.

Sammy Jo...

Turning back to his house, he strode quickly inside and snatched up the sheaf of papers awaiting him on the kitchen table. He rolled up the papers and shoved them into his back pocket. Halfway to his truck, his mouth quirked grimly as he realized she would likely kick his rear end back to Serenity, cursing him all the while, as soon as he started talking. She wouldn't want to hear one more "deal." He couldn't blame her.

But this was the deal of a lifetime.

The hot night breeze fanned Sammy Jo's flushed cheeks as she sat beside the charred oak. The scent of burned wood still permeated everything. Inhaling deeply, Sammy Jo tried not to mind too much.

"You would hate this," she said aloud, shooting a glance toward the heavens and her misguided father, rest his soul.

Sammy Jo's mouth twisted in self-deprecation. All these weeks and months doing her darnedest to save the place from the likes of Cooper Ryan and *wham!* Her worst enemy had been waiting in the wings, ready to strike. Peter Whalen had just bided his time until Sammy Jo burned through her last option.

But she wasn't out of the game yet.

Standing, Sammy Jo brushed off the back of her jeans. Trigger climbed to her feet and looked up at Sammy Jo expectantly.

"It's time to face the music," Sammy Jo murmured to the dog, whose tongue lolled out of the side of her mouth. Cooper had been looking for her earlier. Now it was her turn to look for him.

Before Sammy Jo had taken three steps toward the house, the rumble of a truck's engine cut into the still night, stopping Sammy Jo in her tracks. Twin beams of headlights bounced down her lane. She braced herself, half expecting Peter Whalen to step out of the cab and grin like a devil, gloating in his triumph.

But it was Cooper's black truck that headed toward her. Her heart leaped in spite of herself.

Spying her, he pulled to a stop beside the tree. Trigger barked and wagged her tail in greeting as Cooper climbed from the cab and came around the truck to where Sammy Jo stood.

"I've been looking for you," he said, bending down to scratch the Border collie's ears.

"Actually, I wanted to see you, too."

He shot her a glance, difficult to read in the darkness. "As I recall, you told me you'd kill me if I ever stepped foot on your property again. Or words to that effect."

Sammy Jo's throat closed. "I don't really think it's my property anymore."

"It ain't over 'til the fat lady sings," Cooper said softly.

Sammy Jo's gaze swept over him. His shirt was white, glowing in the evening shadows. He was leaning negligently against the truck, legs crossed at the ankles, arms crossed at his chest. A faint strip of moonlight gleamed off his belt buckle. Tonight, his ubiquitous cowboy hat was missing, leaving his dark hair to ruffle in the faint, evening breeze.

"I went to L.A.," he said. "To finalize some business. And I met with my ex-wife, Pamela."

"Oh?" Sammy Jo scarcely dared breathe. What was this all about? Any previous reference to the notorious Pamela had been said with anger or disgust. Much as Gil had referred to Sammy Jo's mother.

"It was the first time I could look at her without thinking what a bitch she was. Not that she isn't a bitch," he added, his teeth a flash of white in the darkness. "But I don't know. It was different this time. I just didn't care anymore."

"Why are you telling me this?"

"Because I haven't been fair to you. I've made a lot of remarks about women and marriage and things." He sighed. "None of it really had anything to do with you."

Sammy Jo wasn't sure what to make of this confession. "Well, I've got something I want to say to you, too."

"About?"

"My remarks about being your...mistress," she struggled to get out.

"Oh, let's not go into that. Please. I'm tired, and I don't want to fight."

"Neither do I," Sammy Jo assured him quickly, "but I thought—"

"Don't think." He suddenly shifted to his feet and reached for her, his hands clasping her forearms, dragging her close to his warm chest. Sammy Jo resisted out of habit, but then she collapsed against him, wanting him so much, it was an all-consuming ache. Squeezing her eyes shut, she fought the burn of something hotter than tears. Love. She loved him, and she would be a fool to tell him so.

He kissed her. Hard. She reveled in it, her head falling back, her body limp. He laughed, a low rumble of seduction, and she shook her head.

"Oh, Cooper, don't."

"I can't help myself." His hands slid down her back, over her hips and buttocks. He dragged her close until there was no doubt about what he was feeling. A smile tugged at her lips. She loved this.

"Kiss me," he demanded, and she placed both hands on his face and held him captive, her mouth ravishing his, her tongue darting in his mouth in hot exploration.

He swept in a startled breath. "...Sammy Jo!"

In no time at all, they were lying on the grass, a tangle of jeans and unbuttoned shirts, and anxious fingers and mouths. Trigger whined and moved away.

"She's learned," Cooper breathed raggedly against Sammy Jo's lips.

"Trigger?"

"Uh-huh." He groaned as her tongue stabbed into his mouth again, slick and melting. "Sammy Jo, too," he murmured, dragging a silent laugh from the depths of her.

"Hurry," she whispered to him.

"Why?"

"I don't know. Just please ..."

With quick, expert hands, he removed her boots and jeans. Her underwear followed. Then she lay on the ground, hair wild around her, bra and blouse half-on, half-off. Untamed and ravaged-looking in a streak of silvery moonlight.

The sight of her broke Cooper's control. He ripped off his own clothes and fell on her hard. Sammy Jo's fingers clenched into his hair. There was something primal, needful about this lovemaking that she reveled in. She loved him. *Loved* him. It felt as if this might be her only time to show him.

His mouth found her breasts as his fingers slipped inside the moistness between her legs. Sammy Jo moaned at this delicious invasion, winding herself around him.

I love you, she thought, the words circling through a haze of pleasure. *I love you....*

Cooper groaned as her own fingers delighted in a discovery of their own. "What are you doing to me?" he muttered.

"Nothing you aren't doing to me," she whispered.

"Sammy Jo...?"

"What?" Her heart nearly stopped at the tension in his voice.

He didn't answer. Instead, his mouth moved lower, and still lower, until Sammy Jo's hips arched upward as eager for him as he was to taste her. She cried out.

I love you . . . I love you . . . I love you.

The world spiraled, and then Cooper twisted to his back, dragging her atop him, thrusting inside her at the same time so that Sammy Jo rode him hard and fast, in a sweet rhythm that brought them to the brink so quickly they both cried out in ecstasy in one glorious shout.

Afterward, Sammy Jo lay panting on Cooper's chest while he wound silken strands of her hair around his fingers, his own heart still pounding as if he'd been in a race.

"Sammy Jo," he murmured.

"We've got to stop meeting like this," Sammy Jo blurted out shakily.

That sent them both into fits of laughter. Time seemed suspended. She could have stayed this way forever, but slowly, steadily, embarrassment reached Sammy Jo and after long, loving moments cradled in his arms, she became conscious of her complete nakedness. Her ever-vigilant conscience came to screaming life, reviewing this wild escapade and warning her harshly again that she would pay for her indulgences.

"Did you mean it?" he asked huskily, his voice a satisfied purr.

"What?"

"How quickly they forget." He pulled her mouth to his. She could feel the grin that stretched his lips. "You said you love me."

Sammy Jo went completely still. Shocked. Suffocated. "What?" she asked, mortified.

"You said, 'I love you.'"

She leaped to her feet, grabbing her clothes, staring at him in dawning horror. Cooper leaned on one elbow, watching her, a frown darkening his expression. She couldn't look at him. At his male beauty. She couldn't stand his knowing.

Had she really said those terrible three little words aloud?

"Now what?" he asked, baffled.

"I'll be your mistress," she said quickly, biting off the words. "I want the ranch. I want it that badly. But I'm not in love with you."

He swore a word that singed her ears, sharply and violently. Trigger growled low in her throat. "Liar."

Sammy Jo ground her teeth. "I'm ready to strike that deal."

"Forget it. I bought the ranch," he told her flatly, reaching for his pants. From the back pocket he withdrew a rolled-up sheaf of papers. He tossed it at her feet.

"You bought it?" The blood drained from Sammy Jo's face as she stared down at the roll of papers. The edges ruffled in the breeze. With shaking fingers, Sammy Jo buttoned her blouse and snapped her jeans. Her boots lay haphazard on the ground, forgotten in her haste and distress.

"I saw Matt Durning at Valley Federal today, and he told me some things I didn't think—"

"You went to Matt today and bought my ranch?" Sammy Jo interrupted furiously.

"Would you let me finish?"

Snatching up the paper, she shook it in front of Cooper's nose. "What is this? What does this say?"

He swore again, yanking on his clothes with restrained fury. "It says, you owe me two hundred thousand dollars. I bought out your loan. You can pay me back whenever you want."

"*What?*"

"Your contract's with me now. Not Valley Federal."

Sammy Jo froze, uncertain whether she should be furious or relieved. But remembering his lazy amusement over hearing her speak her soul . . . *I love you.* . . . She opted for fury. "I don't need any more of your help!"

His hand clasped her arm so quickly she gasped. "Now this is the end," he snarled, equally as furious. "I bought your ranch to keep some eager investor named Peter Whalen from snatching it up for a song. Ring any bells? As I understand it, he's not your favorite uncle. Not by a long shot. Now, if you'd rather he owned the Triple R than me, I can rip this up now. Right here. And we'll burn it right along with the oak tree!"

He was shaking her. Cooper was actually shaking her arm. Sammy Jo jerked it away from him.

"And I don't want you for a mistress," he growled.

"Good. Because I just decided I don't want you for my lord and master, either!"

She stomped off in the direction of the house, certain she was making another huge mistake, but burning with humiliation, nonetheless. She started running, oblivious to the fact that her feet were bare and the hard ground was giving away to gravel as she approached the house. She'd told him she loved him! What power she'd given him. Now she had to make him believe it wasn't true, or . . . or . . . or . . .

Or what? she asked herself. She might get hurt? She might lose everything she possessed?

Hadn't she already?

Gasping for air, Sammy Jo collapsed against the fence alongside the house. She staggered to the back paddock, leaning over the rail, hating herself. Cooper was beside her in an instant, his breath hot against the back of her neck.

She whipped around, ready for battle. He stared at her, chest heaving. "It's because you admitted you love me," he said quietly. "Isn't it? That's what you're running from. You're running from yourself."

"What do you want from me?" Sammy Jo demanded, her voice catching. "You know, I just can't have this kind of casual affair. It's tearing me apart!"

"I know."

"Then why do you keep showing up here? I'd be better off if you just left me alone."

"You need me, Sammy Jo. And I need you."

She backed away from him. She needed distance. Her fingers encountered the lock to the gate and she let herself inside the paddock. There were no horses anymore. No cattle. She left the gate open and Cooper followed her inside.

"Look, Cooper. I don't want my uncle to have the Triple R. You bought it, it's yours. I don't want to owe you money."

"You can pay me in installments."

"I don't own any livestock anymore!"

"We'll make that thieving friend of yours, Tommy Weatherwood, sell them back to you."

"Cooper . . ?" Sammy Jo sighed.

"Sammy Jo," he returned.

This time when he tried to drag her into his arms, she jumped back. No more of that. No more falling for his peculiar kind of magnetic seduction. She saw him grin again, that dazzling flash of white.

"I'm not going to fall into your trap," she told him flatly. "I'm not."

"I want to marry you, Sammy Jo," he said. Her jaw slackened. "Did you hear me?" he demanded to her silence.

Her mind buzzed in wild circles. "For the ranch."

"No!"

"You're not making any sense!"

"For you. I want to marry you for *you*, Sammy Jo!"

He stepped forward and she shrank back, and that was Sammy Jo's fatal mistake. Her heel slipped in mud, mud that had collected from a teeny pinprick hole in the water trough at the corner of the fence. One moment Sammy Jo was flailing her arms, struggling for balance, the next she fell backward with a huge, cold splash, her rear end dropped to the bottom of the trough. Shrieking with surprise, Sammy Jo grabbed on to the sides of the trough. Her legs dangled over the edge.

For a moment, Cooper stared at her in shock, then he buckled over and started laughing so hard Sammy Jo was sure he might split a gut.

With an effort, she dragged herself from the trough. She was wet from her neck to her knees. Cooper was beside himself with hysteria. He howled with laughter, making absolutely no effort to hide his mirth.

Sammy Jo fought a smile. It really was funny. And for reasons she didn't want to look at too closely, her heart was singing. She grinned at Cooper like an idiot, and he swooped her into his arms, his shoulders shaking with laughter.

"Okay, okay. It's funny. I'm soaking wet!"

"You deserved it. You know how many times you've hit me and pushed me and nearly drowned me."

"You're exaggerating," she said.

"Am I?" He held her away from him and studied her face. In the moonlight she saw his expression change. "I see those dimples," he said softly. "You know, I don't see them nearly enough."

"I don't smile a lot," Sammy Jo admitted.

"Why are you smiling now?"

She chuckled. "Because I just made a raging fool of myself! What do you think?"

"You didn't tell me what you thought of what I said. About marrying you," he clarified when she automatically opened her mouth to question him.

"Oh. That."

Cooper sighed. "It's not every day I ask a woman to marry me. I never thought I'd do it again. But you're not exactly jumping for joy," he observed dryly.

Sammy Jo shivered and Cooper's arms tightened around her. But she wasn't cold. Not physically. "I'd like to know why you want to marry me. I mean, you said it's for *me,* but..."

"I love you, Sammy Jo," Cooper said clearly, amazed at how easily the words came to his lips. "I've loved you since you first slammed into Valley Federal and gave Matt Durning a piece of your mind."

"He deserved it," Sammy Jo muttered, feeling suddenly shy and awkward. Could she believe him? No! Was she crazy? Yes!

"I loved you when you schemed to marry Brent Rollins to save your ranch."

"You hated me for that!" she protested.

"I hated the lengths you had to go to, but I loved you. I just was afraid."

"Afraid?" Sammy Jo asked, drawing back to search his face. "Are you being straight with me, Cooper?"

"You are so damned suspicious, woman," he growled, kissing her hard. "Come on. I'll take you inside and warm you up."

Sammy Jo liked the way he said that. "You know, I'd do practically anything to keep Uncle Peter from getting the ranch."

"Even be my mistress," he mocked gently.

At the door, she stopped short. "Do you really want a wife? Really?"

"I want you, Sammy Jo. Only you."

Now, in the half-light glowing from the living room, Cooper's blue eyes staring into hers, Sammy Jo read the truth. He did care about her. He'd said he loved her. Her lips parted in wonder, her heart slamming inside her chest.

Swallowing, she said, "I meant what I said."

"What was that?"

"Back . . . by the oak tree. I didn't know I said it, but I meant it."

His eyebrows drew together. "I can't remember what you said. Refresh my memory."

"I said . . . I said . . ."

"You said," he encouraged, his mouth drawing into a sexy smile.

Sammy Jo planted her hands on her hips. "I said I'd never let you be my lord and master!"

Cooper whooped with delight. "Say it! Say it!" he demanded, tickling her with hands that found every sensitive spot.

"Stop it!" Sammy Jo panted, laughing hysterically. "Stop it!"

"Say it!"

"I love you, you sadistic monster!" She tried to kick his shin. Cooper practically threw her over his shoulder as he hauled her screaming and shrieking form inside. Tossing her onto the couch, he held her arms down and kissed her neck, face and shoulders until tears of mirth stormed down her cheeks.

"I love you, too," he told her. "We'll be married this weekend."

"Too soon." She pulled his mouth down to hers for a searing kiss.

"Not soon enough. We'll have the wedding right here. At the Triple R."

"And we'll invite Uncle Peter!" Sammy Jo giggled.

"I'm serious, you know. I really do want to make you my wife."

Sammy Jo smiled at him. Her heart was so full of new, fresh hope she could scarcely believe this wasn't a dream. "I will make you a good wife," she promised solemnly.

"You'll be a pain in the rear end," he predicted. "Thank God."

And Sammy Jo, with all the love she'd never been able to lavish on her family, pulled her husband-to-be toward her by his lapels, kissed him lightly on the lips and said, "We're going to be very happy."

"And you'll beat the tar out of anyone who says otherwise." Cooper chuckled.

"Darn tootin'," Sammy Jo murmured, as she and Cooper sealed their bargain with a kiss that quickly turned into another wildfire of passion.

*   *   *   *   *

Barbara

DELINSKY

A COLLECTION

New York Times bestselling author Barbara Delinsky has created three wonderful love stories featuring the charming and irrepressible matchmaker, Victoria Lesser. Worldwide are proud to bring back these delightful romances – together for the first time, they are published in one beautiful volume this September.

THE REAL THING
TWELVE ACROSS
A SINGLE ROSE

Available from September   Priced £4.99

W★RLDWIDE

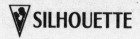

▼ SILHOUETTE

⟩ SPECIAL EDITION ⟨

COMING NEXT MONTH

JUST HOLD ON TIGHT! Andrea Edwards

That Special Woman!

Gabriella Monroe could rear a teenager solo, but she'd much rather do it with the benefit of a helping masculine hand. But since when did a man's love guarantee shelter from life's storms?

DANGEROUS ALLIANCE Lindsay McKenna

Men of Courage

Libby Tyler knew that loving a marine meant sorrow and loss. So how could Captain Dan Ramsey restore her faith in love?

A VOW TO LOVE Sherryl Woods

Vows

When they met as teenagers, Penny Hayden stalked away from Sam Roberts because she'd discovered he'd only taken her out as a favour to her matchmaking grandfather. Years later, history was repeating itself!

MAN OF THE MOUNTAIN Christine Rimmer

The Jones Gang

Jared Jones was surly and nothing but trouble, but Eden Parker was woman enough to renovate his broken dreams and shattered heart.

WILD IS THE WIND Laurie Paige

Wild River

Genny McBride always made Rafe Barrett forget everything but the passion she aroused. But this time he was determined no one would get hurt, which meant he had to catch the assassin after them.

THAT OUTLAW ATTITUDE Noreen Brownlie

Returning to the Wyoming mountains meant Caitlin O'Malley had to face the only man she had ever truly wanted and the memories of the tragedy that had torn them apart.

COMING NEXT MONTH FROM

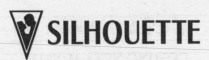 SILHOUETTE

Intrigue

Danger, deception and desire—
new from Silhouette...

SHADOW OF A DOUBT Margaret Chittenden
TO DIE FOR M J Rodgers
KEEPING SECRETS Jasmine Cresswell
TORCH JOB Patricia Rosemoor

Desire

Provocative, sensual love stories for the
woman of today

LUCY AND THE STONE Dixie Browning
PERSISTENT LADY Jackie Merritt
BOTHERED Jennifer Greene
THE TROUBLE WITH CAASI Debbie Macomber
ONCE UPON A FULL MOON Helen R. Myers
WISH UPON A STARR Nancy Martin

Sensation

A thrilling mix of passion, adventure
and drama

HOLDING OUT FOR A HERO Marie Ferrarella
BORN TO BE BAD Naomi Horton
CHEROKEE THUNDER Rachel Lee
SOMEWHERE OUT THERE Emilie Richards

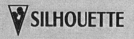

SPECIAL EDITION

QUESTIONNAIRE

A few months ago we introduced new-look covers on our Special Edition series and we'd like to hear your comments.

Please spare a few minutes to answer the following questions and we will send you a FREE Silhouette novel as a thank you. Just send the completed Questionnaire back to us today—no stamp needed.

Don't forget to fill in your name and address, so we know where to send your FREE book!

Please tick the appropriate box to indicate your answers.   [✔]

1. **How long have you been a Silhouette Special Edition reader?**
   Less than 1 year [ ]   1-2 years [ ]   3-5 years [ ]
   6-10 years [ ]   Over 10 years [ ]

2. **How frequently do you read Silhouette Special Editions?**
   Every month [ ]   Every 2-3 months [ ]   Less often [ ]

3. **From where do you usually obtain your Silhouette Special Edition?**
   Silhouette Reader Service [ ]   Supermarket [ ]
   John Menzies, WH Smith, Newsagent [ ]   Woolworths/Department Store [ ]
   Other (please specify) _____

4. **Please let us know how much you like the new covers?**
   Like very much [ ]   Like quite a lot [ ]   Don't like very much [ ]
   Don't like at all [ ]

5. What do you like most about the design of the new cover?

_____

_____

6. What do you like least about the design of the new cover?

_____

_____

7. Do you have any additional comments you'd like to make about our new-look Special Edition titles?

_____

_____

8. What other books do you read?

_____

_____

9. Are you a Reader Service subscriber?

Yes ☐   No ☐

If Yes, what is your subscription number? _____

10. What is your age group?

16-24 ☐   25-34 ☐   35-44 ☐   45-54 ☐   55-64 ☐   65+ ☐

THANK YOU FOR YOUR HELP

✉   Please send your completed questionnaire to: ✉

Silhouette Reader Service, FREEPOST,
P O Box 236, Croydon, Surrey CR9 9EL

NO STAMP NEEDED

Ms/Mrs/Miss/Mr: _____   CSE

Address:_____

_____

_____ Postcode: _____

mps MAILING PREFERENCE SERVICE